ZIGZAG CANYON

THE LEGEND OF GOLD GULCH

RON FELDMAN &
MIC McPHERSON

SUNSTONE
PRESS

SANTA FE
NEW MEXICO

2/17/2001

To Ed + Linda

Kindred Spirits

Ron Feldman

*Dedicated
to the memory
of Zane Grey*

Printed in the United States of America

10 9 8 7 6 5 4 3 2

Library of Congress Cataloging in Publication Data

Feldman, R. (Ron) , 1944-
     Zigzag Canyon : the legend of gold gulch / R. Feldman & Mic McPherson --
1st ed.
        p. cm.
     ISBN 0-86534-212-1 : $14.95
     1. Gold mines and mining--Arizona--Fiction. 2. Apache Indians-
-Fiction. I. McPherson, Mic, 1953-   . II. Title.
PS3556.E4595Z34   1994
813' .54--dc20
                                        93-38633
                                          CIP

Published by Sunstone Press
        Post Office Box 2321
        Santa Fe, New Mexico 87504-2321 / USA
        (505) 988-4418 / FAX: (505) 988-1025
        Orders only (800) 243-5644

TABLE OF CONTENTS

INTRODUCTION

In the years after 1800, there was an invasion of lands that now comprise the southwestern United States. Indians who had lived in these lands for centuries included the Apache tribes — themselves, relatively recent invaders.

This new invasion of the 1800s was led by a special breed of man, known as mountain men. They preferred wilderness to civilization. They were driven by a craving for exploration and discovery. They exploited the land's abundant natural resources to pay their way. Many were lured by the siren-call of gold.

These same motivations still drive some men today. Modern-day prospectors, lured by gold and adventure, are still in evidence throughout the Southwest.

Though the Apache preceded the mountain men by several centuries, their coexistence with other Native Americans was a tenuous and generally unfriendly one. Apaches were tolerated only because of their military might and prowess. The very word Apache meant "thief" or "enemy" to neighboring tribes.

Apaches maintained a unique culture. Braves were considered vastly superior to squaws. Non-Apaches were regarded as less than human. Stealing from other Indian tribes, or Mexicans who had begun to settle in the region, was the most honorable means of making a living. It was also an important way for an Apache brave to gain status within his tribe.

Fighting was honorable as an often necessary part of stealing raids. Hunting, too, was esteemed for young braves because it taught patience, stalking, stamina . . . and killing, skills that would be useful in later life.

Apaches knew the lands they roamed carried gold, but considered it useless except as ornamentation enjoyed by squaws. They gave it the derogatory name "squaws metal."

Apache peoples knew several places where gold was plentiful in what is now Arizona. The first of these, known to modern day prospectors as the Lost Adams Diggin's, is the primary focus of this novel. It is near the Arizona/New Mexico border in central eastern Arizona. Two other lost mine legends enter this story. The Lost Sanders Mine is located one hundred five miles west-northwest of Clifton, near the Sierra Ancha Mountains. The famous Lost Dutchman Mine is one hundred twenty-five miles west of Clifton near Phoenix, in the Superstition Mountain region.

There is no physical connection between the three mines that make up this golden triangle. Each is a mystery in its own right. But the solution to the mystery of The Lost Adams Diggin's is bound up in the legends of all three . . . .

PROLOGUE
AN INNOCENT BEGINNING, 1814

Two young Apache braves entered the narrow canyon. They walked a short distance following its zigzags through solid rock walls that in places had been undercut by rushing floodwaters in times past. The overhanging rock walls forever shadowed the canyon floor from the sun's warming rays.

Soon they rounded a final bend and came upon a high cliff. A crystal torrent rushed over its looming height. The water fanned out before crashing into the shallow pool and created a heavy mist. Sunlight danced on the sparkling water and, where the mist rose, a wide rainbow cast a colorful arc across the canyon walls and falling water, its beauty reflected in the pool below.

The pool held more than this passing reflection. Glints of turquoise, azurite, and gold danced on the rippling water and dazzled the two braves' eyes.

The braves plunging into the icy water and gathered handfuls of colorful stones and pieces of gold. The larger of the two Indians walked through the icy falling water into a small cleft behind the waterfall. A moment later he emerged, holding a fist-sized crystal of almost perfect transparency. Only a slight smokey hue dimmed its brilliance.

The youth raised the crystal above his head in silent meditation for several minutes.

"*The Great Spirit has brought me to my vision crystal,*" he proclaimed.

CHAPTER 1
NIGHTMARES AND VISIONS, 1837

"**S**o much blood!" The big man shuddered as he woke from a fitful sleep. He trembled as the memory of his dream filled him with terror. Nothing he had experienced compared with the emotions this dream raised.

At six-foot six-inches and nearly three hundred pounds, Mangas Coloradas was a giant among his people, revered for his strength and cunning. He could not understand why his sleep was so tormented.

Mangas slept in physical comfort, his large head resting upon a small, hard pillow made of deerhide stuffed with horsehair, his enormous frame stretched out beneath heavy sleeping furs sewn from elkhide by Placid, his wife of only a few months. She had cost him five good horses in dowry — an unusually large compensation — and her name was ill-fitting. On their wedding night, after vigorous lovemaking, Mangas gave her the more suitable name, Dancing Horse.

Mangas' lodge was large and comfortable. His tepee was almost ten feet tall, larger than those of most warriors and almost as large as the ceremonial lodges. Elk and dear hides sewn together into beautiful patterns were draped over twelve slender and straight pine poles, each nearly twelve feet long. The large ends of the poles formed a rough fifteen foot circle. The small ends of the poles were lashed with the same kind of sinew used to make strings for powerful Apache bows. Bows used for hunting and for war. Bows with which he and all Apache braves practiced deadly skills.

Warriors of his tribe said Mangas was blessed by the spirits. This was significant in an Indian's life. It meant Mangas had an edge more valuable than any advantage in physical prowess, though that, too, he had.

Mangas knew that when the Great Spirit sent dreams and visions they were of great importance. What was the meaning of his dream? Wishing only to sleep, Mangas closed his eyes and drifted into unconsciousness . . . . The dream returned.

Juan José, spiritual leader and chief of all Mimbres Apaches, lay motionless on the ground. Looking down on him, Mangas saw blood pouring from his chief's mouth, much more blood than any living body could possibly hold. Near his beloved chief, Mangas saw the hazy outlines of other Mimbres. He could not identify individuals but he knew these were his people: his family, his friends and his loved ones. They lay, dead or sleeping he did not know, directly in the path of this gruesome flow.

A piercing dread filled Mangas' heart at the sight of his people lying so still in the path of what he sensed was approaching danger. "I must do something," he thought. Utter catastrophe would befall his brethren should that frightful blood-river reach them. Yet Mangas could not understand why this torrent of blood, issuing like a proclamation from Juan José's mouth, should threaten these people whom the great chief loved.

Mangas felt urged to scream a warning to awaken the slumbering multitude, but as he opened his mouth, a sudden and deafening thunder drowned out his voice. This was a strange, unnatural thunder, as if the Storm Spirit spoke in many voices at once. Then, rising above the thunder-voices like the wind rises above the rain, came the sound of hideous laughter. Shrill and horrible resounding with cruel pleasure, it seemed to mock the fate of Mangas' people, a people whose chief's life-blood soaked the dusty soil where he lay.

Again, Mangas awoke in terror, gasping for breath, his body covered in icy sweat. Within his great chest his heart hammered more furiously than the time he had run a deer to death. His stomach roiled in distress. This dream had been sent by spirits. In Mangas' mind there was no doubt of this fact, for he was a medicine man.

Mangas sat up and beat his clenched fists against his thighs.

"No! I am a warrior, the son of a warrior," he said stoically under his breath. "I will not let a dream reduce me to quivering like a squaw!"

Resolutely, repeatedly, he forced the unwanted images from his mind.

"O Great Spirit," Mangas prayed. "Why have you sent such a dream to trouble my sleep?"

Only empty silence answered him. Then, from a distance, came the unmistakable cry of an eagle, a cry Mangas had never before heard in the stillness of night. This piercing cry only added to the mystery. Mangas frowned into the darkness and brushed sweat from his forehead and lip. He sought answers. He found none.

Wishing only to erase the dreaded image of his dream, Mangas reached for Dancing Horse. Mangas needed his woman. He would use her to try to forget.

Dancing Horse, her mind muddled by sleep, was alarmed by Mangas' rough urgency. Nevertheless she responded obediently to his need. Her graceful, supple body possessed surprising strength. This night she thanked the spirits for that.

While a lesser woman might have cried out Dancing Horse was a daughter of a warrior race and her strength ran deep. She bore his onslaughts soundlessly, as was expected of a proud daughter of a proud race. She would give him no cause to believe her weak. No warrior wanted a weak woman to bear his sons. She must never voice complaint nor whimper in pain. Yet, as Mangas took her, the brutal force in his body frightened her.

After he finished, Dancing Horse lay silently wondering what strange, dark spirit had possessed him to use her so. She would never ask, and he would not tell her. She was his woman. She belonged to him. But he did not belong to her. He need not explain himself. Her duty was to satisfy his needs and see to his comfort, as he required. It was his prerogative to treat her as he wished. Thus it had always been, thus it was, thus it would always be, or so she believed.

If she ceased to please him with her body or actions, he had the right to cast her out of his lodge, and take another wife and there was jealousy in the camp for she felt the envy of many squaws.

But she did not realize her security. Many warriors would be happy to have her, and Mangas knew this. She was strong, skillful, graceful, and a great beauty. Her pleasant and accommodating nature further enhanced her desirability. If Mangas no longer wanted her, others would fight for the privilege. This was certain.

Yet, momentarily she pondered the possibility of losing her support. With no grown son and without a husband, an abandoned squaw would starve, it was the way of her people. These thoughts ebbed in her mind as she fell into an exhausted sleep.

Physical needs satisfied, Mangas gazed appreciatively at Dancing Horse as she slept. His eyes followed the soft, even rise and fall of her breasts and swept to the perfect curvature of her upturned hip. He felt the satisfaction of a man who had chosen well.

"A fine woman for an Apache warrior," he marveled. He hoped she would become pregnant soon. Strong sons would strengthen the Mimbres and enhance his position in the tribe.

Interrupting these musings, vivid images of his night terror welled up, unbidden. So much blood! And that cruel laughter! Who was laughing? Who could laugh in the midst of such a gruesome spectacle?

"I must know!" He hissed between clenched teeth, his anger roused by lack of understanding. Kicking aside his warm coverings Mangas arose in the predawn chill. He wrapped a heavy fur around his shivering naked body. After standing motionless for several minutes he reached abruptly toward a pouch of curious design, which hung on the tepee pole slanting over his bed. Mangas removed the pouch and faced the glowing embers on the central hearthstones.

The pouch was cut of the softest, finest doeskin and differed little from other drawstring pouches Mimbres often carried, save that it was larger than most. The lumpy object it contained gave it an angular contour.

What made this bag unique were myriad designs incised, painted, and sewn upon the soft pale leather. The painstaking detail of these patterns suggested many hours of exacting labor. Most were common objects such as birds and animals, a few were fanciful, their meanings known only to their creator. This mystically ornamented pouch was not just any medicine bag, this medicine bag belonged to Mangas Coloradas, a man of destiny.

Muttering prayers and incantations, the big warrior pleaded for help from his spirit guide. Fervently, Mangas asked to be shown meaning behind his troubling dream, to know what the Great Spirit wanted of him.

Mangas reached into the drawstring pouch and withdrew his vision crystal, an angular piece of quartz almost the size of his fist. To others, this stone appeared to be nothing more than a pretty crystal — interesting yet unremarkable. But to Mangas, this was a talisman and glowed with a life of its own. He was sensitive to its secrets. It caught his eye and held it, revealing worlds within and worlds beyond.

Mangas concentrated, taking deep, even breaths as he sought the center of his spirit, that place of consummate serenity, the source of his deepest understanding.

His pulse and respiration slowed and his blood pressure dropped dramatically. He sank into a trance. To an observer he would have appeared lifeless, sitting before the embers of his hearth fire cross-legged in the cool stillness of night.

Indeed, the giant Apache was no longer truly to be counted among the conscious. Mangas' soul and awareness drew away from his body — to search the spirit-world for answers . . . .

Gazing into the clouded, crystalline depths Mangas saw the passage of time and how that would change his life. He saw his destiny: He would be chieftain of the mighty Mimbres Apaches, the most powerful Indian tribe in what his Mexican neighbors called Apacheria — a wild land extending many days journey to the south, west, and north.

In his vision, Mangas Coloradas — whose name was Spanish for *Red Sleeves* — saw the blood of many white men on his hands, just as had been foretold by the Spanish priest when Mangas was an unnamed child. Many things were revealed that night. But it was as if the bloody vision had no purpose.

On that subject the crystal was cold and silent.

Finally, blue light, a powerful harbinger of doom, flooded this empty silence, surrounding Mangas, engulfing his very being. Sensing that this sign somehow concerned his tribe's immediate fate, Mangas prayed for understanding that he might somehow prevent the catastrophe he feared it forebode. But concentrate as he might, he could

draw nothing more from his crystal. The spirits remained silent . . . .
Neither his fellow Mimbres nor even the very spirits, it seemed,
ignored Mangas questions so this silence was all the more disquieting.
Exhausted with the effort of meditation, he finally submitted to not
being given understanding.

As his mind began rising toward conscious awareness, a new
vision erupted, startling him.

*Mangas stared into the face of a white man, not a Mexican or a
Spaniard but an Anglo, a face that glowed in a golden-orange light. The red-
bearded visage solemnly stared back at Mangas. The Anglo's reflected
scrutiny made Mangas uncomfortable. Never had anyone invaded Mangas'
visions in this manner, staring eye-to-eye with him.*
"Who are you?" Mangas demanded. "What do you want?"
*There was no response. The vision began to fade, leaving Mangas filled
with an inexplicable sense of loss. Mangas called out, "Wait! What is it that
you seek? What do you see?" There was no answer. Mangas wondered if
perhaps the red-bearded man knew the portent of his own terrible dream.*

As the first gray tendrils of dawn's light crept across the eastern
sky, Dancing Horse awoke — cold! Mangas was gone from his place
beside her. This was not unusual; he often arose in the night when he
was troubled or when he was called by the spirits to seek knowledge
in the stars or in his vision-crystal.

Feeling the morning chill, she quickly stirred herself, intending
to build up the fire and brew him some hot, restorative tea. Still
drowsy, she stumbled against his near-lifeless body, lying crumpled
beside the ashes on the hearthstone. She blinked the morning blur
from her eyes and studied him. He did not look well. He breathed
raggedly and his lips were blue with cold.

She hurried to cover him with their sleeping furs then blew upon
the remaining embers. Feeding in bits of tinder, then larger pieces of
wood, she brought the fire to life.

Over this small blaze she boiled water, then measured sage and
mistletoe from her store of medicinal substances. She added these to

boiling water and set the mixture aside to steep.

Casting a cautious eye on her husband who lay unmoving by the fire, she placed a bowl of the strong, hot tea beside him. She hurried outside to relieve herself, gather firewood, and refill the water bag. When she returned, Mangas sat hunched by the fire, sipping his hot drink. She saw a haunted look in his eyes as he stared, unspeaking, into the dwindling flames.

Dancing Horse said nothing and averted her gaze. Making as little fuss as possible, she stoked the fire to further warm the tepee, prepared his breakfast and handed it to him. As he ate mechanically, seeming scarcely to taste his food, Dancing Horse busied herself tidying their tepee, avoiding any task that might cause undue noise.

When he had eaten, Mangas rose, dressed, and silently walked outside. Dancing Horse breathed a sigh of relief. Much as she loved and admired this giant warrior, she feared his uncertain temper, especially on mornings following his spirit journeys.

She reminded herself that silence was a small price to pay for status. "No other Apache woman is as fortunate as I!" she told herself with a sudden, bright smile. Reminded of the night's activities by a throbbing in her groin, she thought, "Or as satisfied, either."

She hummed cheerfully, going about her daily tasks with a lightness of spirit, no longer mindful of the noise she made. Dancing Horse had always wanted to belong to a man of consequence. The towering warrior who now walked through camp with a troubled brow was surely such a man.

CHAPTER 2
NIGHTMARE REALIZED

The Englishman spat into the fire, chuckled softly, and took another long pull at his bottle. "James Johnson," he addressed himself aloud in the morning stillness, "you was born with a nose for profit. Just plumb lucky you are." Again, he chuckled and told himself, "'Specially since you ain't particular how your profit's made!"

Johnson's scarred, peeling scalp and blond, thinning hair — where he had scalp for hair to grow — and a patchy beard framed his perpetually sunburned face. Peeling skin flecked from his beak-like nose, accentuating an aura of disease.

He rubbed his watery blue eyes, then massaged the scarred skull above his left ear, where scalp should have been.

At age thirteen, James Johnson had been with a wagon train moving through Missouri. Late one afternoon, while the others were busy making camp, he and three young friends had gone exploring.

The full moon was high when the youngsters returned from their explorations to find the camp under attack. No one had expected Indian trouble at night. They had been told Indians attacked only during the day. Trouble was, those particular Comanches hadn't heard of that "fact."

By the light of the moon twenty or more braves rode, full gallop, into the midst of the unprepared camp. Within minutes they had killed most of the invaders and were busy torching everything that would burn.

Johnson and his friends briefly watched what was happening from a low hill, then ran, terrified and grieving, into the night. They found a craggy, dry wash where they hid, huddled together, shivering through the wee hours and into the cold morning, wondering about their future.

As the new day broke, Johnson and his frightened companions were startled awake from the exhausted sleep that had finally claimed them. On the banks of the crooked wash and encircling them stood blood-stained, war-painted and obviously drunken warriors. There was no escape. Only the braves' drunken state saved Johnson's life and half his scalp.

Johnson watched the Comanches slowly mutilate and then scalp his companions. The horror was too much. His mind and body went numb. Then it was his turn. The most bloodied Indian lifted him by his long hair, and the razor-sharp flint knife scraped his scull. The shock was intense. The pain was beyond words. He opened his mouth to scream but passed out without uttering a sound. Late that afternoon he regained consciousness and was shocked to alertness by intense pain. The warriors were gone but that memory never faded from his tortured mind.

Johnson didn't know, and wouldn't have cared, that scalping was a practice started by the French, who paid for Indian scalps in the Canadian Territories. All Johnson knew was that he had been scalped by an Indian. Through the years, his hatred grew into a blinding obsession. Indians were not humans. They were a scourge on the land, nothing more. He felt outrage that such savages dared to oppose the white men moving into the vast western lands.

This night, sitting beside his campfire in the hills near Santa Rita, New Mexico, Territory of Mexico, looking to the east under the rising full moon, Johnson remembered that night. "...Missouri," he mumbled, "... I ain't never going back there."

He felt safer in this wild country with the border of Sonora, Mexico only one hundred miles to the south, and the land known by the local Mexicans as Arizona or Apacheria even closer to the west.

He spat into the fire again and watched his spittle sizzle on a burning log. Then he chuckled and spoke aloud, "Damn Injuns! Never thought I'd see the day I'd get paid for revenge. By this time tomorrow there'll be a lot less of them red devils! And I won't leave the job half done, neither!"

He was delighted with his own cleverness. A few days earlier, smelling an easy — and personally pleasurable — way to make money, Johnson had devised a plan that would be easy to carry out and had little chance to backfire.

He came up with the idea on the morning he stopped in at the Santa Rita trading post with a load of beaver furs, hoping to make a good trade for whiskey and provisions. There he overheard the Mexican government's Indian agent, *Don* Santiago, telling about the new bounty Mexico's government was offering for Apache scalps. He never dreamed revenge would be pleasurable and profitable. A cruel grin flashed across Johnson's face.

Far to the south, in Mexico, both hostile Indians and outlaws taxed the Government's power to maintain peace. Authorities had issued a bounty on scalps from unfriendly Indians. Of course, once the scalps were lifted — who was to say whether they came from friendly Indians or warring tribes?

A bounty hunter could collect one hundred pesos for a brave's scalp, fifty pesos for a squaw's and twenty-five pesos for the scalp of an Indian child. One peso was a good day's wage. These bounties represented a small fortune.

The Indian agent, *Don* Santiago, had no quarrel with his Apache neighbors. In fact, the former Spaniard had developed warm friendships with several Mimbres braves. He was concerned because Mexico's government was encouraging eradication of Apaches; he was more concerned because he realized the government might intercede, sending troops to do the job.

"My fears lie not with our Apache neighbors. I have developed friendships with several Mimbres," Santiago explained to those who were gathered in his store. "It is the Federales I fear. When I was a young boy we lived in a mining town near Durango. Outlaws and Indians terrorized the roads that led to our town of Rosalita. The outlaws hijacked the ore shipments and the Indians preyed on the supply wagons," Santiago continued. "The *Dons* of our town sent a message to the government for help and, 'help' came. The ore shipments were no longer hijacked, and our supply wagons made it through the mountains to our town . . . but the Federales wreaked havoc in Rosalita. They raped our women, stole the supplies that came to town, ate our food, and took over our homes. When there was nothing left for them to take, they moved on."

Johnson saw that Santiago was unwilling to turn against his

Apache neighbors. Still, the Indian agent had provided Johnson with just the argument he needed to recruit other, less tolerant towns-people, for the plan he was beginning to develop.

"Santiago, what makes you think the same thing won't happen here, in your beautiful Santa Rita?" Johnson challenged. He turned to the others. "You know good and well that if you folks don't get rid of them heathen Indians yourselves, sooner or later the Federales will. You just heard *Don* Santiago telling what they'll do to your town and to all your pretty young señoritas when they do."

Santiago paled. Until then he hadn't really believed the Federales would come to the peaceful mining town of Santa Rita. He hadn't even wanted to consider it. He now realized it was a very real possibility. His unguarded rambling had the townspeople gathered in his store grumbling among themselves, prodded on by the outsider, Johnson.

The day after the exchange at the trading post, Johnson called a town meeting. With gossip racing through town about what the two men had said, worried people came to hear more. Johnson plied them with cheap whiskey as they gathered in the town plaza. "Drink up, men. There's plenty more where that came from," he announced.

Johnson bragged that he intended to take advantage of the Mexican government's bounty, with a plan in which they could all make some money. He suggested the people of Santa Rita should have a feast for the neighboring Apaches, "Right here, in the town plaza." Once the Indians were gathered in the enclosure the Mexicans would surround them, massacre them and collect scalps.

In 1835, *Don* Miguel Peralta, a well-educated Spaniard, traveled north from Sonora, Mexico. He brought a group of Mexican peons, all expert miners, to work the expanding copper mines of Santa Rita. His wife and daughter made the arduous journey at his side.

Experienced miners were hard to come by. The mine owners were anxious to have men who knew the various jobs and were impressed by Peralta's letter of commendation from the King of Spain. Although Mexico had recently fought for and won independence from Spain, the mine owners had given great consideration to such a credential.

"This document says you are a man of honor," the miners' spokesman said. "You and your family are welcome here." Within minutes Peralta and the miners had worked out a mutually profitable contract.

Supervising his men in the mines, Peralta kept his family well fed. Over the years he had saved a sizable amount of money. He fathered a second daughter and, with his wife again pregnant, hoped for a son to carry on his family name.

Don Miguel Peralta now stood among those listening to Johnson in the town plaza. Finally he had heard enough. "Why should we allow this Anglo outsider to come into our town and declare war on our peaceful neighbors?" he protested bitterly. "I will have no part in this evil deed! During the two years I have lived in Santa Rita the Apaches have kept peace and have been good neighbors. They are not like the savages of Sonora, who constantly terrorize our brothers there. It would be sin to do violence to those who have done no wrong, and doubly sinful to betray our Apache friends as proposed by this scarred Anglo."

His words echoed the emotions and calm reasoning of many townspeople. In the end, though, calm reason lost out to the promise of easy money. Inescapably, fear and blind hatred of Indians — which now consumed many of Peralta's neighbors — won out.

"Have a good look at what those 'peaceful' vermin will do," Johnson exploded. He bent forward, removed his cap, and gestured at his half-skinned skull. "Them what did this to me were 'peaceful' Indians. Folks had told my people, 'they'd never hurt a hair on your head'."

The unintended irony of his words brought forth a nervous murmur of laughter. Puzzled for a moment, he finally caught on to what he had said then he laughed too, for the first time finding humor in his partial scalping.

"Why, if that Mexican trader returning to Santa Fe hadn't come along I'd have been dead just like all my kinfolk."

The crowd went silent for a moment, pondering the massacre he had described and the one he proposed.

"Anyway," Johnson continued, "the Mexican government says them heathens has got to go and they'll pay us good money to do the job for 'em. They know them heathens ain't no good. They spoil your land. They don't know how to farm it like you good Christian folks do. They're unholy and don't deserve to have what God put here. If we don't do the job Mexico will send Federales to do it. Them Federales will kill them heathens right nice. Only we won't get nothing for it! Instead of bounty, you fine folks will be forced to house and feed a bunch of lousy soldiers until there's nothing left in this town for them to take! Ask *Don* Santiago what happens when the Federales come to town!"

Johnson's accented and illiterate English was hard for the interpreter to follow, but his message was persuasive. Listeners knew there was a measure of truth in what he had said. What if the Mexican government did send Federales to 'suppress' the Indians? Santiago was not the only one at this meeting who had seen what could happen when Federales came. Feeding and housing unwanted soldiers had brought bankruptcy, hunger, and shame to more than one town in Mexico. No one wanted this to happen in Santa Rita.

During the discussion that followed Santiago brooded in silence. He was sure disaster was going to befall his Apache friends unless he did something to stop Johnson and the others.

Finally, after much bickering and discussion, Peralta and the other dissenters were silenced. The townspeople arrived at a black decision. They would invite the nearby Mimbres tribe to a great feast of friendship in the town plaza. The invitation would be extended by Santiago, the Mimbres trusted friend. Apaches were certain to attend in great numbers. Johnson proposed a scheme to poison the food. Once the Apaches were dead or dying the scalping would be easy.

Santiago listened in dismay. He began to devise his own plan to provide the poison and to agree to take the invitation to his friends. These acts would keep the conspirators from suspecting him when things went wrong, as they were certain to if his plan worked . . . .

After the meeting broke up, the conspirators set about making plans for the feast.

The next day, Santiago gave Johnson a small vial of poison,

which the Anglo would add to the food just before it was served. But after thinking about it, Johnson decided poisoning might be too dangerous. There was too much chance some Apaches would survive, or worse, retaliate before the drug did its job. "Besides," he mused, "shootin's more fun."

Later that day Johnson and several outspoken Indian-haters conspired on their own plan. That evening he related these new plans to Santiago.

This scheme was a little more complicated and a lot more colorful. Instead of poisoning their guests, they would urge the Indians to eat wholesome food and to drink good wine and cheap whiskey with abandon. Then, when the guests had gorged themselves and were suitably drunk, Johnson and his allies would besiege them with cannon-shots and rifle-fire. It would be a massacre.

Santiago's hopes to thwart Johnson's scheme were ruined. What the Indian agent had given Johnson was not poison, but syrup of ipecac. It would have made the Apaches nauseous, then violently sick to their stomachs. They would have left town disgusted and angry. Santiago had hoped that over time the hard feelings would fade. He would place the blame on Johnson, telling the Indians Johnson poisoned the food and telling Johnson the poison had gone bad. Meanwhile the massive violence against the Apaches would have been averted.

Santiago knew Johnson's new plans ended any hope of avoiding the massacre, but he said nothing. Realizing how vicious Johnson was, Santiago never told anyone about his deceit, he hoped it would never be discovered.

Already Johnson could taste revenge. He planned nights of debauchery — whiskey and loose women in abundance — with the money Indian scalps would bring. These thoughts, and anticipation of the impending slaughter sent him into a fit of shrill, mocking laughter.

"Yup." He grunted happily, taking another drink, and then corking his bottle, "Tomorrow won't be a bad day at all . . . 'cept for them damned heathens!"

Still chuckling, he arose and headed off toward bed. Tonight he would sleep soundly, dreaming of pleasures he would purchase with his share of the profits.

October 17th, 1837 dawned clear and bright. As those privileged to attend the friendship feast at Santa Rita del Cobre prepared to depart, the Mimbres' camp bustled with activity. Mimbres from outlying camps arrived at Chief Juan José's camp in scattered groups. The mighty Apache would present themselves at the white man's feast strong in number.

Times were good for the Mimbres. They had no fear of neighboring tribes or the ever-encroaching Mexicans. Other tribes dared not challenge the Mimbres under chief Juan José, whose tribe was large and whose braves were skilled warriors. The settlers had kept their peace also, a peace they promised to maintain and were about to celebrate.

Game was abundant. Trading with the Mexican settlers brought steel knives, horses, wool, and other useful goods to the Mimbres. These things made life easier for the Indians, and they grew rich.

These new invaders brought with them something else, too. Change. Inexorably, it would eventually bring to an end the Mimbres' way of life. But that was all in the future . . . .

On this morning, Mimbres men, women, and children donned their finery — patterned and died hides decorated with intricate woven designs of fine cloth, laced with feathers and turquoise — and draped themselves with ornaments. Women strove to control their hungry, impatient children. The children had gone without breakfast, their frugal mothers unwilling to deplete uncertain food supplies before a promised feast.

Chief Juan José, like most of the braves, was dressed in his finest. Pale elkhide draped his shoulders and thighs. Brightly dyed plant fibers accented the long braid that hung down his back. Fringed leather and beautiful red and green polished stones adorned the edges of his garments. Though simple, his attire was stunning, starkly in contrast to the beaded and bejeweled trappings of the women.

Contrary to the men's statement of simple elegance, the women — to the white man's eye — were overdressed to the point of absurdity.

Layer after layer of fancy skins covered them until they all looked very much alike. Most white men wouldn't be impressed but Juan José looked with pride upon the Mimbres women. A squaw's abundance of clothes reflected the success of the man she belonged to and was, therefore, a status symbol. His people were rich.

The great chief looked out upon his people and felt his heart swell with pride. Surely the Mexicans could not fail to be impressed by their handsomeness and magnificent dress. Indeed, the people of Santa Rita should be honored that he, Juan José, respected and beloved chieftain of the Mimbres Apaches, had accepted their invitation to this feast of friendship.

Mangas Coloradas was like a dark cloud on this otherwise bright and cheerful morning.

"Mangas and that habitual frown he has been wearing lately are becoming tiresome," thought Juan José. He walked over to his young friend and asked, "Have you changed your mind about letting Dancing Horse attend the feast?"

"No, she will remain here with the others who will watch the camp." Mangas replied. "A great heaviness hangs upon my spirit. I feel a strong apprehension. Do you think it is wise to bring so many of our people into Santa Rita, my chief?"

Chief Juan José stared into the much taller man's face. For a moment the tendons in the chief's neck stood out in sudden anger, Mangas expected to be chastised for his criticism. Then his life-long counselor and friend spoke in a quiet voice.

"Have you knowledge that we should not attend this feast?" Juan José asked.

Mangas shook his head and was silent.

"Then relax, my friend," Juan José said. "The Great Spirit guides our people. We should not fear the Mexicans just because we do not understand their way of life. Let us have no discord on this fine day! So long as you choose to live in my village I ask you to support and advise me. That is the calling of a medicine man. Unless you have knowledge that we should not attend this feast let us enjoy this great occasion."

Understanding that Juan José had chastised him, if ever so gently, for questioning a chief's wisdom Mangas responded, "I meant no offense. All know Chief Juan José is the wisest of men, who loves and protects his tribe as a father does his children. There is not one here who would not lay down his life for you."

"I know this to be true," said the older man. "Now, join us as we go to Santa Rita and enjoy the festival!" Chief Juan José continued, "Our good friend, *Don* Santiago has introduced me to an Anglo called James Johnson. Johnson is in charge of a group of men who trap beaver and look for squaws metal. As a gesture of good faith and continuing peaceful coexistence I have promised to give Johnson and his men protection and sanctuary while they are on our lands. If Johnson is at this feast, I will introduce you to him. He is easy to recognize. Comanche braves took half his scalp."

At last, the group of Mimbres Apache departed for Santa Rita del Cobre, with Mangas Coloradas walking straight and tall beside Juan José. Mangas was haunted by nagging doubts about the sincerity of the gesture of friendship. Yet he was careful not to frown.

From his vantage point atop the wall at the west side of the plaza, Johnson watched greedily as the Indians approached. He counted as they came through the portal at the east end of the plaza, but he counted pesos, not people. Pesos, dollars, it made no difference to him. Money was money. It was made to spend. "Hundred, two hundred, two hundred fifty, two hundred seventy-five . . . ." With pleasure he tallied scalps, "Near four hundred of them red bastards. Near twenty thousand dollars!"

Licking his lips, Johnson checked his weapons and ammunition supply for the umpteenth time. Others hidden around the plaza were nervously doing the same thing. Still others lounged around at assigned positions, pretending nonchalance, casting an occasional surreptitious glance at the approaching Indians.

In the town square, tables that had been set up the night before now sagged under enormous piles of food and drink. Kegs of strong wine and cheap whiskey were on every table, but other beverages were in short supply.

Santiago, Peralta, and many other townspeople were in the church with the Padre, praying for a miracle and forgiveness.

The designated hosts greeted Chief Juan José and his people cordially. The chief's eyes swept the crowd in the plaza, looking for the face of his friend, *Don* Santiago, but Santiago wasn't there and soon Juan José was distracted by the festivities. He took a seat and joined the hungry children, eagerly attacking the food.

The Mimbres were easily lulled into a sense of security by the jovial welcoming committee who served generous portions of food and promptly refilled empty glasses with whiskey. Feasting was an Apache custom and one they relished. Juan José's people happily abandoned themselves.

After more than an hour, all but Mangas had eaten as much as they could. Most were well on their way toward drunkenness. Their bellies full to the bursting point, children curled up and slept near their sated mothers. Braves who had not already succumbed to drunkenness happily continued to consume the whiskey so generously provided.

Still uneasy, Mangas had eaten lightly and had not touched the whiskey. With a mounting thirst and only the noxious whiskey offered, he rose and wandered unnoticed down a side street in search of water. As he crouched to drink at a horse trough, he heard a deafening roar. The conspirators had opened fire on his people.

In the enclosed space of the town plaza there was no escape. Sudden death hailed down upon the unsuspecting Mimbres from the rooftops and from the top of the plaza wall. The assailants fired rifles, pistols, even howitzers loaded with marble-size iron balls, into the crowded plaza.

Mangas froze. The thunder-voices! At last, and too soon, he knew the meaning of his dream. Seized by the same overpowering dread he felt in his nightmare, he ran toward the town square. By now the gunfire had ceased, giving way to groans of the dying.

As he gazed with horror at the carnage before him, a burning anger welled from deep within his soul. He was armed only with hands and teeth; still, his first, hot, instinct was to kill. But cold reason checked this impulse. If he tried to seek vengeance now he would only die the same senseless death as those who lay slaughtered in the plaza. No. He would wait. He must be certain the deaths of Juan José and his people were avenged.

He feared no pursuit from the butchers, who were busy scalping the dead and dying. As he turned to flee, not from the living but from the dead, he heard the sound of a fierce, maniacal laughter, the echo of a sound he had heard before. Dream, nightmare, reality — all were the same now.

Mangas turned his sharp gaze toward the source of this hair-raising cackle. Laughing wildly, a scarred man moved deliberately from one body to the next, harvesting scalps as he sliced and spat. From where Mangas stood in the shadows of the plaza wall, he had a clear view of the man's hideous sunburned face.

Mangas turned again and ran, grimly retracing the path he and many who now lay dead had taken that morning. He held his fast pace as the trail climbed into the high mountains toward the Mimbres camp.

Running had always brought Mangas a feeling of peaceful bliss. Not this time. His thoughts alternated between disbelief, rage and grief; finally his mind went numb. But there was no peace in the numbness, nothing would bring him peace this day.

As the town disappeared behind him, he began plotting revenge, vowing that Mexicans would regret this treachery for many generations to come. And he swore a second, equally solemn vow: "There awaits a slow tortured death for the scarred Anglo, James Johnson."

CHAPTER 3
SOLEMN HOMECOMING

Mangas returned to a peaceful camp. Those Mimbres who had not attended the feast were going about the daily tasks of caring for horses, gathering firewood, and filling water bags. Mangas' personal anguish faded, as sympathy for his kinsmen swelled, realizing the grief his news would bring. As he stood watching the others, considering the words he must choose to tell what had happened, Juan José's young sons rode into camp, returning from an elk hunt.

The younger brother led a horse pulling a travois that sagged under the weight of a large and beautiful bull elk, thoughts of the feast such a kill would bring flitted through Mangas' mind . . . . Juan José's sons were eager to show their father their kill. Several young boys gathered around them and the two unsuspecting hunters were soon giving an animated account of the kill, bragging about their obvious success.

Mangas recalled many similar scenes, one of his own youth. He envisioned the celebration that always followed the successful hunt, the quiet solitude of the hunt, the moment of the kill. An image forever spoiled.

His spirit failed as he anticipated what his solemn news would mean to Juan José's sons and to the others in camp. Just then, he spotted Nana, his trusted friend and longtime companion. Until this day Mangas would never have admitted needing help for anything. He now welcomed the help of this great and respected warrior.

Nana hailed him from a distance, "Hello, my friend! Back so soon from the feast! Was the food and whiskey not to your liking?"

"Gather our people," Mangas ordered in a cracked voice. "I must speak to everyone. Now!"

Why has it fallen on me to tell of this treachery, Mangas thought.

Noting his friend's anguished expression, Nana hurried to do Mangas' bidding. Within minutes, those in camp had gathered. The respected warrior's unexpected early return and Nana's somber call to assembly had them nervously murmuring amongst themselves as they assembled.

"Hear me, my people," Mangas cried. "Hear the terrible thing I have to tell. I cannot ease the pain it will bring you."

The crowd hushed. This strong, robust, quiet man was now pale and shaking. They waited in silence while he groped for the strength to complete the unwanted task.

Mangas drew a deep, ragged breath and continued in a weak, ragged voice.

"Oh my people, listen now to a tale of treachery, Mexican treachery . . . ."

He told of the feast and paused, then forged on, telling of the slaughter and scalpings that had followed. He spared no detail, needing to purge himself of what he had seen and believing also that his people had the right to know exactly what had happened and who was responsible. He mentioned Santiago's absence and he wondered aloud if the Indian agent had known what was going to happen. Mangas hoped he might never again be required to recall the day's events.

In an uncharacteristic gesture, Dancing Horse came to Mangas' side and took his arm to support him against the anger that shook him until he could hardly stand. Equally uncharacteristic, he allowed her to do so.

Dancing Horse, who had secretly resented Mangas refusal to allow her to attend the feast, now realized his refusal had saved her life. Never again would she doubt his wisdom . . . These seemed selfish thoughts in the face of all who were lost; still, she was grateful.

Exactly twenty of the Mimbres from Juan José's camp survived. Neighboring camps had been a little luckier, but few could say they hadn't lost a family member to the conspiracy at Santa Rita.

Amid wails of grief from the survivors Mangas spoke again. This time his anger rose above his pain and he spoke in a loud, clear voice.

"Sons of warriors, listen to me! We will not permit this slaughter to go unavenged! I have seen the face of the man responsible for the evil of this day. I have heard his cackle-laugh as he took the scalps of our people. I promise you, I shall not rest until that man's spirit is sent into sure destruction. Only then can our beloved chief and our people rest in peace. Only then can we wash the disgrace of this day from our memories.

"For every Mimbres brave who died this day, we will kill ten Mexicans. For every Mimbres child who died there, ten of their children will die and for every one of our women, ten of theirs. They will regret the day they betrayed our people. The word 'Apache' will strike fear into Mexican hearts for generations to come."

Enraged with grief and horror, the surviving Mimbres roared their approval of Mangas' words. Among the shouting voices Nana's was heard clearly.

"Lead us, Mangas Coloradas! May your name be as a death omen to all Mexicans."

Others took up Nana's cry, until the very air resounded with their chant.

"Lead us, Mangas Coloradas! Death to all Mexicans!"

Mangas raised his arms for silence and finished, his voice heavy with emotion. "I accept the mantle of War Chief," he said. "I promise you, we will never again be betrayed by the white-eyed ones. From now on, we will be hunters, silent and unseen. The Great Spirit will lead us into battle. Our quarry will not know of our approach. Death will rain down on our enemies as lightning from the sky."

Mangas instructed the assembly to go to their tepees and grieve in silence. He knew there was nothing to be done for those fallen. He explained that the tribe would have to let the Great Spirit take care of their bodies as He saw fit, for a traditional funeral was impossible.

Guards were posted and runners hastened toward outlying Mimbres camps to tell what had happened at Santa Rita. Mangas sent orders urging all Mimbres to move quickly to the rugged high mountain canyons, and to prepare for war. Those few left in Juan José's nearly deserted camp would spend that evening grieving quietly. It was the Apache way.

After he finished his onerous task, Mangas turned abruptly and strode toward his tepee. Having preceded him, Dancing Horse was waiting under the sleeping furs. As she had anticipated, he needed to use her body to ease the memory of an event he could not, would not forget, not until revenge had been completed . . . .

Dancing Horse was in turmoil, grateful that because of Mangas her life had been spared, but grief-stricken by what had happened. As he made his advances she could not find the strength to respond to his needs.

For his part, Mangas, too, felt drained and powerless and his body failed him.

As he rolled away Dancing Horse somehow knew it was more important than ever to begin new life, and as soon as possible. Calling on unknown reserves, she gently caressed his rigid body, helping him relax. Soon he responded to her ministrations and overcame his feelings of inadequacy . . . .

Long hours after they finished their lovemaking, exhausted though he was, Mangas remained awake, holding Dancing Horse in his arms, burdened with unwanted thoughts that coiled like serpents within his spirit.

Toward dawn, the sleep he craved finally carried him into blessed oblivion, until he began to dream. Again he saw the red-bearded one standing before him, tears in his eyes, seeming to see into the depths of Mangas' broken heart.

CHAPTER 4
RETRIBUTION

By the third day following the massacre, Mangas had moved all the surviving Mimbres into small encampments scattered across the rugged, high mountains of central New Mexico. Small groups —usually twenty or fewer — found refuge in secluded canyons and near timbered peaks, never camping more than a few days in one place.

This was a practice they were already accustomed to, and they were very good at it. Moving was their ancestral way of life; they had always followed the game and good climate.

Now they had a new calling. While the women tended daily chores in the encampments, warriors hunted: livestock, wild game, and Mexican settlers. It was open season.

Any perceived threat to the security of the camp meant an immediate move to a new location, under cover of night, silent and unseen, traveling well-memorized trails.

Often small raiding parties would camp so close to a settler's home that the warriors could hear the activities of the Mexican's daily life. This amused the warriors. To the Apache this was a game, a game in which the Mexicans were outmatched.

Apache runners brought Mangas news from a vast territory. No movement of Mexican settlers within 100 miles went unnoticed. Even neighboring Chief Victorio and his people joined the effort, if only half-heartedly. Victorio had counseled Juan José against any alliance with the invaders . . . .

Every full moon, Mangas presided over council at a Mimbres encampment, usually his own. Security prevailed and seldom was council held twice in the same location.

It was time for the third council of the first new year after the massacre, Mangas and his trusted friend Nana spent the afternoon together.

Nana was a short, powerful man with a pleasant, round face. His looks were deceiving, for he didn't look like one of the most dangerous of all Apache warriors. In his twelfth year when he and Mangas hunted and killed a bighorn sheep, Nana had proven his prowess.

Mangas was the only Apache who could best him in a wrestling match and Nana's hunting skills were unmatched, even by Mangas. These skills would serve him well in the decades to come, when men, not animals, would be his prey.

Twenty-three years had passed since he and Mangas had gone on their journey to find manhood. Each had left Juan Jose's camp alone, as instructed, and traveled separately. But two days later when Nana came to a hot springs near the banks of the Prieto River, he found Mangas already there. Both knew hot springs held a unique spiritual meaning for their people, and therefore they felt compelled to stay, believing their being together was the Great Spirit's will.

This was unusual, though. Usually young Mimbres braves set out on their journey into manhood alone, and passed or failed the test in solitude. Yet both Mangas and Nana had been drawn to this special place. The Great Spirit must have had a reason. Never questioning the Great Spirit's purpose, the two friends fasted in silence.

During his second night without food, Mangas had two visions. In the first he saw himself and Nana sitting in the hot springs pool under a golden light. This vision assured Mangas he and Nana were meant to be together and that their destinies would be forever intertwined.

In his second vision Mangas saw himself standing with upraised arms, his sleeves drenched in blood. Somehow he knew it was Mexican blood, so he took for his name the Spanish words meaning Red Sleeves — *Mangas Coloradas*. Never again would he answer to his childhood name, Dan-Ha.

Nana had no visions or signs until the following morning. At sunrise he gazed upward and saw a massive bighorn ram on the towering cliffs. The ram seemed to look right at him as it bleated repeatedly, na-na, na-na. He had his new name.

Having received their man-names they were allowed to end their self-imposed fast. Nana made a trap and caught fish from the Prieto River, while Mangas gathered berries for their private feast in the wilderness. After they'd regained their strength, Nana planned a hunt that was destined to forever mark them as great hunters among their people.

Before sunrise the next day, Nana positioned Mangas in a hiding place behind a rock on a narrow trail. This trail traversed a rugged cliff. Just below where Mangas was hiding the trail narrowed where it passed over a high precipice. Just beyond that narrowing Nana hid in the brush growing along the trail, above the cliff.

At dawn Nana watched through the foliage as the big ram came down the path to drink at the river, as he had the day before. When the ram strode past the rocks concealing Mangas, Nana sprang from the brush directly into the ram's path and let out a piercing scream. His plan was to startle the ram, distracting it long enough for Mangas to drive home a long flint-pointed spear.

But the big ram had an instinctive and effective strategy of defense; when confronted, attack. When Nana sprang and screamed, the ram faced him, stood on its hind legs with its front legs slashing. With the full force of its powerful haunches driving it forward and with three hundred pounds of muscle and bone building momentum, the ram charged. Only at the last instant did Nana collect his wits and sidestep the crazed animal. The ram found nothing to impede its progress and had no room to stop before plunging over the cliff.

After three days of feasting on the ram's flesh, the two bundled the head and hide and started home. Mangas carried the massive horns and skull on his broad back, while Nana draped the heavy hide over his shoulders. Both strained under the weight of their trophy.

They were in a hurry to show off their prize at the nearest Mimbres camp, situated at the junction of the Blue and San Francisco rivers thirty miles to the northeast. Heading north from the hot springs up the Prieto, they discovered a shortcut. It was a hidden zigzag canyon leading to the east.

Following this canyon, they came to a beautiful waterfall with gold and colorful gemstones in the pool below. They collected samples. It was here Mangas found a large quartz crystal. His vision crystal.

Their journey was strenuous. On the third day of travel they reached the Mimbres encampment. Taking a bighorn sheep was a great hunting accomplishment. For two such young braves to kill one bare-handed was unheard of. They were given hero's welcomes.

There was a feast and runners carried the news to all nearby Mimbres encampments. Many saw this achievement as a portent of the two braves' future greatness.

In honor of such an impressive first kill, each was given a horse. A week later they rode into Chief Juan José's camp, one hundred miles to the southeast, where they were honored again.

Reliving these memories and retelling their story to other braves and young children had brought great satisfaction to them over the years. But not now. Now their attention was turned to more pressing matters.

When all were assembled, Nana called the council meeting to order. Mangas' eyes held a predatory gleam, like those of a ravenous wolf preparing to kill. "What news is there from our raiding parties?" he demanded.

One by one the leaders gave their reports. "Our raids have been completely successful, Great Chief," stated Cuchillo Negro — whose Spanish name meant Black Knife.

He was an older warrior and a small man, revered for his skills in stalking and ambushing. He had eagerly accepted the charge to organize raiding parties that would gather the supplies Mangas' people needed for waging war. His primary targets were freight wagons on the road to Santa Rita.

"Our warriors have brought back weapons and have captured a considerable quantity of food, blankets, salt, and clothing." The others murmured appreciatively and Cuchillo Negro continued.

"Those foolish men who are supposed to guard the caravans sleep deeply. One would think they were deaf old women, so slowly do they respond to our attacks! Pah!" he spat contemptuously, "Coyotes make short work of their stinking carcasses." Those around him enjoyed his vehemence, chuckling as they contemplated the defilement of the guards' bodies by the coyote, harbinger of bad luck.

After a short pause, Nana spoke. "Juan José's sons and my other scouts report that those who live in Santa Rita are suffering greatly. Our brother is right, they are like old women. They depend on the supplies Cuchillo Negro and our other brave warriors have so easily stolen."

Nana turned to Mangas and continued, "As you have instructed, Great Chief, we have concentrated our efforts against supply trains destined for Santa Rita. The settlers are weak. They will not long survive. Already small groups have left our lands, headed for Santa Fe. Their fields and copper mines stand empty. Soon the only inhabitants of Santa Rita will be the ghosts of our people. Whispers from their spirits will torment any White Eyes foolish enough to remain. Surely they already know the wrath of the Mimbres Nation."

Mangas acknowledged their reports and then issued new instructions. "It is time to move our efforts into a greater area. Cuchillo Negro, you and your warriors will continue to intercept supplies heading to Santa Rita. Nana, move your men into the western regions of our territory, into the White Mountains. Go and observe. Attack only when there is no danger to our people. Report any important changes in the settlers' activities."

Nana nodded his understanding. "We need more guns and we have run out of bullets and powder for those we have. We must learn the Mexican's way of making bullets from leaden objects. Then we can better use his own weapons against him," he said.

This recommendation was met with a murmur of agreement and Mangas was quick to approve his friend's suggestion. Then Mangas raised his hand to signal that the council was over. "We will meet again at the next full moon. Until then, good hunting."

The warriors took a final meal, gathered weapons, and moved off into the wilderness, armed with the desire and skill to carry out their assignments.

This war soon spread until all Apache tribes were resisting the Mexican settlers and the occasional Anglo explorer, the newest invaders on their lands. These hostilities lasted nearly seventy years, with Mexican forces and later the United States Cavalry losing one battle after another.

CHAPTER 5
SANTA RITA, 1838

Late spring found the formerly bustling streets of Santa Rita deserted. Even the cantina was quiet. Supplies were exhausted. People scoured their larders for the last scraps of food. The town's cheerful and congenial atmosphere had been replaced with one of gloom and divisiveness.

Santiago was devastated as he looked at the dying town around him. Using the Indian agent's story of what the Federales had done to his hometown of Rosalita, Johnson had convinced the townspeople they should kill the Mimbres. Santiago had tried to stop it from happening. He had almost succeeded. But in the end, Johnson's hatred and greed had destroyed first the Mimbres and now Santa Rita.

Some of Santiago's friends, among them Chief Juan José, had been butchered like cattle in the town square. He couldn't stand to look at the faces of those who were responsible. His business was ruined and Santa Rita was falling down around him. Not even the Federales could have brought more ruination on this once thriving city.

He had stared helplessly at the bodies, which the others in town referred to as "dead vermin." But the bodies he had helped to bury were mutilated men, women, and children. It was more than the gentle Santiago could live with. The burial crushed him, finally, totally.

There was nothing for him to do. He would not leave the safety of his dying town for any reason. He knew about Apache torture and figured he was a candidate for the worst they could offer. After all, Santiago had personally delivered the invitation to his friend, "Juan José, great chief of the mighty Mimbres Apache Nation, will you and your people join the people of Santa Rita in a feast of peace?" The words stuck in his memory like a bone in his throat. He couldn't breathe. He couldn't forget.

His fear and grief were all-consuming. Finally he barricaded himself in his living quarters behind the trading post where he died of malnutrition.

Lamp oil was in short supply and Peralta sat in his spacious but dimly-lit house — contemplating events since the massacre. "What can we do?" he wondered aloud.

He felt totally helpless. As the lamp flickered, Peralta's thoughts wandered back to the day of the massacre. It had been months; it seemed like a lifetime.

"Could I have done something to stop the massacre?" he asked himself. His thoughts returned to the pivotal town meeting and the Anglo's persuasive speech.

Peralta knew then, and bitterly remembered now, how Johnson's inflammatory speech had been, at best, an agglomeration of half-truths. He remembered the night after the massacre and grew even more bitter. Johnson and the others who had raised the scalps had immediately hurried out of town, eager to cash in their spoils, leaving the grizzly task of cleaning up the town plaza and providing "Christian" burials for the mutilated bodies to the remaining townspeople. None of the conspirators had returned.

Peralta reflected that those who so quickly departed were the only ones who benefited from that unholy feast. The townspeople who stayed behind now bore the high cost of the betrayal.

Some who had supported Johnson's plan remained in Santa Rita. They refused to accept any blame for the town's current predicament, using every report of an Apache raid as a basis for justifying the massacre. "See how those heathens are! They killed seven good men in that last caravan. Thievin' heathens stole all our supplies and now we are starving. Too bad Johnson couldn't have killed more of 'em!"

At first, Peralta had tried to reason with them. Finally, he realized the futility of his efforts. He stopped listening to the hollow whine of their self-righteous ravings.

Those who had argued against the massacre couldn't understand how anyone could fault the Apaches for their retaliation. At least the "heathen savages" weren't slaughtering women and children, at least not yet.

Those who favored the massacre couldn't understand why Peralta and the others were so bitter toward them. Santa Rita was a town divided, and a town with no means of support.

Peralta had taken no part in the betrayal of his Apache neighbors. He believed he had done his best to prevent it. Yet he shared fully the burden of retribution. He had no job, some of his neighbors hated him, and most of his friends either had moved out of town or were planning to. His wife was advancing in her third pregnancy and he could not feed or properly clothe her or their daughters. He had money, but there was nothing to buy with it. They had to do something.

Peralta called his wife and daughters together around the heavy wooden table where they had once enjoyed ample meals. His announcement was brief. There was no discussion.

"The Apaches have cut off all shipments to the mine and to the merchants. We have no tools to work the mines and there is no other work here. The shops are empty. There is nothing to purchase with the pesos we have saved. We are out of food. I see no choice. We must load our belongings on a donkey cart and travel to Santa Fe," he paused. "God be with us," he added, almost whispering.

Peralta and his wife knew but did not speak of the dangers the family faced. They knew Apaches were stopping the freight wagons and could, if they chose, make great sport out of killing them all. Peralta couldn't bear to think of the possibility of their death at the hands of the Apaches, but it was certain they would all starve if they stayed in Santa Rita. He led his family in a prayer before they began the painful task of choosing which few treasured belongings would go with them.

CHAPTER 6
SURVIVORS

Gotch Ear was a half-breed. His mother, Claw Woman, was an Apache. His grandfather's propensity for strong drink led to perpetual drunkenness and poverty. When his mother was just entering puberty her family was cast out from the tribe because her father habitually stole from other tribesmen. Among Apaches this was often a killing offense. But some felt compassion toward him. He had been a good warrior until the demon of Mexican liquor overtook him.

Before the banishment, Claw Woman's father stole anything he could get his hands on, immediately taking it to the settlers and trading for liquor. After the banishment, his wife and daughter, having no other means of support and no other hope, went with him. The family settled in a hovel near a military outpost. They survived on garbage and the occasional charity that came their way.

When she was barely fourteen, Claw Woman was sold to a Mexican trader for two pesos and a barrel of rotgut whiskey. On occasion the trader beat her and often lent her, for a fee, to his friends. When she was fifteen, her body swollen with child, the trader cast her aside. She had no family or friends to turn to so she headed toward Santa Fe and the military fort she remembered there. She threw herself on the mercy of the soldiers, begging for food, shelter and any kind of work. She could have sold the use of her body to the lonely soldiers for the things she needed but after the abuse she had endured, she chose instead to slave for meager rewards.

There were plenty of difficult and dirty jobs around the fort. Claw Woman willingly tackled any task offered and quickly proved herself trustworthy and able. She cooked and cleaned for the soldiers, who showed their appreciation by using her as their communal slave. Nevertheless she was happy for the food and shelter they gave her, her only alternative to starvation.

When her son was born, Claw Woman gave him an Apache name, "Kochera". To the soldiers it sounded like "Gotch Ear." This amused them, because the baby's left ear was deformed.

Claw Woman died of smallpox at age twenty-seven. Gotch Ear was then twelve, and was left without family or people. In the years before Claw Woman became ill, she taught him all she knew of her people, including what she remembered of the ways of his Apache ancestors.

She taught him her native tongue, in which she was well-spoken. She told him about Apache rituals, beliefs, and traditions. But she never explained why they no longer lived with her people. She never talked about his father or his grandfather.

Shortly before her death she sent Gotch Ear into the mountains. "It is time for a boy to become a man," she said in a voice that was both tender and firm. "To do this, you must go alone to a special private place. The spirits will guide you. Go where you feel drawn. When you sense you have found your place of solitude, there you must fast. Wait and pray for your spirit guide to appear. If your prayers are answered, you will receive a vision and your spirit guide will come to you. Apache spirit guides are often animals. My father's was an owl . . . " her words trailed off into a whisper, then she continued, "Once your spirit guide has come to you, you will be counted as a man." This was the first and only time she mentioned her father.

Gotch Ear was surprised to hear his mother speak of him. This unusual occurrence and her quiet, almost reverent attitude convinced him this "rite of passage" was an important event in his life. He understood from the look in her eyes that he could never count himself a man without making this journey.

With her blessing, he set out filled with nagging apprehension about his half-breed ancestry and the task before him. With his mixed blood would the Apache spirits find him acceptable? Would he even have a spirit guide?

Fear blossomed into full-blown anxiety as he traveled into the mountains overlooking the fort. He came to a place where he could watch across the wide valley to the west as the setting sun faded behind distant peaks. There he waited, fasting as his mother had instructed through two nights. He weakened and wondered if, and how, he would become a man.

He asked himself, "What if I lose my strength and die without seeing my spirit guide? Should I give up before I become too weak to survive?"

Finally, at the end of the third day of fasting and praying, young Gotch Ear received his vision. As he sat trance-like, staring into the vast void of the evening sky a barely discernable speck appeared.

The speck circled, dropping lower and lower, until the boy could see it was an eagle — "Chieftain of those who ride the winds."

As he watched the great bird soar, tilting and gliding on the wind, Gotch Ear's heart filled with a longing to join the soaring creature in flight. "Such a sensation," he thought, ". . . the purest of pleasure."

His tears fell unbidden and unnoticed as he cherished the sheer beauty of the eagle's flight.

Suddenly, the giant raptor plummeted from the sky with the speed of an arrow, slowing abruptly at the last moment, and with outstretched and fluttering wings spanning more than twice Gotch Ear's height, landed with a gentle thump in front of the astonished youth.

Turning its head from side to side the eagle regarded the boy first with one brilliant eye and then the other. The bird's eyes seemed to pierce Gotch Ear's soul. After what seemed like an eternity the eagle spoke to him, and although the boy's ears heard only an eagle's cry, his heart heard his spirit guide's message.

"Greetings, little brother. Do not look so surprised. I know you felt our kinship as I sailed on the winds."

Gotch Ears gave a hesitant nod. The majestic bird continued, "Listen and attend, spirit brother. A time will come many years from now, when another of our brothers will guide you to a place unique in all the world. Remember this. Watch for a sign. Do not forget, do not forget . . . ."

With a piercing scream, the eagle lunged into the air, spiraling higher and higher until it was once again only a speck, until again the sky was empty.

Gotch Ear stirred from his trance, rubbing his eyes in disbelief. At the onset of his vision the sun had been high in the sky. Now sunset was approaching.

"Did this really happen or was it a dream," he wondered aloud, speaking only to himself. Had he dreamed the whole thing? His eyes fell on the Golden Eagle feather at his feet. Awe-shaken, Gotch Ear picked up the feather and slowly rose on hunger-weakened legs. He held the single feather toward the fading golden sky. The last rays of evening's light intensified the feather's golden hue. The hair on the back of his neck prickled as he twisted the feather's shaft between his fingers. He felt its power and knew he was no longer a boy.

Gotch Ear returned home to find his mother weakened from smallpox. His story of the visit by the eagle, "Chieftain of those who ride the winds," cheered her and brought a rare, warm smile to her face. He knew her spirit guide would soon take her to the Great Spirit.

In the following years Gotch Ear roamed the reaches of central eastern New Mexico hunting, fishing, and exploring. Years of tracking game animals, from rabbits to elk, gradually developed his inborn talents. He became completely familiar with most of central New Mexico. When he turned fifteen he found his first work as a guide. He enjoyed the experience. Gotch Ear had found his life's calling.

As Gotch Ear moved into manhood, two other young men were growing up at an orphanage in Santa Fe. Andrew Adams and Maurice Landrew — when he pronounced his name the "r" sound was subdued and it sounded more like he was saying Londoe — had both been orphaned at a young age. Life at the orphanage was harsh but offered a rudimentary education. Both boys learned considerable Spanish while there and Adams managed to educate himself well beyond the basics required. He could read and write well in both Spanish and English.

Landrew had a more difficult time with schooling. He spoke only French when he came to the orphanage, and since no one else there knew more than a few words of his native tongue he found it harder to learn. He managed to learn enough Spanish to get by and eventually, thanks to Adams' excellent tutoring, his oral English skills exceeded those of his teachers.

Like all children at the orphanage, they were expected to earn their way. Monday through Saturday, their lessons lasted from two to four hours. Monday through Friday, before and after lessons, they worked long hours, either at the orphanage or at various shops around town. It was a rare weekday when they had any time to themselves. Saturday afternoons they could spend as they liked, playing, visiting, or more often simply resting up from the exhausting week. Sundays they fasted and studied the Bible from dawn to dusk.

The children hated Sundays and the required fasting. They all agreed no type of work was as bad as sitting attentively all day, listening to a lesson given in Latin, a language they were not taught and were not expected to understand.

Several times Adams asked why Latin wasn't taught. His question was ignored. From sheer boredom he taught himself enough Latin to pose the same question in Latin. His "insolence" earned him three days of fasting.

A teacher once chastised Adams for an incorrect response to a question posed during a lecture. Adams responded as none of his fellow students dared to. He rose on shaking twelve year old legs and rebuked his teacher.

"You asked me what I thought the answer was, Sir," he insisted. "I told you what I thought."

The teacher turned crimson above the top of his tight collar. He slammed his fist on the podium. "Young master Adams," he bellowed, "your insolence is most unfitting. You are not here to argue or give us your opinion, you are here to learn. In the future, answer as you have been *taught* and keep *your* opinions to yourself."

It had never before occurred to any of the other boys that they could express or even have an opinion about anything. The incident marked a turning point. No longer did they feel helpless and insecure like trapped animals. Adams' courage had opened a door for them all.

From that day on, Adams got along better and better with his peers and worse and worse with the authorities. The youngsters admired his courage to think for himself, to speak up and stand up for what he believed in. Unfortunately for Adams, the authorities found these same qualities less admirable.

Within the year, he was expelled from the school as unmanageable. Perhaps he was. He took up residence at the livery stable, where he made room and board in the usual way.

Within a week, Landrew showed up. The young Frenchman flashing a smile at his friend and said, "I figure if you can make a living tending livestock I can, too."

The livery operator liked the boys. Soon they were doing all the daily chores around the stable. Adams was strong enough to handle all but the most arduous tasks. Landrew had a way with the stock that made the livery man envious.

The owner let his full-time hired hand go. He saved a good deal of money, and told the authorities he was willing to "keep" the two boys. Besides room and board, he gave them the use of spare horses when they were available. The deal satisfied everyone.

Adams and Landrew slept in the hayloft. The owner's wife prepared three square meals a day and an occasional unauthorized snack — which her husband chose not to notice. It was a good life, the best life they had yet known.

The two worked at the livery until they were sixteen, often talking about trying to establish a livery operation "out west" by themselves. Just when they were old enough to consider it seriously, a Mountain Man named Smith came to town. Smith changed their plans and their lives.

CHAPTER 7
MOUNTAIN MEN

"**B**oys," Smith preached, "what we should do is head south. I hear tell those Mexicans are finding gold down there in New Mexico and west of there in what them locals call Apacheria. I'm tired of long winters where a feller can't see the ground, let alone pan for gold. Down south there are plenty of beaver, too. The winters ain't so long and cold, neither. Why, a man can pan for gold all year long. I've got a good bit of money from all those beaver hides I sold over at Bent's Fort, and I've got a plan."

The Mountain Men who listened to Smith all knew of Bent's Fort. The Bent brothers had built a personal fortress deep in the wilderness on the bank of the Arkansas River, midway between the far-western reaches of United States civilization and the remote old Spanish town of Santa Fe, New Mexico — first settled before 1613 by Spanish Missionaries. One brother was a good politician and soon established liaisons with leaders in Santa Fe. Their fort soon became the hub of a great trading enterprise, benefiting Mountain Men, Santa Fe, and the western-moving frontier of the United States.

Smith outlined his plan. "We'll get a group together and head south, prospecting the Rio Grande River. I'll buy the grub and all the other supplies, except tobacco and whiskey. Anybody that throws in with me keeps his share of what hides we collect. We'll pan for gold when we can. I keep half the gold, the other half gets split amongst the rest of you. What do you say?"

John Smith was a burly, blond man who walked with a limp. In long-gone, tamer days, he had broken his foot while working at a lumber mill. It hadn't healed properly. Since then he had been "Mountain Manning." He'd seen men lose fingers and toes in the cold winters up in the mountains of Colorado, then a western frontier of the United States, and he knew more than one man who'd died in the bitter winters there.

So far Smith had been lucky, but he and those gathered around him had known plenty of hardship. The previous winter, 1837-1838, had been particularly savage and long. Partly in celebration of spring, the men were attending a *rendezvous* on the flanks of Pike's Peak, in southern Colorado.

Twice yearly Mountain Men, Indians, and traders gathered at these events in the wilderness, which were month-long parties where they discussed business. Rendezvous were the main social events in the lives of these normally reclusive men.

On the second day of the 1838 spring Rendezvous, Smith presented his plan and made his proposition to a group that was complaining about the lack of beaver in Colorado. He found eager listeners.

"How can we lose? Won't hurt to give it a try — for a spell, at least," they agreed.

They were a motley crew. Some spoke English, some French, some Spanish; but all spoke two common languages — Mountain Man and Gold. "Mountain Man" was a well-developed language and despite their varied origins and experiences they easily communicated. Besides their background in the wilderness one thing drew them together, something stronger than shared experience.

They were bound by a common desire to discover the undiscovered, explore the unexplored, know the unknown. They shared a common lust and like the ancient siren's song, this lust would draw them inexorably to their fate.

The free ride Smith promised was a considerable incentive and seventeen men readily threw in with the affable trailblazer. They were happy at the prospect of warmer weather and the opportunity to see new territory.

This was the first time any of them had traveled in a large band though, and there were problems. Mountain men usually traveled and lived alone, hunting, trapping, and fishing for everything they needed to survive. Most kept no livestock at all and when they did it was usually only one horse to carry furs and "essentials." Traveling south down the Rio Grande River it took the group only a few days to recognize several obvious problems with Smith's plan.

Each man was accustomed to fending for himself. Meals and

livestock tending were a serious problem. Nobody wanted to cook for and clean up after the others, yet "every man for himself" meant they spent all day waiting around camp as each man found time to prepare and eat his meals. They soon realized that, like it or not, they would have to settle on one cook and three communal meals served at a set time each day.

Another major problem was the livestock. Nobody wanted to tend "all those critters." They had come to prospect, trap, and explore. But they were doing little panning or trapping and their progress down the river was slow. They were beginning to act like a bunch of grumpy riffraff and all agreed something had to be done to solve these problems and hasten their progress. Smith proposed a detour to Santa Fe to hire some help.

Each afternoon as they made their way toward Santa Fe they panned sands along the shores of the Rio Grande and discussed gold. Smith was an expert panner and he often roared, "Look here, men! See that tail of yellow? That is sure enough gold. And look at the way the sun glistens on the snow up on them peaks to the east. Them is the Sangre de Christo Mountains. There's likely gold up there but that country's too rough for my liking."

The others were eager to learn Smith's successful panning techniques. They watched closely, marvelling as he easily swirled the pan — partially filled with gravel and water — in a small circle, while tipping it slightly to one side. With his expert coaxing the swirling water easily lifted the lighter pieces of gravel over the rim and out of the pan. Soon only the densest particles remained.

"See how that works?" he explained. "If you're steady and careful you can get rid of the rock without losing any gold." As he added water to a pan full of gravel for the fourth time, he noted, "usually, there'll be some of this here black sand." He gestured with a finger to the tail of black that was forming as he slowly swirled the water in the pan. "When you see black at the back of the moving sand and gravel and you don't see any gold following the black stuff, you're done. It's time to try another pan of sand. Hardest thing is picking out all the big pebbles first. Well, that and the cold water." He dumped the pan, walked a few feet downstream and repeated the process he had just demonstrated.

Most mornings the group broke camp and moved farther downriver, looking for beaver and gold. As days passed, they became better at the art of panning, and more men found traces of the precious metal.

Whenever they came to a sizable side creek, several group members would detour up the tributary for a few days. Usually they found a few beaver but they never found much gold.

This disappointed Smith, who proposed that once they took care of their business in Santa Fe they should head into the unexplored reaches of western New Mexico into Apacheria — country that Smith and most other Anglos called Arizona.

"I hear tell the country around the Gila River is unexplored. We'll go there," he said. "If there's any gold about, we'll be the ones to find it. We'll hire us a cook and somebody to tend the livestock in Santa Fe. Then we'll head west."

Gold fever consumed Smith. "Just wait until we hit the mother-lode, boys. We'll have it made."

Time after time, his pan revealed nothing. Yet he remained undaunted. "Just wait. We'll hit pay dirt, then we'll all be rich!"

But it was not potential wealth that lured John Smith on. He was an explorer and an adventurer. He spent his hard-earned money to feed and clothe a small army of men because he loved prospecting: New lands, new adventures and new gold. Dreams of discovering that elusive fist-sized nugget filled his sleep, but he didn't crave the riches gold would bring, he craved the thrill of discovery. The excitement of the search was everything — only a chosen few understand what motivated him.

Leaving the Rio Grande River and heading up the Santa Fe River, the party came upon a man and two young girls laying flowers on two fresh graves — one of typical size, the other a small mound. Smith ordered his men to detour widely around them and to make camp, "A ways upriver." He whoaed his horse at a respectful distance from the sad trio and waited.

When it seemed appropriate he called out in his best Spanish,

"Hola al campamento!"

He repeated his greeting in English when the man, who looked and dressed like a Mexican, didn't respond to his first greeting. "Hello in the camp!"

Only when the older girl tugged at the man's sleeve did he rise in silence and turn slowly toward Smith.

Smith recognized that he was indeed addressing either a Mexican or a Spaniard, and spoke again in Spanish, *"Señor,* I see you are in mourning. I offer you my condolences. Is there anything my men and I can do to help?"

The man finally responded, in clear English. "Pardon me, sir. You are very kind. If you have food for my children, I will pay you. Later this day I will wish to visit with you. Right now, I must make peace with God and try to help my daughters understand what has happened."

Smith nodded. "My men are making camp a short distance upriver. I will return with jerky and biscuits within the hour. You will have a wake feast and you'll not pay for it."

He touched the brim of his hat, and rode off.

At the new encampment, he told the others about the bereaved man, instructing them to make themselves as presentable as they could. Then he gathered a sack of ready-made victuals — mostly biscuits and jerky — and rode back to the hungry children.

"I'm John Smith, Mountain Man," he introduced himself. "There are eighteen of us. The others will be along shortly to pay their respects."

He hesitated, and the man spoke. "I am *Don* Miguel Peralta. I have just buried my wife and our firstborn son, *Señor* Smith."

After the other men came and showed their respect for the newly buried dead, Smith invited Peralta and his daughters to join them in their camp. Around a fire, later that evening, Peralta related the events that had brought this tragedy. He knew little of the Mountain Men's ways, but sensed these men were kindred spirits. He was certain they would have opposed the massacre and he had a burning need to tell his story, as though telling it might somehow ease the burden.

Peralta's words rushed out, unabated. "Unlike men who have

lived among the Indians, many settlers in Santa Rita feared them blindly. When that Anglo came to town with his plan to take advantage of the foolish government offer to pay for Apache scalps, those who feared Indians were happy to help him kill our Apache neighbors. I argued against it, as did many others in town, but we were not heard. We could not stop the massacre.

"The surviving Apaches declared war on all Mexicans. They completely cut off Santa Rita's supplies. We lacked tools to work the mines. Even if we could have, we could not ship the copper ore to the smelters.

"Food from our meager gardens was soon exhausted. I had money but supplies did not come and soon there was no food to buy. I couldn't just wait in Santa Rita while my family starved, so I decided to try to make it to Santa Fe. We found some food and shelter in settlements along the way, but they are suffering the Apache's wrath, too, and we traveled in constant fear. I was certain that once we made Santa Fe we'd be safe, but the journey was too hard for my wife. She went into labor early. After our son was born, she bled to death. He never even fed at her breast. She looked at him, smiled and was gone. He lived a few hours, but he was just too tiny and we had no milk . . . I could do nothing."

Peralta slumped into a thick silence, cradling his sleeping daughters. One by one the men left the glow of the campfire and crawled into their bedrolls. Smith stood next to Peralta.

Peralta looked up at the much taller man and issued a warning against traveling west. The Apaches were waging war all over that country. He spoke again of the Anglo, whom he blamed for the massacre and the resulting hardship. Unfortunately he did not describe the Anglo, nor did he speak Johnson's name.

Smith and his companions left Peralta what food they could and moved on up the river. "*Señor* Peralta," Smith said, "we will hurry to the first mission and ask for a priest to come meet you and your family."

Smith kept his word. Then he and the others forgot the little family around the graves — or tried to. Later, in Santa Fe, they heard all about the massacre. Details Peralta had left out of his short and confusing description. They were again stunned by the account of atrocities the people of Santa Rita had committed. Everyone agreed that Mexico's government held the greatest measure of blame. The evil and greed the story related was nothing new to them, these were some of the reasons they had chosen to live apart from what others called "civilization." Thus reminded, they took care of the business that had brought them to town as quickly as possible and headed back into the wilderness.

Late one evening at their camp near the Gila River, John Smith sat contemplating matters. Watching the dying embers of their fire, he spoke up, "I gave married life a try once, just after I turned twenty. Had me a real looker, too. She weren't too bad to live with neither but that damned boss, down at the sawmill . . . . Came like to killing that man. I wouldn't do the job his way. I'd already broken my foot working there and three other men had lost fingers. I weren't about to lose no fingers. A man needs all the parts what God give him."

The men laughed appreciatively at Smith's colorful storytelling, all except the new cook, an unhealthy looking, sunburned man with a partly skinned skull. He wasn't a prospector, Smith was sure of that, and he didn't seem to appreciate Smith's remarks. James Johnson had fallen in with Smith's group at Santa Fe. Obviously this new cook had no sense of humor.

"Anyhow," Smith concluded, "I finally had all the regular, work-a-day, life I could take. I collected my wages and headed into the hills. Ain't been back, ain't going back!"

Although deep in hostile territory, Smith was at ease as he sat and talked with the others, laughing fearlessly, suspecting no danger.

Cuchillo Negro crouched in the shadows watching Smith and his band, joyfully contemplating the prospectors' deaths. Smith was making something of the loss of a finger. Cuchillo Negro had plans that would cost him much more than that . . . .

Johnson had joined the band to further his continual quest for easy money. What he'd claimed for scalps taken at Santa Rita had dribbled all too quickly through his fingers.

Unlike the Mountain Men he now traveled with, this man cared little for adventure. His lust was simple, easy money.

Had Smith known of Johnson's role in the Santa Rita massacre, he never would have hired him. In fact, had any of these men learned of Johnson's role in organizing the affair it's likely they would have strung him up right then and there. They had lived and traded with Indians. They felt a kinship with the nomadic people and their way of life. None among them would have been involved in such treachery. Furthermore, after seeing firsthand how Peralta's family and life had been destroyed, they held a special contempt for all who had conspired at Santa Rita.

Following the slaughter in the town square, Johnson had cashed in his scalps for a hefty sum in Santa Fe. He then set out to enjoy his fortune, promptly attaining a state of admirable drunkenness, which he maintained over several days and nights. He had no idea how long it lasted. He had started with enough money to stay drunk and supplied with women for months. But he couldn't resist the promise of more easy money at the poker table.

He was no card player, even when sober. It took less than an hour for the other players to divest him of everything but his pants. He would have lost those also, if they would have let him bet them. He awoke the next evening, literally in the gutter, half-naked, reeking of alcohol, amid his own vomit, and excrement.

To clothe himself and feed his surprisingly empty stomach, he reluctantly took work at the livery stable. "Should have spent some of that scalp money on food," he mused. A few days of shoveling was more than enough. When Smith and his men came into town looking for a cook, Johnson was all ears.

"How hard could that be?" he thought.

"I'm your man. James Johnson's the name. I cooked for a wagon train once," he lied. "Came through Missouri. What's the job pay?"

Taking Johnson at his word, Smith signed him on with his burgeoning expedition.

But Johnson couldn't even build a decent fire, to say nothing of his limited cooking skills, and by the time Smith realized the deception, Santa Fe and civilization were far behind. Johnson just laughed and cussed anyone who complained about the meals he prepared,

"You bastards wouldn't know good food if you fell in it!" he proclaimed.

In time Johnson learned to add enough water to the beans to make them marginally edible. Sometimes he even cooked them long enough to "get the lumps out." Johnson's work was not all that hard, and he was so bad at cooking that the rest of the group preferred not to trust him with any other tasks. This suited him just fine. It gave him more time to think of ways to get even for all the abuse they gave him.

Besides Johnson, two others had joined the party in Santa Fe, Andrew (Andy) W. Adams and Maurice (Maury) Landrew. Landrew, a thin boy with a long nose, was surprisingly good at handling the mules and horses that carried the groups' supplies. Adams, who smiled freely, was also good with the stock and, since the two insisted they were a team, Smith hired them both.

They hadn't thought of asking for any wage, but when Smith offered it they accepted cheerfully. The job offered three meals a day and a "free ride," or rather, free hike, into the uncharted wilderness.

Smith also hired a guide, Gotch Ear. He was a young half-breed with a deformed ear, who claimed he knew the lay of the land. The three young men hit it off right away. Often in the afternoon and early evening, as the others settled into camp and panned for gold, the three went exploring. Gotch Ear was a tireless hiker. He was impressed by Adams' stamina and perseverance. No matter how rough the climb or how fast he moved, Adams, breathing hard and sweating profusely, managed to stay right on his heels. Gotch Ear soon quit trying to best him. Together the three companions explored the lands near the banks of the headwaters of the Gila River.

They were a contrast in purpose. Gotch Ear hiked to explore and learn the country, always looking for landmarks — drainages, mountain peaks or unusual formations. Adams hiked just for the fun of it, seldom looking beyond his feet. Landrew, who was more observant of landmarks hiked mainly for youthful companionship.

Adams and Landrew had signed on just after Johnson, who used his seniority to badger them into doing much of his work, such as gathering firewood and carrying water. At first they protested. But when they did he reduced their meal portions and they soon learned not to quibble. Before long, Johnson was doing less than anyone in camp.

It was an easy life he had created for himself. Each night he slept beside a fire that Adams and Landrew kept well fueled. He napped each afternoon, and he continually nipped at a bottle of rotgut from a large stash he had secreted in the bean sacks stored in the pack saddles. His only real concern was that the others might discover his whiskey.

The only thing he couldn't manipulate was the explorers desire to move camp nearly every day. "A man just gets himself settled in, comfortable-like, and it's, 'Let's get a move on, men! Need to make some miles before dusk'," he complained loudly and often.

When he was feeling particularly disagreeable he would spit into the afternoon meal. The thought of others eating his spittle soothed his temper and gave him a perverse pleasure. The others always knew whose obscene cackle echoed from the cook-fire. There was no mistaking his shrill, mocking convulsions. But they had no idea what he found so amusing. Had they discovered the reason for his laughter they likely would have slow-roasted their so-called cook over the evening's fire. A little fun could go both ways.

Johnson knew the others disliked him and would welcome any reason to do him harm. But he didn't care. The little vial he had carried all those months, since deciding not to use it in Santa Rita, could still come in handy. One day . . . .

The gold fever which consumed Smith, more and more infected his companions as they traveled west, down the Gila. After they had unknowingly passed the confluence of the San Francisco and the Gila Rivers "color" (gold-dust) became more common in the washed sands. They talked excitedly of a "mother load" awaiting them somewhere just ahead.

"I figure this gold came from those mountains up north," Smith explained. "If we keep going down this river 'til we stop finding gold we'll know the source is behind us. The Gila must not be the source. We started way up by the headwaters and never found much 'til we saw those mountains there," he said, gesturing north, toward the

White Mountains.

His reasoning was flawed. The source for the gold they were finding was the San Francisco River. They had passed the confluence of that river without knowing it because they had detoured far to the south of the Gila's channel to avoid the rugged canyon walls and high water, which made for tough going along the river bottom.

"We're getting close, boys. I don't think anybody has prospected here. There'll be good hunting and lots of gold. All we have to do is keep going," Smith preached encouragingly.

By now they were more than twenty miles into Apacheria, one hundred twenty miles west of the nearly deserted town of Santa Rita. Their belief that a great gold discovery lay just ahead spurred them deeper into what they knew were hostile Indian lands. This was the territory Peralta had warned them not to enter.

Heedless of the warnings, they crossed the Gila and continued west following the river's north shore. That evening they came to the confluence of the Gila and the Prieto Rivers.

"This looks like a good place to make camp for a couple of days," Smith said. "It'll give the animals a chance to rest and we can use the time to do more prospecting."

He had barely finished speaking when a panner who had rushed into the knee-deep and placid waters of the Prieto, cried, "Gold! Look! More than we've ever seen."

"This here river is the place to look," Smith laughed, as the others fell over each other, running to see the color. "We'll work our way north, starting in the morning.

CHAPTER 8
NANA'S ASSIGNMENT

The full moon was again rising above the high mountains to the east as the sun sank in the west. As was custom, the Mimbres had arranged their tepees in a circle, except Mangas.' His tepee stood alone on a small rise east of the main camp.

Before starting these war-council meetings, Mangas watched the rising moon through the door of his tepee, where he meditated alone. As the moon cleared the mountainous horizon he gazed into his vision crystal, looking for guidance.

Later his hand fondled charms, pebbles, feathers, and other small tokens that had been brought to him by warriors for his blessing. From some he had fashioned amulets to bring their owners special protection in coming battles.

At sunset scouts, braves, and tribal elders began to assemble around a small fire in the center of camp, awaiting Mangas' appearance. According to their custom, they waited in silence. Sometimes, when the spirits called him to do so, Mangas would join the others chanting a sacred song. This night he joined them silently.

Before beginning council business, Mangas told each man of the spirits' message for him. Most of these messages foretold events of everyday life. Twin sons would be born to old Cuchillo Negro. This was a very good omen and brought hearty congratulations and good-humored ribbing from those gathered. The younger braves offered exaggerated bows to the "frisky" old man. Another brave was told that many years hence he would die bravely in battle. Other readings were less momentous.

When Mangas finished delivering the messages he handed out the various charms and amulets he had fashioned for the braves. There was one for every man there, and several special ones for others who were absent. It was past midnight when they finally began discussing the business of war.

Mangas listened to reports from all the leaders. He was especially pleased at the report about Santa Rita. "It will be empty soon," he said in a satisfied tone. "Our war against the Mexican invaders is going well. Is there any other news?"

"A group of about twenty men has come into our lands, traveling further and further down the Gila," Cuchillo Negro reported. "They trap for beaver and play in the water. Perhaps they are those called prospectors who look for squaws metal. I followed them down the River until they headed up the Prieto."

Mangas acknowledged Cuchillo Negro's report. Then he spoke to the group. "We will continue to concentrate our efforts against the traitors in Santa Rita," he directed, "until all have left that town or have died there."

A young brave who had lost part of his family in Santa Rita protested, "but why do we not kill them all?"

Mangas replied, "Those whom we allow to escape are chosen by the Great Spirit. Perhaps some are innocent of the wrong. Perhaps not. But innocent or guilty, all who escape live in fear and will forever tell other Mexicans the consequences of betrayal. They do our work!"

Aware that Nana was anxious for a greater role in the war, Mangas rather casually handed the fate of Smith's party over to him. "We will let the intruders on the Prieto live for now. They will provide a good opportunity for some of our young braves to sharpen their war skills, especially the skill of patient observation, a skill which is so hard for young men. Turning these white men into red men will be as much sport next moon as it would be this moon, won't it?"

Laughing at their chief's little joke, the others heartily approved his plan. The council meeting concluded.

As directed, Nana took a band of twenty young braves to observe the party of trespassers. "Simply to watch," Mangas had said. "At least for a while."

The young braves found the cook particularly interesting. They didn't know who he was, but they were amused that an Anglo man would do squaw's work.

Nana spent hours each day tutoring his charges. The first few days, before sunrise, he positioned individuals at vantage points where they could watch the white men's camp. After a few days he allowed the braves to choose their own hiding places.

The idea was for several braves to find positions with a clear view of every possible trail out of camp. If the explorers started to move camp, the observers would inform Nana of the direction they were heading.

Nana explained how important it was to have a concealed escape route. "You must learn to use the lay of the land," he said. "Look at that ravine behind us. If anyone were to come toward us from any other direction, we could be out of sight in minutes by going down that ravine."

To the young braves, spying was tedious and boring work. Those not observing passed the day gathering food and maintaining a quiet existence in a hidden camp little more than a mile from Smith's men. Because of the proximity of the explorers' camp Nana allowed no fires or active loud games. The days were dull and the nights were cold and uncomfortable.

Nana assigned braves to choose their positions around Smith's camp. Then to keep himself entertained while training the inexperienced braves he would set out to find each observer without the youth seeing him. When Nana found one, he would carefully move in close enough to pelt him with a pebble. When the brave turned, startled, Nana simply smiled at him. The older man never spoke nor chastised; the humiliation of surprise discovery was enough.

On days when Smith moved camp, braves ran ahead, flanking the party while staying out of sight. The explorers were constantly watched from afar.

As the days passed the young warriors improved their skills of observation. Several were showing promise. Nana was happy with their growth. He was particularly pleased that the three young men from the camp who hiked every day had never spotted any of his braves.

"Nana, must we keep up this game forever?" Juan José's youngest son asked late one evening.

"Are you so anxious to see white man's blood on your hands?" Nana asked in reply.

The sixteen-year-old youth paled. He was an Apache, the son of a vaunted warrior. He had sworn a blood oath of vengeance for his father's murder. Nevertheless, neither he nor any of the other young braves in the group had killed a man, not yet. The first time was never easy.

Nana understood this. Killing these men would be hard, even for him. In his heart, Nana knew the death of these innocent men would not bring his fallen kinsmen back. Nevertheless, these men were invading Mimbres' lands. Still, he realized it would be easier for the young braves if those they would soon kill had done the murdering at Santa Rita . . . .

As the prospectors traveled further up the Prieto River they came closer to the sulfur smell of the sacred hot springs where Nana and Mangas had been given their names and had killed the bighorn sheep. Following along and watching, Nana reminisced about the story of two young braves and a bighorn sheep. Even now, so many years later, Nana clearly remembered the greeting Juan José had given them when they entered his camp and showed him the gold and the stones they had collected in the hidden zigzag canyon.

"My sons, these gleaming stones are called squaws metal by our people," Juan José said. "They are soft and of no use to a brave. But they are greatly prized by our women for decorating their clothing and for jewelry. When you desire to take a wife it is fitting to give her mother a gift of squaws metal."

He went on, and his manner became more serious. "The zigzag canyon you found is a sacred place," he continued with a stern warning. "White men crave squaws metal more than anything else on our lands. They must never know what you have found in Zigzag Canyon. If even one finds out about the plentiful squaws metal there, more will come in endless numbers. They will violate our sacred places and destroy our way of life. This has already happened to other tribes in places far to the south. Our places of squaws metal must be kept secret."

Nana reflected on the admonitions of Juan José as he and his young charges observed the white men now camped on the banks of the Prieto, and traveling daily closer to Zigzag Canyon. He somehow knew that if these men were allowed to continue, they would discover that hidden place where the squaws metal white men coveted was so abundant.

CHAPTER 9
GOTCH EAR'S DISCOVERY

Since his fifteenth birthday, Gotch Ear had been guiding travelers on the upper reaches of the Gila River. He guided soldiers, settlers, and other adventurers — like the party he presently led — through wild, largely uncharted country. This was an impressive accomplishment for a young man. There were no roads, the few existing trails were often difficult to find, and sometimes harder to follow. But most important, these were Apache lands and only the Apache traveled here in safety.

By the time he turned twenty, Gotch Ear was an expert guide. Yet he had never ventured far into Apacheria. When he hired on with Smith's party, just outside Santa Fe, he had agreed to take them down the Gila River as far as they wanted to go. When they wanted to change course and turn up the Prieto, however, he balked and tried to dissuade them. "There is great danger here, greater still if we turn away from the Gila and travel north. This is Apache land, the lands to the north are sacred to the Mimbres and I am not familiar with that country. I advise you to follow the Gila!"

Gotch Ear went on to describe certain Apache tortures he had heard of, but Smith and the others made light of the tortures he ascribed to the Apache and ignored him.

Heedless of his warnings, the party continued up the Prieto, heading north into the heart of Apacheria. These gold-hungry men would not be dissuaded from their exploration. Several times, in the quiet afternoons as they prepared to pan the sands of the river the question of hostile Indians came up. They would discuss the question until the swirling water in their pans washed away the sands and revealed a glittering tail. Then they only talked of gold.

Gotch Ear considered abandoning Smith's party and returning to New Mexico. He had never quit in the middle of a job before, but he was tempted to now. Yet for reasons he did not completely understand, he remained with the group. Later he realized he also was caught up with the obsession to explore, to seek the source of the beautiful yellow metal. Perhaps the alluring yellow gleam reminded him of the golden glow of a feather he had once held toward the glow of the setting sun . . . .

Around the campfire the conversation centered on the gold they were finding, the mother-lode they expected to discover soon, and all the things they would buy with the riches it would bring. Gotch Ear had lived among Mexicans all his life and, unlike the Apaches, understood how profitably gold could be used among all white men.

The Apache way was not to trade but to steal, thereby a brave could demonstrate his cleverness and manhood. The idea of trading something as worthless as squaws metal for something of real value was still outside the Apache reasoning. In time this would change and Gotch Ear would be one of those who helped usher in a new Apache awareness.

Following the Prieto, the prospectors stayed as close to the river channel as possible, panning for gold at every opportunity, and especially in the afternoons and early evenings, until the light failed. Their efforts were often rewarded. They quickly found more gold on the Prieto than in all their previous panning along the Gila and Rio Grande.

They left the river only when they came to narrow impassable places. Most of the time the going was easier than it had been on the Gila, but occasionally willow groves and beaver dams made progress difficult.

Sometimes Gotch Ear advised shortcuts where they could circumvent a looping bend in the river by going over a ridge — let the river meander, they had a goal. These climbs, though sometimes difficult, provided a welcome diversion from the slow and almost blind progress through the willows, insects, and mud alongside the river.

Gotch Ear estimated the group was now about twenty miles from the Gila. They were following a well-established game trail as it crossed a low ridge on the east side of the river. As they climbed up and out of the river channel onto the sloping ridge, they had a good view of the surrounding countryside. Smith and the others hardly paused to look around. They were always in a hurry to get back to the river where they could again search for gold.

Gotch Ear marvelled. "No wonder these men need guides! They hardly notice the country they pass through." Pausing to familiarize himself with the lay of the land, he noted a meandering ribbon of water flowing between glittering pools, a tributary to the Prieto entering from the west. Even from a distance, he could tell the water was clear and occasionally he smelled sulfur on the air.

From this vantage point he could see that north of them the canyon of the Prieto closed in on both sides of the river. He knew they would soon have to choose between climbing out of the canyon and over the high cliffs or dropping back into the river bottom to get their feet wet again. While the rest of the group took a break, Gotch Ear scouted on ahead.

He found no path that would take them easily out of the canyon on the east side. On the west side he found a trail leading to a high bench above the cliffs. However when he explored ahead for several miles, he found no trail leading back down to the river. He could see that the beautifully timbered river bottom opened up again not far north of where it narrowed. He decided the best route would be along the river channel through the short narrows after which they would have easy passage again.

Gotch Ear returned and found the others well-rested. He described the canyon, the lay of the land, and suggested they follow the river bottom. Smith agreed.

Where the river channel turned to the east, the game trail they were following dropped over the ridge and back down to the river bottom. Smith proposed they make camp. "Looks like a good area to spend a few days," he said. "We can let the livestock fatten up a bit on all that good grass downstream. I noticed there's a pretty little creek on the other side of the river, about half a mile west of here. Smelled sulfur earlier; suspect it's a hot mineral spring. A couple of you fellers can check that out tomorrow. I reckon even mineral springs could have gold. We'll just take us a *siesta grande*, right here."

Noting that Smith had seen the stream, too, Gotch Ear chuckled to himself, "I guess they aren't all totally blind."

Blessed with adequate run-off from the mountains to the north and periodic rains, the Prieto River Valley was lush with willows, grasses, poplars, cottonwoods, and spruce trees. Willow bark provided food for the beaver and larger trees provided material for the dams they built at frequent intervals along the river bottom.

Standing in the midst of such abundance, none could guess that within fifteen years the beaver would be all but exterminated along the banks of the Prieto and all its tributaries by greedy and short-sighted trappers. They couldn't know that a substantial decline in rainfall would soon alter the delicate natural balance, thereby creating an entirely new desert ecosystem.

Nothing in the area would escape the effect of these changes. Most of the plants that had once thrived along the river would find conditions intolerable, become stressed, and die. Fires would be common. Eventually cacti and other desert species — prickly pear, yucca, agave, juniper, sage, and a few other hardy plants — would be the only important species along the lower reaches of the Prieto. As the beaver dams disappeared, grasses and other soil-holding vegetation which now thrived beside the placid waters behind the dams, would also disappear. Where seasonal runoff had been largely moderated for centuries by thousands of small dams and vast soil deposits that could hold temporary excesses of water, seasonal flooding would become severe. After intense rainstorms and during spring snow melts there would be nothing to hold or slow the water. Resulting floods would easily wash away accumulated mud leaving behind only sterile sand and gravel. In isolated spots, willows and a few cottonwoods would survive, but even these would show stress. There would be little mud from which trees could extract needed minerals.

Beaver, trout, and mink were once abundant, but no animals that depended on continuous flow of fresh water would survive. Only insects, a few reptiles, smaller species of mammal, and an occasional bighorn sheep would endure.

The drying conditions that would contribute to these changes had already begun prior to the spring of 1837, but young Adams and the others didn't know this. They saw nature as eternal and unchanging. For now, they saw a world where a life-sustaining river flowed freely between banks populated with beautiful trees, a canyon where the evening stillness was interrupted only by gentle whispering of breezes moving through leaves. This serenity was punctuated with an occasional cascade of water rushing inexorably over logs of a beaver dam or an occasional outcrop of bedrock.

It was a time before human intervention had brought any visible changes into such wild places. Man's intervention and the resulting changes were something most of these men had deliberately left behind when they took up life as Mountain Men. They neither understood nor considered the possibility that the pristine conditions they saw here might not be eternal. They had sought and found a place where the earth still gave freely of her riches, providing gifts for the taking to those whose fate brought them to the right spot . . . .

They could not anticipate the imminent change in their plans that a half-breed scout's news would bring — nor, indeed, the future changes in this river and its environment, changes that time and man's interventions would cause.

The men happily accepted Smith's plan to spend a few lazy days in this inviting spot, hunting beaver and panning for gold. While most of the group went off to pan the river's sands, Gotch Ear again explored the trail ahead. This time he followed along the bottom of the river channel, relishing the opportunity to be alone. He found most of these men likeable enough, except for the cantankerous creature who cooked for them, and he especially enjoyed Adams' and Landrew's company. But too much company grated on his nerves, perhaps because he never felt completely comfortable among other men, Indian or white.

A ways out of camp he paused, admiring the stunning beauty of the seemingly unbroken cliffs towering over the placid river. As he stood admiring the serenity, a dust devil whistled across his path. Gotch Ear, coughing and sputtering, pulled out a worn bandanna to wipe the dust from his stinging eyes.

As Gotch Ear repocketed his bandanna he looked up. Still blinking, he froze. Perched on a rock not twenty feet in front of him was an eagle — a golden eagle. The magnificent bird stared fearlessly at him.

Gotch Ear barely breathed — his life seemed suspended in the face of such majesty. Reverence filled his heart. This was the earthly embodiment of his Guardian Spirit.

With a piercing scream, the eagle sprang abruptly aloft, circling slowly upward into the sky. Then just as abruptly it dove toward a dark cleft in the rocks of the sheer cliff along the east side of the river. When it reached the cliff the eagle disappeared, as though it had penetrated the solid rock.

"What can this mean?" Gotch Ear said aloud. Startled by this magical eagle's sudden appearance and disappearance, the usually quiet half-breed continued, "Where could he have gone?"

Scrambling toward the spot where he had last seen the eagle he discovered a curious thing. As he moved upriver, what had appeared as a solid wall of rock opened almost as if it were a door, to reveal a side canyon leading east, out of the Prieto.

Gotch Ear walked up this narrowing canyon until he came to what appeared to be a second wall of rock. This, he quickly discovered, was not really a solid wall either. Concealed in the shadows of the canyon and the mottled pattern of the rock face, he spotted a cave. A moderate stream and pleasant echoing sounds issued from this opening. Gotch Ear stood, puzzled, trying to make sense of what he saw and heard. Then came a harsh cry.

Looking upward he saw the eagle floating, high above him. Against the breathtaking backdrop of cliffs, its feathers blazed in the light of the setting sun. Gotch Ear was certain such splendor was not of natural origin.

"Surely this is the sign promised by my Spirit Guide, on the day I left my childhood behind," he whispered under his breath. Naive in the way of the spirits, Gotch Ear decided the eagle's appearance that led him to this special place meant he was supposed to bring the prospectors here. "I have to tell the others. We must explore this canyon."

Sending a fervent prayer of thanksgiving to his spirit guide, Gotch Ear hurried back to camp to share with the prospectors his belief that this canyon held the secret and the wealth they sought.

At first, as Gotch Ear described how he had been led to his discovery by a spirit, the others laughed. "Why, the very idea of some half-breed having a vision! You must be touched in the head if you expect us to believe such nonsense."

The others laughed at Gotch Ear's story, Johnson did not. He knew all too well how seriously Indians took their religious beliefs. Hadn't he watched for hours as his friends were ceremoniously dispatched of their scalps during a Comanche "religious" ritual. Hadn't he heard the chief chant repeatedly, throughout the ordeal, "My friend the weasel has led me to these invaders." Johnson and half his scalp survived that ceremony. His fear of Indians, and his hatred ran deep. Johnson more than believed. He knew.

Although they joined the laughter some of the others felt uncomfortable upon hearing Gotch Ear's fantastic tale. They also knew.

Early the following morning, twenty-one men headed up the Prieto. Before the first fingers of sunlight lit the western escarpments, this jovial group turned east and headed into a hidden zigzag canyon. None of the prospectors admitted believing Gotch Ear's story; they told each other they were just going along to humor him. But they found things just as Gotch Ear had described them.

When the party arrived at what looked like the opening of a cave, Gotch Ear, moving ahead, disappeared into the shadows. Moments later he returned, holding several gold nuggets in his outstretched hands. The others scurried with great excitement through the opening. There they discovered not a cave, but a narrow ravine only wide enough in places for a single man to pass. The channel zigzagged through twenty-foot high overhanging rock walls.

As if drawn by a magnet the intrepid explorers slowly, almost reverently, entered the twisting channel, heedless of the frigid water through which they waded. As the first light of dawn began to show on mountains to the west, the prospectors came upon the source of the gentle echoing sounds that filled the twisting ravine.

It seemed much further to them, but they had walked only about one-hundred feet into the passage when they came to the base of a spectacular waterfall cascading over a towering cliff. Their progress was blocked. They gathered in awe, all eyes following the rushing water as it fell into the pool formed by the falling torrent. Myriad glints sparkled at them through the water. Gold! There was pandemonium as they scratched to grab the precious nuggets, some the size of buckshot. They had found what they were seeking in abundance beyond their wildest dreams. Here was enough gold to grubstake them all for the rest of their lives!

A few miles to the east was a region that would later become a major copper producing area of the world. This canyon, which would later be named Gold Gulch, drained from that area.

For millions of years this small creek had carried erosional products from that mineralized region toward the Prieto River. Through the ages, huge volumes of weathered and eroded rock were carried down this creek to the Prieto, the Gila, the Colorado, and finally the Sea of Cortéz.

Wherever the water slowed, along the way, the denser gold settled and was concentrated. The heavy pieces of gold moved only grudgingly away from the weathering mountains and down this stream, taking sanctuary in every deep pool. It was particularly concentrated in the pool below the waterfall, awaiting rescue.

Soon the nuggets scattered near the surface were recovered. Groups of men returned to camp for shovels, buckets and pans, eager to recover every morsel of gold from Zigzag Canyon. They were spurred on by the occasional echoes of gleeful whoops from those still digging with their hands. En route to camp, in their thoughts, the buckshot-size nuggets had already grown to the size of acorns.

Johnson was awakened by the boisterous conversation and excited activity of the returning prospectors. He didn't miss the importance of what was happening and quickly began plotting.

This was a major find. Because of the confined space and frigid water, the men worked in shifts. Eight worked the gravels, while eight others built a shelter. The others rested, tended daily chores, and guarded against Apaches and other prospectors.

Adams and Landrew continued to tend the livestock and do camp chores. The prospectors agreed that Johnson, too, should stay in camp. They didn't trust him.

The livestock had a good feeding area near the camp they had already established and there weren't any better campsites closer to the dig so they decided to make a permanent camp right where they were. They would stay here until they had recovered what gold they could with their hand tools. They expected to be working the hidden canyon for several weeks, and they began construction of a lean-to cabin. If supplies ran low, some of them would have to make a trip to the nearest settlement, more than sixty rugged miles away. There the men could trade their beaver hides for whatever they needed.

Johnson, happy to stay put, was working on yet another plan for quick and easy profit. "Let them buggers dig away! Old Johnson, why he'll just take it easy in that nice snug cabin they're buildin' him."

He spat into the fire, where the stew was warming, and fondled the vial in his trouser pocket. "Yes," he mused, "and after they've gathered a tidy lot of gold, old Johnson'll have a little something extra to add to their supper." He grinned at the thought. "And when they're dead and all that gold is mine, I'll find myself some more damn Injuns to kill."

This tickled his twisted mind and he cackled uncontrollably, nearly choking himself. When the others returned to camp for supper they found him surprisingly cheerful. James Johnson's luck had changed again, and for the better. Or so he believed.

CHAPTER 10
NANA REPORTS

When Nana saw the explorers constructing a cabin he knew they intended to make a permanent camp on the bank of the Prieto River. It was time to act.

He had long been puzzled by the peculiar afternoon activities of the explorers — huddling along the banks of the river like a group of squaws who were washing clothes — and now his scouts reported whoops and hollers of those who went into the zigzag gorge.

Now he fully understood what they had been doing. They were prospectors: Those who look for squaws metal, those whom Juan José had warned him must never find the hidden zigzag canyon. It was too late to stop these men from discovering the squaws metal, but it wasn't too late to keep their discovery a secret. Already Nana was forming his plan. He would use the shiny metal they craved to set a trap for them.

The young braves were camped west of Smith's men, above the sacred hot spring, where Nana and Mangas had been given their names. "Do not disturb the white eyes," Nana ordered. "They will be here for a long while. I will report to Mangas. Move back farther from their camp and wait for my return. I am certain Mangas will allow us the pleasure of dispatching these men after I tell him they are prospectors and have entered the sacred zigzag canyon. Our chief holds special contempt for those who love squaws metal. Remember, it was a prospector who led the massacre at Santa Rita, a man who laughed as he took the scalps of our people."

Nana set out for Mangas' camp certain his friend would act on the news he carried.

It was another restless night for Mangas. Again a powerful dream interrupted his sleep. He rose and sat, cross-legged, in front of the fire in his tepee, holding his vision crystal before the dimming fire. Dancing Horse watched through sleepy eyes as he sat before the dying embers. She watched his expression change and listened with surprise as Mangas spoke from his trance.

When he uttered, "Santa Rita," she knew he was revisiting the massacre. When Mangas whispered, "Johnson," his features revealed the hatred and intense fury that came over him whenever he thought of "the butcher." Later she saw his expression change abruptly to one of delight. She was certain his vision foretold fulfillment and revenge.

As Dancing Horse's eyes were closing and she was drifting into sleep she heard him whisper in an inquisitive tone, "Red bearded one, who are you? Why will you not speak to me? Why will you not approach me? Why do you gaze silently at me?"

His whispered questions brought her back to full alertness. Even before he was chief, because of his size and his imposing presence, Mangas seldom was ignored by anyone. When he asked a question, no one refused to answer. To do so would be to risk the great man's wrath. Yet, although the bearded one of his vision apparently would not answer, Mangas showed no anger in either his voice or in his expression. This puzzled Dancing Horse.

She watched as he withdrew from his trance. She awaited his embrace. She had learned to anticipate his violent passion on nights like this. But tonight Mangas surprised her. He was gentle and considerate, making love to her tenderly just as he had on the night he first took her as his woman, administering to her needs then his own before falling asleep in her embrace. Dancing Horse did not know why his vision had affected him as it had but she knew good things were to come.

Later that night, asleep in her arms, Mangas dreamed of a special place. He was certain he had been there, but — as often happened in his dreams — he did not recognize it at first. The hated Johnson was there, and Nana, and a broken crystal. Slowly he recognized it was the zigzag canyon he and Nana had found so many years before.

His dream became a new vision. He was looking into the zigzag canyon of gold, not as a young man carrying a sheep's head, but as a mighty warrior. Blood covered his hands and arms. The red-bearded one stood before him, gazing into his soul. Mangas moved to touch his vision companion, but as he moved forward, the distance between them remained unchanged. Mangas found himself running, following the bearded figure up the familiar canyon until the bearded one merged with the falling water, faded and passed into the night.

Mangas emerged from his lodge uncharacteristically late the next morning. He spotted Nana waiting for him at the communal fire. "Greetings, my friend. Have you tired of watching those white explorers?"

"Killing is better than watching, my chief," replied Nana. "It is time to be rid of them. They have found squaws metal and appear to be settling in for a long stay. I have watched them digging in the sands of the Prieto every evening. Now they have gone into the secret zigzag canyon to the pool where squaw's metal glints in the sun's light. They are near the sacred place of our manhood."

"I remember those places well," replied Mangas, "I have just seen the canyon again in a vision. A red-bearded Anglo haunts me from that place. Many times, I have seen him. He looks deep within me but he does not speak . . ." Mangas voice trailed off. He motioned his friend to continue.

"These men entered the hidden canyon with great shouts. Now they grub in the dirt like pigs. Only the two who tend the mules and the one who does squaw's work do not behave this way. The squaw worker is a repulsive man spurned by the others. His hideous laughter erupts for no reason, and he constantly scratches his head where some scalper left his job unfinished. He must be possessed of an evil spirit." With this, Nana gave a shudder of revulsion.

Mangas came to full attention, "What!" He leapt to his feet. "Partly scalped? Laughs like one possessed of an evil spirit?"

Taken aback by his friend's intense reaction, Nana swallowed hard and nodded.

"Johnson!" Mangas spoke this name as he would a vile curse. The big man's features writhed with the intensity of his hatred. In the next few seconds the massacre in the plaza of Santa Rita flashed through Mangas' mind.

Mangas strode abruptly to the horse corral. He shouted orders for braves to outfit his two best horses with weapons and provisions. "Now!" Mangas thundered.

Nana secured three horses. Within minutes they were riding at a cruel pace toward the prospectors' camp, Mangas leading one spare horse and Nana leading two. They headed west along the Gila, riding at a hard gallup. Nana's mount finally collapsed under him. Mangas slowed his horse while Nana changed horses and caught up with him, then they continued at the same hard pace. Soon Mangas was riding his only replacement mount, a big bay mare. Dead horses left behind held no significance this day. These were men on a mission, impatient and pushing themselves and their mounts as hard as they could.

Long before they reached the hot springs, Nana's second horse fell. Mangas' second mount carried his enormous bulk more than twice as far as any horse he had ever ridden. Finally, her great heart burst and she stumbled to the ground, dead. Mangas was saddened by the death of such an exceptional animal, another day he would consider it more carefully.

Mangas continued afoot, running at his unusually fast dog-trot pace. Nana slowed his horse to match Mangas' speed. Mangas never considered asking for Nana's mount. It was Mangas' choice to bring only two horses. He would run all day if need be, but he would never ask for his friend's horse. Likewise, Nana would never insult his friend and chief by offering his horse. This was not the Apache way.

CHAPTER 11
PREPARATIONS

When they neared Smith's encampment, Nana brought his mount beside Mangas and pointed first toward the hot springs, then toward the white man's camp.

Mangas recognized that Nana had made a wise choice in settling his braves at the spiritual hot springs, only a mile from Zigzag Canyon. The springs were on the other side of the river and not visible from the river bottom. As they neared Nana's camp, the air was filled with the unmistakable odor of sulfurous gases, mixed with the odor of Nana's sweating mount and their own bodies.

Nana's poor beast, lame beyond help, was led off to be butchered. They didn't need a horse now. Nana and the others had been following the invaders on foot; they would finish their business on foot.

Nana sent for all the scouts to return to camp. Mangas called his group of warriors together. There were twenty-three Mimbres — more than enough to handle the ill-armed and unprepared men camped on the banks of the Prieto.

Soon strips of horseflesh were sizzling over a small clean-burning fire. Then Mangas did a curious thing. He ordered the men to save the cooked horse meat and gather berries and roots. "Later we will have a feast," he said. "Eat nothing now. Remain here quietly until I return."

Mimbres' feasts were normally spontaneous and Mangas' delay of this one seemed unnatural to the young braves.

Mangas worked his way back down the Prieto until he could cross over to the ridge, much as Smith's group had done when they came up the canyon. He followed the game trail leading to the prospectors' camp and hid close behind the newly constructed cabin.

When the cook came out to relieve himself, the veins and tendons bulged in Mangas's huge neck. He wanted to charge down the hill and disembowel this man he had hated for so long. He thanked the spirits for giving him the strength to restrain himself. He vowed that such a special event as this man's death should be shared. And he pledged that Johnson's death would not be quick.

When he returned to the hot springs he again assembled the warriors. Silently they gathered, amazed at the quivering tension in Mangas' body and the fierce expression on his face.

"Johnson!" Mangas hissed savagely, gesturing. "The man responsible for the massacre at Santa Rita is there! The one who laughed while he killed our people, took their scalps and defiled their bodies."

At his words the other warriors were infected with Mangas' thirst for vengeance.

The fire of Mangas' anger appeared to diminish after he spoke, but Nana and the others knew this calm calculating facade was Mangas at his most dangerous.

Now he surprised them again, speaking in subdued tones. "Let us eat! Out of respect for those who died in Santa Rita we will feast in silence. We will speak no more until the morrow."

Early next morning, Mangas again gathered the braves. "We have had our feast, a feast in memory of our fallen brethren at Santa Rita. Now we will have our massacre! We will corral and kill these men like sheep. All except Johnson. Chief Nana tells me Johnson always remains at camp, sometimes alone, which is all the better. While the rest of you have the honor of following Nana into battle against these trespassers, the sons of our beloved Juan José will go with me to capture Johnson. When the others are dead we shall again feast while we take our time attending to him!"

Throughout that day Mangas and Nana conferred, perfecting Nana's plan. "We will tease them into the rough and indefensible area above the falls," Nana suggested. "Our braves will be waiting in hiding there."

"You know how to lead them into this trap?" Mangas asked.

Nana had been thinking about it for days. "Yes I do. I will go to them and tell them the area above the falls contains much squaws metal, that it belongs to the Apache, and they must not go there."

Mangas knew the white man's lust for gold and he knew Nana's plan would work. He praised him. "You are wise, my friend. These men are like children. They will not be able to resist that which is forbidden. Just as our brothers were tempted to the slaughter in Santa Rita we will tease these whites into an area where they can easily be dispatched."

While the Mimbres planned the massacre, it was business as usual at Smith's camp. They had long since stopped trapping in favor of panning and were only concerned that their food was running low. Security had fallen off. Having seen no sign of Indians during their many weeks in the wilderness, none of the prospectors thought much about hostile Indians or even other prospectors or trappers.

Adams and Landrew were washing up after breakfast — Johnson had been keeping a very neat kitchen since the discovery of gold, but as usual they had been bullied into another of Johnson's jobs. With another windfall in sight, Johnson was eager to please the rest of these men with his best manners. His meals were now served on clean plates.

Johnson sat complacently, belching and picking his teeth. Life had become quite comfortable for the scarred Englishman. Much of the work that should have been his, he pawned off on the young mule skinners. Landrew, in particular, was easily coerced into various chores. Others thought him somewhat dull of mind but in reality he simply chose the way of least resistance, finding it easier just to go along. Even Adams' assertiveness waned in the face of Johnson's constant bullying and threats of starvation rations.

As had become their habit now that a permanent camp was established, the others left for the diggings earlier in the morning, eager to take every bit of gold from the sands of the narrow ravine. Each day was a challenge. They worked feverishly to exhume as much gold as possible before the sun's rays failed and the gold's gleam faded. They calculated that within a week they would finish panning all the sand in the narrow gulch. They didn't even consider working the vast sandbar where Zigzag Canyon opened out before its waters joined those of the Prieto. There was just too much gravel to move to do the job by hand — and where would they put it?

As they worked the pool below the falls and the sands further down the canyon they were suddenly startled by a shout of greeting. Standing on a bench that jutted from the cliff above them stood a lone Apache brave, a dark-looking, powerfully built man. He called to them in heavily accented and broken English.

"Greetings. I am Nana of the Copper Mine Apaches, I come on behalf of my chief to bring you a message. You are on Apache land. You hunt our lands and you fish our streams. You take Squaws metal from the sands here. This we will permit. But do not go above these falls."

He gestured toward the falls above them, and began his deceptive announcement: "The land above these falls is sacred to our people. That is the source of this yellow metal. It is for our people alone. You must not go into that sacred place where the yellow metal is so abundant. Our chief has spoken."

With a parting gesture, Nana disappeared.

The men regarded each other in open-mouthed astonishment. More than one was unable to repress a shudder.

That evening's discussion was lively. Several men wanted to pull out entirely, leaving the gold right where it was, buried under the hearthstone in front of the cooking fire. These were the sensible ones, those who had some understanding of the Apache. They didn't believe Nana's words of reassurance for one minute. They sensed their only chance for survival was to abandon all and outdistance the Apaches, if they could.

Had Johnson known who waited in the darkness surrounding the camp, or that "Mimbres" and "Copper Mine" were two names for the same tribe, he would have pulled out immediately . . . but that would have done him no good. Every possible escape route was already well guarded.

Those who advocated immediate departure were shouted down by others unwilling to abandon their gold. "After all, we've been given permission to continue working below the falls," Smith pointed out. "Gotch Ear says the homeland of these Apaches is several days travel from here. We are safe enough, at least for the time being."

As hired help, Adams, Landrew and Johnson had no say in what the group would do. Smith and the others listened to what Gotch Ear had to say but seemed not to hear his words. As before when Smith's group refused to heed his advice, Gotch Ear wondered why they had hired him.

Among the others, the conversation took a predictable course. If the diggings were so good in the limited area below the falls, imagine what it must be like above the falls! After all, Nana had said gold was plentiful up there.

Smith came up with an idea that seemed like the perfect solution. "Gotch Ear says them Apaches live several days from here, so Nana can't report to his chief for a few days. We can please everyone. We'll go above the falls, take our fill of the easy pickings up there and head out of here the day after tomorrow. Sounds like we can gather more gold up there in a few hours than we could if we worked another week where we've been. We'll head back down the river before they have time to return."

This plan seemed agreeable with everyone except Gotch Ear. He made no further comment. He had repeatedly warned them, "Apaches are dangerous and not to be trifled with." He knew the others would not listen to him, especially now that the lure of even more gold filled their heads.

He waited until the others were bedded down, then left camp, following the now well-beaten trail toward Zigzag Canyon. But this time he didn't turn up the hidden canyon, he continued up the Prieto and never looked back. Only his stealth saved him. Had he been careless he would never have gotten past Nana's concealed guards, unobserved. By morning, Gotch Ear was miles away. He knew the others would be killed and he knew there was nothing he could have done to prevent it. His only goal was to save himself and then try to find his mother's people.

The prospectors slept little that night, nervous because of Nana's warning, but excited with the prospect of new adventure and the promise of more riches with the new day. In the morning they arose early. Forgoing breakfast, they hurried toward their reward. No one even noticed Gotch Ear was gone.

They scurried up Zigzag Canyon, most immediately climbing past the falls without even a second thought. They were puppets, and Nana had pulled their strings, leading them into the forbidden land with the one thing they could not resist. Just as Nana had said, they began to find large nuggets scattered in the myriad shallow pools found there.

Mangas and Juan José's sons, hiding on the ridge above the camp, watched with malicious delight as the white men took the bait and hurried toward Nana's trap. Mangas knew what awaited them there. His own thoughts were fixed on the man in the cabin below.

Adams and Landrew had set out before dawn, with instructions to begin rounding up the free-roaming livestock for a hasty departure. They were very good at catching the livestock unaware and they started sneaking quietly toward the plateau behind the camp. Soon they located and easily captured several animals, tying these to trees to recover later. Then, hearing the movements of an animal on the benched cliffs above them, they decided to investigate.

"Well, Maury," Adams whispered. "It could be a burro. Good excuse to do a little climbing, anyway!"

Grins flashed in the pre-dawn chill and they forgot all about livestock. Landrew was all for the diversion. He had learned to enjoy mountain climbing. Since settling into the permanent camp the two had done considerable exploring on the rugged ridge behind and to the east of Smith's campsite.

This day they climbed high above the camp in the dim morning light to a bench of rock that led toward the canyon, where the older men would soon be digging in the sand.

"Maury," Adams said. "Looks like we can follow this bench over to the diggin's. Maybe we can watch them from up here."

Carefully they made their way through the deep shadows along the narrow bench as they crossed the almost sheer west-facing cliff. Several times they thought they had come to an impasse, but found they could climb a little lower and then continue. Three times they followed a narrowing bench that angled up and across the cliff face, then climbed down to another ledge that continued toward the mouth of Zigzag Canyon.

By dawn they were high above the canyon's mouth on a rocky bench with a sparse covering of grass and a few small bushes. They hid, lying on their bellies in the tall grass, figuring to spy on the prospectors as they plied the sands below. From their vantage point they had a good view of the lower part of Zigzag Canyon and their camp.

As they lay on this grassy ledge in the morning shade, the two were unaware that Mangas had already dispatched his warriors. Adams and Landrew thought it a good joke to watch in secret as the prospectors worked feverishly, especially since they were supposed to be working themselves, gathering livestock.

In the middle of the night, with the waxing moon low in the western sky, Mangas deployed his warriors. Then, in the early morning's darkness, he and Juan José's sons had positioned themselves on top of the plateau south of the prospector's camp. As the prospectors slept, ten young braves took positions and waited above the falls; the rest waited with Nana on the west bank of the Prieto, just upstream from Zigzag Canyon, sheltered in darkness by an overhang of rock. In the morning, after the prospectors had entered Zigzag Canyon Nana and nine warriors would cautiously follow, closing the trap. But for now they waited.

Adams and Landrew were first alerted to the ambush when they spotted Nana and his group moving out of the brush, across the Prieto, and into the narrow canyon below them. The two watched helplessly, sensing what was about to happen and unable to do anything to stop it. To try to warn the prospectors would certainly get them both killed and just as certainly it wouldn't save the others.

Hiding in the upper part of the canyon, braves watched from positions that were within easy arrow shot of any who might move past the falls and pass below them. Since the only possible escape was either up or down the cliff-walled canyon the braves were certain there was no possibility any of the prospectors might escape their trap.

Adams and Landrew watched with mounting dread as most of

the prospectors scrambled over the escarpment and headed eagerly into the forbidden area. Five of their companions cautiously stayed below the falls, believing they might somehow be safe if they heeded Nana's warning.

As the more adventurous prospectors spread out in small groups at the gold laden pools, Mangas' well-trained but inexperienced braves waited. They were under orders not to move against these trespassing whites until they heard Nana begin his attack in the lower part of the canyon. They could wait. It was their day for revenge. A good day to kill. For these irreverent invaders, a good day to die.

The prospectors working the sands saw nothing out of the ordinary. Had they carefully searched the shadows with a suspicious gaze, they might have caught a glimpse of the braves hiding among the boulders and brush, waiting patiently for the appointed time. But the prospectors remained oblivious of the gauntlet they were entering.

CHAPTER 12
ANNIHILATION

Landrew and Adams watched in frozen anticipation as the Apaches approached the narrow opening to the zigzag ravine. Nana's hand signals directing five braves to take positions above the prospectors in the lower canyon was clear even to them.

Their hearts raced as the five painted Apaches inched their way onto the narrow shelves along both sides above the zigzag ravine, above those working the sands below. They could see the bright crimson paint and charcoal black streaks accenting the warriors' faces. Landrew shuddered. There was nothing pretty about an Apache in war paint.

The five warriors watched the busy prospectors, shoveling sand and working their contraptions. The sounds of the water crashing into the pool drowned out any noise the ambushers might have made as they positioned themselves.

Nana and the four braves remaining below the widening of the canyon waited in positions to the sides of the opening of the narrow passage, their bows and arrows poised for slaughter. On Nana's signal the braves above began cursing and throwing fist-sized stones at the hapless men. Startled, the prospectors looked up . . . .

Trying to find protection from the rocks raining down upon them, they sought refuge under overhanging portions of the ravines' walls. This was useless. The braves easily out maneuvered them by moving to new positions. They were always able to find a place where they could see the prospectors' legs. For several minutes, they took great pleasure in pummeling the cowering prospectors.

Finally, convinced they could not escape this stoning, the battered men ran for open ground. As they fled through the mouth of the ravine, they were met by a shower of well-aimed arrows. They had not violated Mangas' decree. For this, their reward was a quick death.

As the young warriors plundered the bodies of the fallen prospectors Nana scurried up the sloping rock to a new place of hiding above the falls. There he waited in ambush.

Those who ventured above the falls were not so lucky. As agreed, the braves in the upper portion of the canyon waited until they heard Nana begin his attack. At the sound of his battle cry they waited, poised, a few moments longer.

The venturous prospectors also heard Nana's battle cry, followed soon after by the death cries of their fallen comrades. Struck with the horror of what was happening, several began to run toward the mouth of the canyon, then hesitated. Was there anything they could do to help their friends now? Did they really want to join them?

As the echoing screams of death faded, the attack came to them. Slowly and methodically warriors descended upon the ill-armed men like mountain lions stalking their prey. Several prospectors drew knives. Others grabbed their muzzle-loading rifles, but not one was able to take aim and fire a shot. Crippling arrows prevented them from bringing their rifles to bear on the approaching warriors. Several men panicked, fleeing back down the canyon.

By some miracle, Smith escaped the upper trap with only a leg wound. He tottered toward the treacherous sloping outcrops above the falls on two bad legs — one from the old injury that never healed correctly, and the other now crippled by an arrow protruding from his knee. Nana sprang from behind a boulder and gave a bloodcurdling howl. Both Adams and Landrew had a clear view of what happened then.

Smith turned and tried to flee by making his way down the treacherous sloping rock. As he did so, Nana released his tomahawk with practiced skill. Striking just above the blond man's shoulder, the heavy, razor sharp flint blade nearly severing Smith's neck. Blood fountained from this new wound. The prospector staggered clumsily, his head hanging at an awkward angle. He cursed his attacker with horrible gurgling noises. Finally, as the remaining young braves made their way toward the top of the falls, Smith lost his footing and plummeted from the cliff to the canyon floor, fifty feet below. This chance timing saved his body from further mutilations.

Within minutes all the other prospectors who had ventured above the falls had fallen, but none of their deaths came swiftly or easily. Nana's braves took slow pleasure in the final slaughter. They moved from one dying or crippled man to the next to deliver the final thrust of the knife. There was no compassion for these trespassers. They made their final killing advance slow and deliberate, like a pack of wolves.

Adams and Landrew had a clear view of everything that happened in the canyon below them and the narrow canyon above funneled the sounds of that slaughter to their position with unnerving clarity. Sometimes they even recognized one of the tortured men's voices. Both had vivid memories of Gotch Ear's descriptive explanations of Apache tortures and in the ensuing minutes, minutes that seemed like hours, Adams and Landrew could only imagine mutilations to match the screams they heard.

Since all the Apaches they had seen were now above them in the canyon Adams thought it a good time to leave. Leaning close, he whispered, "Should try to get out of here now?"

But Landrew lay mute, unable to respond.

No more that fifteen minutes after the massacre had begun, it ended. Nana and his men traversed back down the treacherous sloping outcrops of rock above the falls as easily as if they were traveling on flat ground. When all the warriors got to where the five more-cautious miners lay they stopped for the job of scalping. Nana took the first of these scalps with much ceremony.

This grisly detail almost finished things for the two young men. Landrew was staring blankly at the scene below, as if he expected the bodies to come to life and scurry back down the canyon and toward camp, arrows and all, like a group of porcupines.

As the pair watched the scalping began. At the sight of the first glistening skull, Landrew suddenly jumped to his feet, vomiting, choking and gasping for air.

Adams, terrified the Apaches might see or hear Landrew, seized a handy stone and clobbered his friend on the back of the head. Landrew collapsed and again lay still in the grass on the ledge. For several minutes Adams feared he might have killed him. As Landrew regained consciousness, Nana and his men were approaching camp. Then they saw a huge Apache walking down the path from behind the cabin. This outsized Indian and two frail-looking companions seemed to appear out of thin air.

Adams looked at Landrew. "We may be here a long while," he whispered. "Can you stay quiet and still?"

Landrew was too sick and too scared to do anything but nod.

Adams and Landrew had a bird's eye view of Johnson's capture and torture. It would have been easier for them if they hadn't.

Inside the cabin, Johnson heard nothing but the rush of the river, the whisper of the breeze through the willows and the crackle of the morning fire. He was busy with preparations for the afternoon meal, and he anticipated his customary morning nap. His only concerns were that he was working on his last bottle of rotgut and he hadn't figured out how he was going to pack all that gold out by himself. This evening's meal would be the one. He could wait no longer. The vial of poison he'd saved from the Santa Rita affair would go into tonight's stew.

He smiled evilly. "Lucky for me I didn't trust poison to kill those heathens quick enough," Johnson thought. "Now I can put it to better use."

Johnson was fondling the small vial when the makeshift door of the cabin burst open, revealing the silhouette of a huge Indian. The cook sprang to his feet. Determined not to show the fear that gripped him, he demanded in his most vicious tone, "Who are you? What do you want?"

The big man answered with a silent implacable glare. Seeing only one Indian, Johnson mustered a grin. Maybe he had a chance. The Indian stepped back. Johnson stepped out of the door holding out his bottle of rotgut. "Want a drink? Good stuff . . . ."

His words were cut short as Juan José's sons sprang from their places of hiding to either side of the door. They grabbed him and forced his arms behind his back in a crushing hold. The whiskey bottle fell from Johnson's hand and shattered on the rocks, but he managed to hold tight the vial of poison. It might yet come in handy.

Although he refused to grasp his fate Johnson's bladder gave way. As the two young Indians dragged him behind the silent red giant and toward a stand of trees, he soaked his pants. The full weight of his predicament settled on him and when he heard the victory cries of the returning warriors and recognized the trophies they waved so proudly over their heads, he knew he was doomed.

At that realization he convulsed in hysterical, hideous laughter. Surprised at this response, one of his captors lost his grip. In that brief moment of freedom, Johnson threw himself to the ground, uncorked his vial of poison, and swallowed quickly.

"There!" he shouted. "I've beaten you heathen bastards again. You aren't going to torture this pilgrim anymore! You can take what's left of my scalp but that won't bother me none. I'll be long gone."

These words were hardly out of his mouth before he realized the last laugh would not be his after all. He had tasted that vile substance before. Once, as a youngster, when he had stolen a peppermint stick the local constable had given him a taste of the rewards of thievery.

"Syrup of ipecac!" Johnson moaned. "That damned Spanish trader gave me vomit potion instead of poison!"

He could no longer speak or think coherently. He was completely overtaken with convulsions. His body emptied and then tried to reëmpty his stomach. Next his bowels acted and in moments he was a wretched, exhausted mess. Unfortunately, he was not dead.

Mangas and his braves took perverse pleasure from Johnson's discomfort. They presumed his convulsions were the result of a coward's fear. But they didn't care what caused them; they merely stood back and enjoyed the show.

When Johnson finished with the worst of this, they stripped him naked and threw him into the frigid, cleansing waters of the Prieto. Then they dragged him roughly to his feet, holding him up in front of Mangas. Mangas stared his hatred into Johnson's eyes, for a long silent moment. At last he spoke.

"Vile scum! Killer of innocent people!" he hissed. "Your time has come. Your death will be a great medicine for all Mimbres and I promise you it shall not come quickly. Before we grant release of your spirit, you will endure all the agonies you inflicted that day at Santa Rita, and more." With that he spat in Johnson's face.

Juan José's sons dragged Johnson, who was kicking and screaming, to the nearby cottonwoods. They bound him with rawhide taken from the horse they had feasted on the day before, tieing him spread-eagle between two convenient trees.

Johnson babbled incessantly throughout these proceedings.

"It weren't me!" he screamed. "I weren't even there. You've got the wrong man. Please, anything! What do you want?"

His cries landed on uncaring ears. The only response was jeers and curses. He hoped death would come soon.

Mangas drew a razor sharp flint skinning knife from its sheath. Speaking prayers and singing incantations while a background of whoops and chanting rose and grew into a rhythmic cadence he moved closer to Johnson. There were no recognizable words to the warriors' chant but the message was clear: "Kill, kill, kill . . . ."

Eerie modulations in Mangas' voice accentuated his exaggerated motions. In a stylized dance he stalked his prey, arching his back, hunching his shoulders, and crouching his body low to the earth. His feet struck the ground toe-heel, toe-heel, toe-heel in rhythm with the chant of his braves.

Johnson now watched the unfolding ceremony dumbly, his mind finally grasping the full measure of the ordeal he faced. He began to lose focus, he hoped he was dreaming.

Without breaking his rhythm, Mangas reached out deftly making a small preliminary cut. Then stepped back to appreciate his victim's reaction. Johnson wailed in agony. Mangas stared back, icy and passive. He felt no compassion for the abominable thing in front of him. Mangas' only regret was that Johnson's torture *might* end with death.

Johnson recovered enough from the shock to dare look down at his chest. Where his left nipple had been, he saw a neat red patch dribbling surprisingly little blood across his quivering belly.

Mangas moved around his victim, contemplating his next move. He wanted to exact vengeance that would follow Johnson into the spirit world, a vengeance he could not escape in death. He bent close to Johnson to tell him in detail what he intended to do. Johnson, his voice already hoarse from screaming, closed his eyes to avoid looking at his tormenter.

Mangas screamed, "No, white man, you will see my face and you will see what we do to you." While Juan José's sons held Johnson's head, with swift and exact strokes, Mangas cut away Johnson's eyelids. Patiently Mangas waited for the bleeding to stop.

"Now you will have an unobstructed view of what we do," Mangas continued. "Your eyes will see and your spirit will know what we do to your body and you will carry your uselessness into the afterworld with you."

Mangas moved to Juan José's elder son and spoke in a low voice. He handed him the knife. The young brave broke into laughter as he stepped forward and with one sharp stroke cleanly removed Johnson's left testicle, throwing it to the ground and stomping it into the dust amid great whoops and hollering. Juan José's younger son then took the knife and completed the task his brother had begun. At last, Johnson had no more voice with which to scream.

Whenever Johnson regained consciousness, Mangas invited another warrior to inflict a new injury. But always something that would not bring death. Each time Johnson's body convulsed in response to the pain. His only sound was a soft groan.

As the sun moved below the western mountains, Mangas again broke into a prayer chant. He danced and chanted until the last rays of the evening's sunlight disappeared. Then, by the eerie glow of the moon, Mangas stepped forward and made one swift slash. Reaching up through this latest unnatural opening, a new one under Johnson's chest, Mangas tore out the still-beating heart, holding it up for Johnson and the others to appreciate. Then, as Johnson finally, forever lost consciousness, Mangas made one final slash, separating the heart from its connecting tissues.

Johnson's body convulsed and then slumped. Mangas held his trophy overhead, his sleeves soaked with his victim's blood.

"Juan José and our slaughtered brothers are avenged, at last. Now they can rest in peace. Let us celebrate. This loathsome affair began with a white man's feast. It is fitting that it should end with one of our own. Capture their burros and mules. We will eat our fill for many days."

As the sun was setting and before the rising moon's light shown on the west facing cliff, Adams led his friend back across the cliff, the way they had come. Adams hoped there would be a place to climb down to the Prieto farther from the camp than where they had climbed up, but in the growing darkness he couldn't find one. If Landrew had been able, he might have chanced going all the way back to where they had climbed up the cliff. But Landrew was so wobbly, Adams dared not try and the two returned to the bench. There they waited through the cold night, hoping the Apaches would soon leave, praying they would not be discovered, wishing they could forget what they had seen.

Below them, warriors' victory cries echoed off the canyon walls while they plundered the camp. They set aside those supplies that were of value to them. The rest were scattered like dust in the wind.

Braves butchered pack animals and built a great fire with wood from the cabin walls and roof. Soon hunks of burro meat were sizzling over a raging bonfire. The festive atmosphere was infectious. None of the braves seemed immune to its attraction, even those who were troubled because they had never killed before.

In the midst of the long hours of celebration, Mangas drew Nana aside. It was a great victory and Nana deserved special credit.

"This is a great moment for our people, my friend," Mangas spoke. "The spirits of Juan José and the others rejoice with us because you made this revenge possible."

"I also feel their eyes upon us and I feel their satisfaction," responded Nana. "The death of that loathsome Anglo and of those with him, has lifted a great burden from all our hearts."

"Yes, my friend," Mangas said. "Now, go and join the others. I need time alone, to speak with the spirits."

As Nana joined the throng milling around the fire Mangas moved off into the moonlight by himself. His tired body longed for the soothing, healing waters of the spiritual hot springs. Yet he was drawn first to visit Zigzag Canyon.

CHAPTER 13
MANGAS' GIFT

Adams and Landrew stayed hidden in the grass on the bench, shivering as much from fear as from the cool evening air. Thirst and hunger were beginning to gnaw at them, and both thanked God the evening chill calmed most of the bugs that had tormented them unmercifully during the day. In the daylight they had been afraid to swat at the insects for fear of being spotted by the Apaches. Now, as it grew darker, Adams could at least swat at the few insects that still pestered them. Landrew no longer noticed the insects, he seemed to be losing consciousness again.

"How long do you figure they'll stay there, Maury," Adams mumbled. "I don't think we've got a chance of getting down alive with Apaches in our camp. But I don't know how much longer we can survive up here."

Landrew mumbled an incoherent response.

When Mangas walked away from the light of the camp fire into the eerie light of the bulbous moon and headed toward Zigzag Canyon, Adams' heart froze. He prayed his death would be more merciful than Johnson's.

Mangas had a hunter's night vision. Guided by moonlight, he soon reached his first destination. Under the terrified gaze of the pair on the rocky bench, Mangas strode boldly into the shadowed, shrouded, and eerie darkness of Zigzag Canyon, drawn there by memories of his recurring vision of a red-bearded man.

Mangas paused at the entrance to the winding portion of the canyon, oblivious to the bodies scattered there. He waited as his eyes adjusted to the darkness, until he could see into shadowy recesses of the canyon where the moon's ghostly glow didn't reach. He almost expected to see the red-bearded one just as he had seen him first in dreams, then in visions.

Finally, after a long pause under Adam's gaze, Mangas sighed and moved into the shadows of the ravine. He was surprised and angered to find the sands of the canyon floor so disturbed. When he had first come here as a youth all those years ago the cool water had flowed ankle-deep across a smooth sandy bottom. Now he stumbled through a series of holes, splashing several times into knee-deep water. Mangas thought, "Our people are content to let things remain as they are. Even Indians who till the soil have a purpose but white men tear great holes in the earth for tiny bits of the useless yellow metal." Those now dead had defiled the canyon, but Mangas took comfort in the knowledge that, in time, nature would heal these wounds.

He nearly stepped on Smith's body as he rounded the final bend before the waterfall. Ignoring this, his eye caught the beautiful play of the moon's rays on the water plummeting into the pool at his feet.

Mangas lifted his head and roared, not in anger, but from deep passion. "Where are you, my friend? My heart would swell with joy to see you, to know what you know."

Before Mangas' outburst, Adams had been contemplating what he should do. Watching the fire and the festivities he decided all the Apaches must be gathered at the feast. Landrew was sick and getting sicker. Adams had been considering abandoning him and trying to make his escape alone that night. But Mangas' passionate cry changed his mind instantly. He didn't know who Mangas was looking for but it was clear the giant Indian expected to find someone in the canyon. Adams thought at first that Mangas might be calling to one of his men waiting in a hiding place in case there were survivors who might come back down the canyon. Or perhaps Mangas knew Adams and Landrew had escaped the initial massacre and was just teasing them. Either way, Adams decided he would rather die of thirst than face the torture he had seen Johnson endure. As Adams contemplated what kind of death he would have, Mangas strode out of Zigzag Canyon and across the Prieto.

Running silently at a slow trot in the bright moonlight, Mangas moved down the Prieto, past the festivities at the plundered camp, unnoticed. Within minutes he was at the hot springs to the west. There, clear warm water ran down the face of an ivy-grown cliff into the sparkling pool below. All was quiet and peaceful.

He stripped and stepped beneath the gently falling water. Gazing at the moss-covered rocks surrounding him, he was filled with a sense of peace. The killing anger flowed away along with the blood that had covered his arms. "I am clean again. The Great Spirit's healing waters have purified me."

He moved away from the cliff into the knee-deep middle of the pool, removed his vision crystal from his medicine bag, and sat, cross-legged, in the warm water. He raised the crystal over his head in symbolic tribute to the Great Spirit. He felt his heart would burst for joy — joy of revenge, joy in knowing the hated Anglo was dead, joy in knowing his slaughtered people could finally rest in peace, joy in living.

Much later, he stood and moved back under the falling water. He stayed motionless, holding the vision crystal high toward the moon's silvery light. Moonlight reflected from drops of water glistening on his massive body. Rainbows of color sparkled in the crystal as he turned it in the light.

Mangas was transfixed by this beauty, standing in the refreshing water, his lips forming a silent prayer for further guidance. As he gazed reverently into his crystal, it began to glow with a red hue. Red — like the color of blood. The color of death. The color of life. His color, after all.

This was a good omen. The spirits were pleased.

Although his arms began to tremble with fatigue, Mangas continued staring into the upheld crystal. His mind wandered to his great and good friend, Nana. He sent up a quick prayer of thanksgiving for providing him with so loyal a friend.

Suddenly there was a sharp crack. The sound issued from Mangas' crystal, as if it had spoken. A chill ran through him as he lowered his shaking hands which grasped the once solid quartz, now two equal pieces.

Mangas, holding one piece in each hand, waited until they began to glow again. Their reassuring red hue calmed him. Another good omen! Another sign from the spirits!

He knew the spirits were instructing him to do something unheard of among medicine men. He was to give Nana a great gift, and more than that, Mangas was to share his medicine with his friend. Without the spirits' guidance, he would never have considered doing such a thing. That was not the Apache way. But tradition was one thing, the Great Spirit's calling was another.

He wondered briefly whether Nana would be insulted. After all, Nana had his own medicine. But the spirits had spoken and Mangas would obey.

He returned to the feast and again sought Nana out. "My good friend," he said. "The spirits have given me a sign concerning you."

Nana paled, but Mangas hastened to reassure him, "Do not be concerned! It was not your death I saw, but a glorious and long life! And something else. The spirits have instructed that I do a most unusual thing. They wish to show you special honor for the victory won this day."

Mangas held up the two perfect halves of the vision crystal for Nana to see. "The spirits have done this. You are to choose one of these sacred stones as your own. From this day forward our spirits are to be as one while we lead our people!"

There was a long silence between them as Nana contemplated his chief's words. Had they not been friends of longstanding, and had Nana not understood the special meaning this crystal held for the great chief, he would have been most uncomfortable. Medicine men did not share their medicine. Yet Mangas said he was doing the spirits' bidding and Nana trusted his friend.

"I would be honored, my chief," he said. "From this day forward, we are equals between ourselves and before the spirits. Nevertheless, I will continue to call you my chief before our people. This way, our people will have no confusion."

Mangas was visibly relieved by Nana's suggestion. "This is good. From this time forward you and I are equals. Our combined wisdom and leadership will make our tribe even stronger. Now, let us join the festivities."

They found the others still carrying on, young warriors trying to outdo each other's feats of daring. To the cheers of onlookers they wrestled, took turns leaping over the huge fire, climbed the nearby cliff by moonlight, and competed in all manner of physical exhibition.

Adams continued to observe the comings and going of warriors around the fire, trying to keep track of them, praying they would soon leave. As the night wore on, he realized the Apaches did not intend to leave soon. He kept a cautious eye on Landrew who seemed to pass in and out of consciousness. He was worried. His friend had become too quiet.

The Indians' celebration continued through the night. Some feasted while others postured, gyrated, and leapt through the flames of the fire until they were overcome with exhaustion. Finally, in the early hours of the morning, the last of the revelers fell asleep. They used the prospector's bedrolls right where they found them, taking special pleasure in knowing the former owners no longer needed the soft padding.

When the camp finally quieted, Adams decided to risk an escape. Landrew seemed to move between unconsciousness and delirium and Adams knew he could never get past the Apaches with his friend. Hunger, thirst, and the pestering insects were driving him crazy.

As he crawled away from his friend, Adams mumbled, more to himself than to Landrew, "I'll get us some food and water and then come back." Maybe he intended to come back, maybe he didn't. He really didn't know.

Soon he was traversing the cliff face. He made good time, always careful to keep a watchful eye on the camp. When he came to a place where he had to climb back up the cliff, he unwittingly dislodged a large rock that bounced down the cliff face and splashed into the river below with a loud crash.

Adams froze, his eyes glued to the camp. Sure enough, one, then two braves appeared at the water's edge. He watched in terror as one of them pointed in his direction and then gestured, waving his arms in the air. Had they seen him?

He hung on the cliff's face waiting for the two to sound the alarm, but they only turned and began to rebuild the fire for the day's feast, "Or my roasting," he thought. His courage gone, he retraced his steps and was soon lying beside Landrew once more, exhausted from lack of sleep and from fear. He determined to stay put until the Apaches left or he died of thirst, whichever came first.

Late the next morning the camp came back to life. Indians butchered more animals and continued their joyous feasting. Johnson's eviscerated corpse was left hanging in their midst, where he had died, his eyes forever fixed on nothing. Again the celebration continued all day and far into the second night.

The third morning they finished their feast with a quick meal. The stench of carcasses, both human and animal, had begun to interfere with the fun. The Indians gathered up the remaining supplies, set fire to the remnants of the cabin, and headed back toward the hot springs.

The fire they left behind had barely subsided when the buzzards and other carrion eaters swooped down to begin their own feast. The carcasses in Zigzag Canyon were already well on the way to being picked clean of flesh, those in camp would soon follow.

Mangas and Nana agreed that the young braves who were now tested warriors needed a period of cleansing, away from the contamination of the white man's camp. Taking the two remaining burros and one mule with them, they spent the next three days in quiet rest at the warm spring where Mangas had purified himself two days earlier.

When the cleansing ritual was completed, Mangas turned to Nana and spoke. "This is sacred ground and a special place to us both. But the sun shall not see you and I here again. In time the spark of the Mimbres fire will have died. Smoke will no longer rise from our people's tepees. Only the coyote will remain."

CHAPTER 14
ESCAPE

Adams and Landrew had slept fitfully the first night after the massacre, unable to force the gruesome images and sounds from their minds. Time and again the flying tomahawk flashed in Adams' mind's eye, and he pictured Smith falling, crimson spurting from his gaping wound. The screams of tortured men and the war cries of the Apaches echoed through his mind, as they had through the canyon. He could not silence the memory of Johnson's hideous laughter or his agonized screams, nor could he forget the chanting of the braves and the big warrior's howl as he raised the cook's heart over his head.

Several times Landrew awoke with a gasp only to fall into unconsciousness again. Each time, Adams feared his friend's cries would give them away.

Mercifully, Landrew slept through the following day. But the insects were driving Adams crazy. Mosquitoes, gnats, and biting flies tormented him, yet he dared not move a muscle for fear of being spotted by the reveling Apaches.

When evening's shadows finally came at the end of the second day, the two were thoroughly bug-bitten, sunburned, and parched with thirst. After sundown, Adams fought back, swatting at persistent insects and rubbing his gnawed flesh. His skin was covered with welts and painful stinging bites. He was almost as frightened with the prospect of spending another day being tortured by bugs as he was by the Indians. Almost.

The Apaches seemed to be renewing their feast in the gathering darkness. Adams was certain he and Landrew would die if they didn't get to water soon. In spite of his earlier resolve to stay put, after dislodging the rock, he decided he would rather risk falling to his death or being killed by Apaches than to die of thirst while cowering on a lonely bench of rock in the God forsaken wilderness.

He awoke Landrew, and barely mustering enough saliva to wet his mouth so he could speak, whispered, "Maury, we have to get to water."

Landrew nodded weakly. Painstakingly they picked their way across and down the cliff face, trying to beat the moon's light that was rapidly advancing across the valley floor toward them.

Adams was convinced they would be spotted if the moon's light exposed them on the sheer rock face. Yet Landrew was unable to hurry, and they had to proceed slowly to avoid dislodging loose stones.

Landrew always seemed about ready to lose his balance. Twice they both nearly slipped to their deaths while crossing a rough spot along their tenuous path. But they were past the point of no return. The moon continued to rise in the cloudless sky and there was nothing they could do but proceed. Besides, after Adams' aborted attempt to get to food and water alone, he had resolved that live or die, he would not abandon his friend again. From a more practical point of view, if he abandoned Landrew now his friend would almost certainly fall. In falling he might alert the Apaches to their presence, even if he didn't cry out.

Adams' immediate concern was that the only path off the cliff took them directly toward the reveling Apaches. To get down they had to come within a few hundred feet of the camp. Adams hoped the Apaches would be night blind from staring into the fire. Nevertheless, he worried because the Indians seemed to move so easily in and out of the darkness.

The moon's rays reached them just as they reached the willows on the grassy bank of the river. Thus far they had not been spotted. Both drank deeply from the cool clear water. Almost immediately Landrew was overcome with retching convulsions.

Again Adams had to fight his survival instinct and the desire to desert his friend. Evidently, his resolves were not so certain as he had believed. After a few seconds Landrew seemed better and drank a little water without getting sick. Landrew rested while Adams tried to decide what to do next.

Although he had not intended to do so, Adams surrendered to his exhaustion and fell into a deep sleep. When he awoke the sun was full in his eyes. Terror gripped him. He pictured an outsized Indian holding a still-beating heart in front of his face.

He jumped to his feet and then froze, standing motionless, listening carefully, afraid to breathe. The only sound was that of the Prieto rippling through the grass and the breeze in the willows that had concealed him as he slept through the morning, only a few hundred feet from the slumbering Apaches. Looking down, Adams saw Landrew sitting in the tall grass beside him, a strange, twisted expression on his face.

"Them heath — heath, Them — heath . . . left about noon," he stammered. "Head — Headed down riv'r."

Adams thought of looking for some scraps of food at the camp but he remembered the big Indian's trip into Zigzag Canyon and worried that there could be an Indian watching the camp. Instead they headed back upstream, sneaking through the willows, heading away from camp, the hunger in their stomachs momentarily forgotten and their thirst quenched by the abundant cool water.

They didn't speak, each contemplating the grizzly spectacle they had witnessed. The scene etched most indelibly was that of the huge Indian, outstretched arms crimson with fresh blood, holding Johnson's still beating heart before the final swift knife stroke that ended it all.

Near the mouth of Zigzag Canyon, they came upon Smith's body. The man who had befriended them, had taken them in, had given them work, and had fed them; the man felled by Nana's skilled tomahawk throw. His bloated body had been moved along by the rushing water until it hung up on a gravel bar. The sight of Smith's decomposing corpse in the water they had been drinking was too much for Landrew. Again he retched uncontrollably.

Adams searched Smith's body for a knife, a canteen — anything that might help them on their journey away from this place of horror. Adams brightened when his hand came on the handle of Smith's big Bowie-style knife, but his heart sank as he pulled it from under Smith's body and he saw the blade was broken off. The search yielded nothing else that would help them survive in the wilderness. But there was a small leather pouch clutched in Smith's rigid left hand.

The bag was heavy for its size. Opening it, Adams found gold nuggets, most about the size of a pea, but there was one larger one.

Almost the size of a walnut, it was the biggest nugget Adams had ever seen.

With this much gold, Adams knew he and Landrew could support themselves for a long time in civilized comfort — if they survived long enough to find civilization.

Adams desperately wanted to enter Zigzag Canyon, where he was certain they would find, among the scattered remains, canteens and weapons to help them on their journey. But again he remembered the Apache's cry into the night: "Where are you?" and decided against venturing up the canyon.

The two moved up the unexplored Prieto, but were able to travel only a few miles before exhaustion overtook them. Having gone without food for several days their strength failed quickly. At dusk they came to a sandbar under a rock overhang. Once the main flow of the river had been on that side of the canyon and had undercut the cliff; now the main portion of the river flowed on the other side of the channel. Some water still trickled through a substantial pool under the overhanging cliff. Adams sat on the sandbar and considered their options while Landrew stretched out on the cool sand. Adams was thinking of the unburied dead, but he had felt compelled to hurry away from that grisly place. In any case, neither he nor Landrew had enough strength for that task.

Adams was fairly certain Santa Fe was east of them. He considered going back and following Zigzag Canyon to the east. But what if an Apache scout awaited them there? They considered going back down the Prieto to the Gila. He knew if they followed the Gila upstream they would find a settlement, but that was the direction the Apaches had gone.

They could do many things, Adams thought, his head swimming. He wished they'd tried harder to find a weapon. A gun, a knife, anything that could help them get food. Adams' thoughts blurred and he dozed.

He awoke abruptly, wet and cold and gasping for air. In his sleep he had tumbled into the moonlit pool. Under different circumstances he might have found humor in his unexpected bath, as Landrew seemed to. There was a crooked grin on the Frenchman's face as he watched the spectacle of Adams thrashing in the chilly water.

Adams' topple brought him back to reality. If they were going to survive they had to keep moving and they had to find food.

He helped Landrew to his feet and they started out again. Later, Adams woke with a start. He had fallen asleep as he walked. There was a shimmering of light in the eastern sky, and he had no idea how far they had come but he was relieved to note they were still traveling up the river.

Landrew hadn't uttered a sound since reporting on the departure of the Apaches the day before. He appeared to be drifting further and further from reality. His hands and knees were scraped and bruised from repeated falls. He seemed hardly aware when he stumbled and did little to protect himself from injury when he did. Adams knew Landrew could not survive without his help. The question was, could he survive to provide that help?

As dawn broke, Adams spied another of the many caves in the canyon, this one just out of the river bottom. He cajoled Landrew inside the low cave. "Come on Maury! There's a cave and we can sleep," he pleaded.

Once inside, they collapsed. Adams pondered the situation.

"No food, no weapons, nothing but blistered feet to carry us the hundred or more miles to civilization! Hostile Indians all around and a sick man for company! A fine mess!" he mumbled.

They slept soundly for a time, safe within the confines of the cave. "Well, at least we're getting enough water," Adams thought, as he stirred a second time to relieve himself. "Now if we could just find some food."

He decided against traveling during the day. "Too hot, too much chance of discovery. We'll travel by night and rest by day," he reasoned soundly.

Late that day he made a decision that probably saved both their lives. He was no Mountain Man. He didn't know how to find food. He knew it wouldn't be long before they would be too weak to continue. He hadn't paid much attention to landmarks during their journey from Santa Fe and he didn't have any idea where they were now. Nevertheless, he became convinced their only hope was to head back down the Prieto to the Gila and then travel east. If they ran into Apaches, so be it. He almost didn't care anymore. It seemed their only chance for survival.

His instincts were good. The country farther up the Prieto was even more rugged than where they were and there were no settlers to the north to help them. If they kept going upriver, he was sure they would die in the wilderness. He sensed this, but he was terrified at the thought of what lay behind them, namely, Apaches, one outsized Apache in particular.

Near sundown when he went to the river to get a drink, he saw something in the soft mud that convinced him they must go back the way they had come. "Gotch Ear warned us not to go up this river and now here I am following moccasin tracks!" His heart was pounding, "We're probably headed right into the heart of Indian territory!" He didn't know he was looking at Gotch Ears' tracks.

He roused Landrew. "Come on Maury, we have to go! Hey! Come on!" Landrew responded with a slack-jawed, vacant expression and silence.

Alarmed, Adam's shook his friend by the shoulders. "Look, Maury. If we don't get a move on, them Indians are going to get us for sure. Now come on!"

A flicker of fear crossed Landrew's face. He staggered to his feet, stooped and swayed as he walked out of the low cave.

"That's it," Adams said, encouragingly. "Now just stick with me, and I'll get us both out of this predicament. You'll see. We'll find someplace where there aren't any giant Apaches to bother us ever again."

Adams coaxed Landrew down the Prieto. If Landrew realized they were backtracking, he didn't show it.

All night Adams kept up a soft chatter, as much to reassure himself as to keep Landrew moving. He spoke of anything that came to mind. He talked of the comforts of a real bed awaiting them in Santa Fe. Then he hit upon a subject that seemed to do the job for both of them.

"Hey, Maury," he said. "When we get to civilization, how about you and me going into business together? With this gold I got off

Smith, we could start ourselves a right nice outfit, I'll bet. How does that sound?"

Landrew didn't answer. Concussion, exposure, dehydration, starvation, and terror had addled his mind. He heard the words, but his brain only partially processed them. He didn't respond because he couldn't. Several times he tried to speak but words would not come.

Although when Adams talked of setting up a business Landrew's pace quickened. So Adams continued talking of the future as he walked behind his friend, rallying him toward civilization. Nevertheless, long before dawn Landrew's condition had deteriorated again. As the sun rose he was moving woodenly where he was guided, soon collapsing into a nightmare-ridden sleep.

The next two days seemed an eternity to Adams, who was not granted the merciful oblivion afforded Landrew. Each night they struggled onward, Adams doing what he could to encourage and help his friend. As much as his voice would allow, he continued his one-sided conversation.

"Yes, Maury, we're good mule-skinners and we're going to build us up a first rate freighting business," Adams prattled. Although he varied the words, he always talked on the same subject. Talking about the future made him feel better and he sensed it helped Landrew, too. So he kept it up, mile after mile.

The days were the worst. Hiding, always hiding, fearful, lest they be discovered. Landrew slept, but for Adams sleep was fitful at best. His stomach cramped with hunger and insects still feasted on his already tortured flesh, especially on the new wounds he incurred each night — scrapes and bruises, most of which he had no recollection of getting. He did his best to ignore the blisters that rose and broke on his feet. Yet the worst torture came when he finally did fall asleep!

Fear of being discovered invaded his dreams. Nightmares awakened him repeatedly just as he was about to scream. The possibility that he might actually cry out in his sleep terrified him.

Each time he was rudely awakened he huddled, shivering with fear, listening to the sounds around him. What if he had really cried out, and not just dreamed that he had? What if someone, perhaps a giant Apache, had heard his cry? Surely the air would erupt with cries of attacking warriors. And so, time after time, he sat lost in his fear, with only the empty Landrew for company, waiting for darkness when they could again move on.

On the third or forth night after heading south — Adams had lost track — they reached the Gila. There they turned east, Adams wasn't really sure where they were going; he just hoped they would soon find a settlement and safety.

His hunger subsided and was replaced by a curious light-headed feeling. Adams felt he was going to float away into eternity. He found himself talking not only to Landrew, but to strange apparitions floating by in the moonlight.

When the next day dawned, he was too far into delirium to fear discovery. He staggered on, clutching Landrew's arm, chattering away. His last memory was of the surprise he'd experienced when some of his apparitions started talking back to him.

CHAPTER 15
RESCUE

As the group of Mexicans was traveling east, following the Gila en route to New Mexico, they noticed movement in the brush along the river ahead. Fearing an Indian attack, they took cover and drew their weapons. Rather quickly they realized this was no Apache ambush, but two young whites in very bad shape.

Neither of the tattered pair responded when questioned. One babbled incoherently about mules and freighting, the other just stared, as if unseeing. The Mexicans loaded them aboard a donkey cart, giving what care they could and continued traveling eastward.

After two days of rest, food, and water Adams recovered enough to speak of the horrors he and his friend had endured. It took nearly a week for Landrew to recover enough strength to begin focusing on his surroundings. The Frenchman would not speak of what had happened. The rescuers, who were sympathetic with his torture, kindly left him alone when he cried out in the night. At those times Adams sat beside him and talked of inconsequential matters until Landrew fell back to sleep. Eventually the Frenchman began to sleep through the night and in the daytime seemed normal, if unduly quiet, to the casual observer.

After many days, the group reached San Vicente, a settlement in far-western New Mexico, which was then nothing more than a frontier settlement, though in years to come it would grow and be renamed Silver City. Adams and Landrew thanked their rescuers, who refused any payment and were genuinely insulted at the offer. The Mexicans continued on their way, leaving the two young men to fend for themselves. Their rescuers were another group of prospectors, following rumors of riches to be found in the high mountains of New Mexico. They had not seen the nuggets in Adams leather pouch, and neither Adams nor Landrew had spoken of the gold and the greed that led to slaughter on the Prieto River.

In the following years, Adams caught the prospecting fever that permeated the country. Landrew, too, was caught up with gold fever. They used the smaller nuggets from Smith's pouch to purchase supplies. When their gold and supplies were exhausted, they turned to freighting, the business Adams had prattled on about during their ordeal.

Freighting was not what either had supposed. There was too much responsibility and Adams soon realized that what he really enjoyed was prospecting.

Soon they were caught up in a repetitive cycle: prospect until their supplies and money were all gone, then freight long enough to earn a grubstake, then go back to prospecting.

Minor discoveries of gold and silver teased them along. Once they hit a small bonanza, enough easy diggings to carry them through the winter, well fed and well clothed. They were even able to buy two mules and two sets of good tack.

But in the end the gold always ran out and they returned to freighting. Working until they made enough money to get back to what they really wanted to do. At least that's the way Adams saw it.

His mind returned more and more to the pot full of gold he knew was buried under the hearthstone of a burned-out cabin beside a twisting river somewhere to the west.

He had watched at night when Smith moved the hearthstone and added the days' diggings to the pot buried there. He'd heard Smith's claim, "Near three hundred pounds so far, boys." The Apaches hadn't torn up the floor of the cabin and the gold was still there, Adams was sure of it.

Time after time Adams attempted to broach the subject of going back for the gold. "Maury, think of all that gold just waiting for us out there in Apacheria! And here we are, scratching for gold dust! Let's go and get it," he pleaded. "We'll have more gold than we could ever use."

But each time he spoke of it, Landrew withdrew into silence. He didn't want to hear about that place and he would never return there.

Landrew did everything he could to forget. Adams did everything he could to remember. Landrew's dreams were nightmares of dread. Adam's dreams were of riches beyond compare.

Each day, in Adam's dreams, the nuggets in the hidden canyon grew larger. The walnut-sized specimen from Smith's leather pouch was soon remembered as a puny example of what was left behind.

Adams became increasingly obsessed with returning to Zigzag Canyon to claim his fortune. Only one thing held him back, and it wasn't fear of Apaches. It was the memory of one Indian that terrified him. What one Indian had done to Johnson and what that Indian had later hollered in the dark recesses of Zigzag Canyon. Adams vividly remembered that cry echoing in the darkness, "Where are you?" Adams was certain that Indian was waiting there for him, should he ever return.

Whenever Adams and Landrew were in town, Adams read any bits of news he could find, and he eventually read a newspaper account that identified the Apache who haunted his dreams.

The account told of a wagon train massacre attributed to a huge red man. Scanning the rest of the story he learned the Apache Chief's English name was *Red Sleeves* — *Mangas Coloradas* in Spanish. "The most feared Apache alive," the article stated.

With a shudder, Adams cast the paper into the fire. He stood staring into the flames, remembering the details of Johnson's death. "Red Sleeves," he muttered. "An apt name!"

By early 1845, seven years after the massacre, Landrew had grown tired of prospecting. The only big money he had ever made was from freighting. The hardest work and most miserable conditions he had faced were while prospecting. One night he broke the news to Adams.

"Andrew, my friend, I have had all the prospecting I want. I'm heading for Santa Fe to go into freighting full-time. Will you join me?" Adams was stunned. He and Landrew had been together most of their lives. Yet he couldn't imagine giving up prospecting.

The next morning Landrew headed out, alone, for the first time in years. When he got to Santa Fe, he spent all his savings on a string of mules. He was good with mules, and he was determined to stick with what he did best.

Using his mules as collateral he borrowed as much money as he could to purchase the necessary freighting equipment. Then he went to work.

But Landrew was no businessman and though there were plenty of jobs he was losing money. He would have done well if he hadn't been paying an excessive fee on the money he'd borrowed. Little by little, he was forced to sell his equipment to pay off his loan. It was all he could do to keep himself and his mules fed. Wagons, harnesses, crates, trunks, and finally mules disappeared. By the fall of 1846 he was out of debt, but had sold everything except six pack saddles and ten mules. He was flat broke and looking for work.

CHAPTER 16
EMORY'S EXPEDITION, 1846

In 1846, the U.S. government commissioned a massive Army expedition to map portions of the vast wilderness of New Mexico, Territory of Mexico, Apacheria (which the U.S. government called Arizona), and California, Territory of Mexico all of which the U.S. hoped soon to win, either by force or by intimidation. The expedition set out from Fort Leavenworth, which was located in what was then western Missouri territory. They traveled as one group to Santa Fe, the last bastian of civilization any of the troopers expected to see until they reached San Diego.

September 25, 1846 dawned wondrously. The high mountain air was clear and crisp. That day the force reached Santa Fe, where they split into three separate parties of nearly two hundred men each. The eventual destination for each of these groups was San Diego, California. The plan called for each to take a different route and explore regions remote from the others. There was considerable danger ahead. But for now they were concerned only with last minute preparations.[1]

Lt. William Helmsley Emory was a tall, clean, sharp-featured young man. His appearance properly conveyed the impression that he was military to the bone. He was well-educated and articulate, the ideal person to be in charge of information gathering for Colonel Stephen W. Kearney's expeditionary force. His specific duties included mapping, sketching, and noting details of every significant item of interest as the battalion passed down the uncharted Gila River and west past the Colorado River to San Diego. He was a thorough officer and a keen observer; even mundane things he encountered on the journey were to be well-documented.

The stated purpose of the expedition was "scientific investigation," and Emory was made second in command. Early on, Colonel Kearney gave him free rein.

Just now Emory was busy with final details before embarking on the journey into the uncharted wilderness south and west of Santa Fe.

"Sgt. Reaves, did you requisition the twelve additional pack saddles and the eight mules I ordered?" he barked, "It's two p.m. already. We need to get on our way."

"Sir, I was unable to find any livestock in town," Sgt. Reaves replied.

Lt. Emory frowned. He quickly decided to see if he could procure the additional livestock and supplies himself. He rode the sixteen miles to Santa Fe and after several inquiries among the locals, an odd-looking young man told him of a Frenchman who had gone broke in the freighting business, a man who still owned pack saddles and mules. "His name's Londeau." The man pronounced it just as Landrew did.

Emory found Landrew at the stables on the north end of town.

"I don't have that many pack saddles," Landrew replied, "but I do have ten good mules and six of the saddles you need. I don't intend to sell none of my gear, but I will hire on as a packer with all my mules and equipment to boot."

Emory didn't quibble. He needed all the help he could find. Another experienced mule-skinner was welcome insurance. Later, when the illiterate Landrew signed his "X" for the paymaster, Emory added a notation about the man's job, misspelling the Frenchman's name, *Londeau*.

Late that day Emory returned to camp with Landrew and his mules loaded with pack gear. Early the next morning Kearney's battalion moved out under Emory's provisional command.

They followed the *Rio Grande del Norte* — Large River of the North — south to Albuquerque, where they came to a natural ford, crossing the river there they headed west. For several more weeks, travel was easy.

Often at night Landrew came into the officer's tent and talked with Emory while the younger officer mapped, catalogued and sketched what he had seen that day. With great care, Emory noted anything he thought was important. Listing particulars down to the smallest detail.

"Are we getting close to Apacheria?" Landrew asked, interrupting Emory's work. "I've been there before," he volunteered. "Didn't have a good time, though."

Landrew's voice shook a bit as he spoke. He found himself wanting to tell the young Lieutenant more, but he was afraid to. He'd kept his mouth shut for almost nine years; he intended to keep it shut forever.

Noting the change in Landrew's voice Emory asked, "Do you know much about that country?"

Landrew gave no answer. His mind had wandered back to the canyon, the massacre, and a blood stained Apache. As one particularly bloody picture formed in his mind, he forced himself back to the present. "Nope," he answered. "Not much." With that, he turned and fled Emory's tent.

Nothing out of the ordinary happened for many days as the battalion marched west. The young lieutenant recorded, mapped and spent much time sketching pictures of flora, fauna, drainages, formations and distant mountains. Landrew didn't understand why Emory bothered to do all those detailed illustrations, although he really liked some of the plant drawings. They reminded him of paintings on the walls at the orphanage.

"Pretty enough to hang in a church," he opined.

Landrew continued to come for evening chats with Emory. At times Emory tired of Landrew's chatter. Other times he found it a welcome break from the tedious work and official talk that pervaded his days.

On October 5th, 1846, members of the battalion rode up to the base of Sierra Soccoro, a high peak in central New Mexico. In several places where the soil had eroded to bedrock, they could see galena and copper ore. Lt. Emory dismounted and collected sample specimens. He speculated that Soccoro Peak had once been worked for gold. His men collected specimens of turquoise and other beautifully colored rocks.

"West of here there's plenty of these green stones," Landrew commented. "The mountains there are full of colorful stones." He offered no other information, though.

On October 6, Emory ordered the battalion to again head due west.

"Señor Emory, we must not continue further west," exclaimed Pablo, a Mexican employee.

Pablo was the leader of a group of mexican peons Emory had hired in Santa Fe because they had freight wagons and teams to help haul the battalions' cumbersome gear.

Hearing Pablo's complaint and noting that the Mexicans had not moved when the march orders were given, Emory rode back to inquire. "What seems to be the problem here?" he demanded.

"Pablo and his friends will go no further west," the Mexican replied, his voice quivering. "We fear the Apaches."

As he listened to the ensuing argument, Landrew wanted to quit and run, too. He probably would have, but he believed he was safer in the company of so many well-armed men. He certainly didn't want to head back into the wilderness behind them, either alone or with the small group of ill-armed Mexicans.

Emory could not change their minds. He solved the problem by offering to buy their wagons and teams. "You and your men may leave or stay, as you wish." The Mexicans agreed to the offer and Emory paid them a fair price. Then after further discussion among themselves, Pablo and his group headed east, afoot.

It was long after nightfall when the exhausted Landrew finally fell asleep. Ever since his escape from the massacre, nightmares were a regular part of his life. Now, as the expedition traveled further into Apache lands, his nights became filled with terror. More than once he awoke with a scream in his throat. On this night his dream was especially vivid . . . .

The iron grasp tightened around his throat and he was lifted into the air. Terrified, he opened his eyes, face to face with the Apache chief who held him at arm's length, as if he were a rag doll, his feet dangling uselessly in the air. He tried to scream but the powerful fingers grasping and almost surrounding his neck choked him and he could only gag. Then, Mangas Coloradas raised his other arm, the one holding the knife, plunged it downward, and then back up . . . .

Screaming and gasping for air, Landrew rose from a pool of

sweat to find half the men in camp gathering outside his tent. When they began to question him about what had happened, he realized he had only been dreaming. Similar dreams had haunted him for years, but none had ever seemed so real.

"Hail in the camp!" A sudden shout came through the darkness, pulling attention away from Landrew. A buckskin-clothed man came riding in, a rifle at the ready lying across his lap. Several men rode behind him.

"Well, if it isn't Kit Carson!" Emory exclaimed. "What are you doing in this part of the wilderness?"

"I have a dispatch from California for Colonel Kearney. Seems it's quite important," Carson explained.

Lt. Emory took the folder and handed it to Kearney, who opened it and read the single short dispatch carefully. Smiling, he motioned for Emory to call the battalion into formation. When they had gathered and were standing at attention, Colonel Kearney announced. "Mexico has surrendered. The American flag now flies over all of Arizona and New Mexico!"

The men cheered, their spirits recharged in spite of the arduous task they still faced. The fear of possible attack by larger forces of Mexican soldiers was now gone, at least until they reached California.

Carson and his men decided to stay and guide the battalion. They had already endured many hardships while trying to find Kearney's group, and Carson reported sighting Apaches along the way. Carson made it clear that Mexico may have surrendered but the Apaches were still a force to be reckoned with. Carson's news of Apache sightings prompted two other Mexican peons to desert the battalion.

Contingencies called for changing the battalion's directives upon the eventuality of Mexico's surrender. Colonel Kearney, Capt. Moore, Lt's. Hammond and Dickenson, Kit Carson, Robideaux, and Landrew would accompany Lt. Emory and one hundred dragoons — heavily armed troopers — as they continued west toward California.

Major Sumner would take the balance of the dragoons and retrace their steps to Santa Fe where they would set up an official liaison office between the mexican settlers, many of whom had ancestry of over two centuries at Santa Fe, and the new Government of the Territory.

With half their original numbers, Emory's group of explorers continued west. On October 19 they camped ten miles southeast of the Gila river.

October 20 dawned sunny and warm. The men marched down a broad flat valley into a narrowing canyon which led to the Gila River, now only two miles to the northwest.

"Londeau," hollered Colonel Kearney, "you and Robideaux take word to the Apaches to come into our camp. They've been watching us for several days. I'm tired of their spying."

"Me, sir?" Landrew's voice was shaking.

Kearney exploded. "Yes, you two Frenchmen get started, now! The Apaches have been at war with everyone. I want to know what this band wants. I wonder why they haven't attacked? Probably our numbers and the howitzers."

Even before Kearney's order, Landrew was so nervous he was becoming physically ill and was having trouble hitching harness straps. He had fallen seriously behind in his work. Now, at the Colonel's order he turned pale and was visibly shaken.

Kearney, remembering Landrew's night terror sized up the mule skinners condition and changed his orders.

"Robideaux, you and Carson approach the Apaches," adding kindly, "Londeau is too far behind in his work."

Landrew was visibly relieved. He didn't want to meet any Apaches ever again. He feared this band was led by the Apache chief with blood-stained arms. The thought made his flesh crawl and his hands shake uncontrollably. He wondered if he was on the verge of a nervous breakdown. He'd been watching the lay of the land and he knew the Prieto was not far to the northwest. He never would have signed on in Santa Fe if he'd known the journey would take him so close to the place that haunted his thoughts and tortured his sleep.

Carson and Robideaux mounted and left immediately. An hour later they returned to camp. Carson reported to Kearney, "Sir, the Apaches will follow directly behind us."

Kearney ordered Emory to assemble the dragoons in readiness for the impending visit. Emory, Kearney, and Carson took the forefront. Tensely they waited.

"We'll need you to interpret for us, Mr. Carson," Kearney said.

With a surprised look, Carson responded, "Mangas Coloradas' English is a lot better than my Apache, General. You won't have any trouble understanding this Indian!"

The troopers watched while forty Apache braves assembled on the eastern horizon, the sun at their backs. The Indians were clearly putting on a show.

A handful of braves stood on both flanks of the formation, dressed in little more than loin cloths. Some carried spears, others had bows and leather-fringed quivers filled with arrows hung over their shoulders. All had one or more knives strapped about their waist and legs.

The rest of the braves rode ponies of every description. These mounted warriors were soon assembled in a neat line between the foot soldiers. The horses were bareback but highly decorated with feathers and beads braided into their manes and tails.

Those on horseback carried the water bags, blankets, and other communal gear. At the middle of the formation on an undecorated horse carrying no gear was a well-dressed and unusually large rider.

"That's Mangas himself, Colonel," Carson pointed him out to the commanding officer. "You'll never have trouble spotting him in a group of Apaches, or any group for that matter."

The Indians, pausing for effect on the bright horizon, waited for some silent signal. The formation broke into a run, moving toward the assembled troopers, holding their straight line. Halfway down the sloping hill the configuration abruptly changed to a neat, single-file. An outsized Apache took the lead followed by the other mounted warriors with the foot soldiers following.

Landrew went numb. He recognized the leader of the group and he thought of James Johnson and his nightmare. Terror overtook him and he could neither think nor move.

Mangas Coloradas rode up in front of the assembled troops and greeted the dragoons. As Carson had said, Mangas spoke easily understandable English. "We swear eternal friendship to the whites and everlasting hatred to the Mexicans. Even small groups; one, two, or three white-men might now pass in safety through our country; if you are hungry, we will feed you or if on foot we will mount you. The road is open to the American now and forever. The white man could hunt and prospect for the squaws metal."[2]

Kit Carson leaned over and whispered to Emory, "I wouldn't trust one of them."

His keen hazel eyes burning in his intense face, Carson turned and whispered to Colonel Kearney, "Mangas, or 'Red Sleeves' is responsible for much bloodshed, especially that of prospectors.".

Colonel Kearney acknowledged Carson's warning, but decided to allow the troops to do some trading with the Apaches. It seemed like an opportunity to garner some good will.

"They have mules, ropes, whips, and mescal. We can trade them shirts, blankets, knives, needles, and the like," the General suggested.

Unfortunately, the Indians had the mistaken notion that this battalion was rich, so little useful bartering took place.

As Mangas and his band prepared to depart, Colonel Kearney and others noticed the Apache Chief's agitation and sensed that he was perturbed about something. Kearney asked Mangas what was bothering him. Mangas turned to Kearney and answered in a vicious tone, "You have already taken New Mexico and will soon take California. Go and take Chihuahua, Durango, and Sonora. We will help you."

Colonel Kearney studied the band of Apaches, who were dressed mostly in Mexican garb. He did not immediately answer Mangas' challenge. From their clothes, he could tell what people this band had been preying on. However Kearney noted the jacket worn by Mangas was made from a Henry Clay Flag.

"No doubt taken from an earlier explorer from the United States," Kearney mused to Carson under his breath.

"Yes, I wonder what countryman gave up his life for that jacket," Carson answered in a whisper.

Just then a pack mule spooked, broke free of his tethers, and took off across the rocky slopes at a dead run.

This small disturbance broke the tension. Kearney and Emory understood only that Mangas had made a challenge. But Carson knew the Apache Chief expected a response to his challenge.

Kearney forestalled Mangas by proposing to take his offer of help against the Mexicans to his "Great Chief." This seemed to please Mangas and without a word, he and the braves with horses mounted, turned, and rode away. Those without mounts followed on foot. These on horseback galloped up the treacherous, rocky slope of the canyon wall as if they were riding across level ground. Those without mounts paced the horses, and showed no evidence of fatigue as they ran up the steep hillside.

When the riders neared the top of the ridge and were out of rifle range, they paused to rest their obviously winded mounts. Without pausing, those on foot ran past them, over the top of the steep high ridge, and out of sight. A few moments later the horsemen disappeared after them.

This deliberate demonstration of physical prowess successfully drove home the danger of the Apache — as intended. Kit Carson knew full well that under different circumstances this relatively small band of peace-proclaiming Apaches could rain death and destruction on the expedition. Further, given the right circumstances, they almost certainly would. He explained this to Kearney who ordered the battalion to make ready for an immediate departure.

Lt. Emory turned to Colonel Kearney. "Should we send scouts to keep track of them?"

"Wouldn't do any good," Carson interjected. "Those on horseback would just lead the scouts a merry chase and those on foot are right up there in the rocks where you last saw them, waiting to ambush any scouts foolish enough to follow. If that isn't enough to convince you, consider this. Those foot soldiers can out-distance your best horses. Then after your boys are afoot the Apaches will have a fine time torturing them while feasting on horseflesh.

"A man would have to be a fool to play the Apache's game! Best thing you can do is stay in one large group and pray old Red Sleeves will keep his word. If he doesn't, we'll soon be dead!"

Such a bleak assessment of the situation from the famous Mountain Man, expert scout, and vaunted Indian fighter brought a communal shudder from those around him. None there questioned his opinion. He was, after all, *the* expert.

With renewed vigor the sobered battalion readied itself to resume its journey. For the next several days all felt the Indians' presence, but they saw no Apaches. On October 25, they continued west down the Gila River. It was rough going as they followed along the south side of the river. After a time Carson pointed out the Rio Prieto where Emory suggested they ford the Gila to "try the north shore for a spell."

Landrew's anxiety mounted by the hour. He tried to dissuade Emory from this plan. He was already closer than he ever wanted to be to the scene of his torturous memories, the source of his endless nightmares.

But Emory paid him no heed. The crossing was uneventful.

The next day brought the roughest trails yet encountered. As the party continued west, trying to stay close to the Gila River, the country grew ever more rugged. They found themselves fighting their way around one deep arroyo after another. Emory considered backtracking and scouting the south shore again, but Carson had already scouted there and reported that it was no better than where they were. (They could not know an easy passage existed, just a few miles south of the river.) Finally, Emory made a decision. "We are getting too far from the river," he declared. "We're more than a thousand feet above it. From now on, until we get out of this mess we have to descend whenever possible. Otherwise there'll be no water tonight."

They advanced slowly for the next sixteen miles. Often a scouted trail turned out to be impassable for the wagons and they had to turn back and try a different route. Sometimes the wagons and howitzers could make it only after the men moved boulders and shoveled gravel. This ordeal lasted all day.

The mules, being hurried all the while, suffered greatly. The expedition lost fourteen of the beasts that day. Most of the casualties resulted when the animals lost their footing. Two freight wagons and one howitzer went over the edge, each taking two hapless animals with it. Several mules bolted in fear and had to be shot before they trampled someone or forced men or other mules off a cliff.

After they had passed the worst parts and the country leveled out again, Emory spoke up. "'The Devil's Turnpike' is what we'll name this pass." He later wrote in his journal:

> "There was a maze of basalt and limestone here where the Gila cut its way through. An influx of water from the Prieto River, the Azul River, [*Actually the San Francisco River — Emory had the river names in that part of Arizona all confused*] and the San Carlos Rivers to the east, swelled the Gila's flow here."

Landrew had been troubled for days. He longed to share his story with the young Lieutenant, and he wanted to tell him about the gold in the sands of the Prieto. Now that the Prieto was behind them, his relief loosened his tongue. He had passed it, and he hadn't died!

Emory, working late into the night to bring his notes up to date was again interrupted by Landrew. The young officer found this visit more interesting than most. Later he recorded what Landrew told him, word for word, in his detailed notes:

> "'The Prieto flows down from the mountains, freighted with gold. Its sands are said to be full of the precious metal. A few adventurers, who ascended this river hunting beaver, washed the sands at night when they halted, and were richly rewarded for their trouble. Tempted by their success, they made a second trip, and were attacked and most of them were killed by the Indians'. My authority for this statement is Londeau, who, though an illiterate man, is truthful." [*sic*]

At Landrew's request, Emory promised not to tell anyone else the story until they reached California. Emory was happy enough to agree. He did not want his dragoons to have any knowledge of a possible gold strike. It was hard enough to keep the troops in line without the temptation of quick riches.

For some time it had been Colonel Kearney's earnest desire to trade with the Apaches. So far he had been unsuccessful. Then, on November 2, from a hill above the expeditionary force, they were hailed by a group of mounted Apache warriors. In Spanish the leader said he wished to talk.

"One of you put down your rifle and come to us," the Indian directed.

Lt. Emory carefully laid his rifle aside and asked Londeau, who spoke good Spanish, to accompany him. Though stunned, Londeau obediently accompanied Emory, numbly walking up the hill toward the Indians. As they approached, the Indian leader espied the handle of a large horse pistol in Emory's belt and told him to put it down before continuing farther up the hill.

Lt. Emory carelessly threw the pistol aside and the two proceeded to the top of the hill. Although the Indian leader was mounted and surrounded by seven warriors armed with rifles and bows, they were received with great agitation.

It seemed the Indians' principal fear was the howitzers. The Apaches were not about to enter such a heavily armed camp. "Not surprising," Emory thought, reminded of the story of a massacre at Santa Rita led by a man named Johnson.

It was ironic that Lt. Emory should think of James Johnson while Landrew stood beside him and in the midst of a group of Apache warriors. Had Emory known the terror welling in Landrew's heart he never would have brought the Frenchman with him to this meeting. He wouldn't have deliberately added to Landrew's pain and the last thing they needed was extra tension in an already dangerous situation.

CHAPTER 17
MANGAS' DEATH — THE SEARCH BEGINS

Adams and another prospector were talking as they sat in front of a blazing fire in a mining camp near the newly renamed town of Silver City, New Mexico, now a Territory of the United States. The subject, of course, was gold. Adams was boasting of his discovery.

"You got a sample of those walnut size nuggets," asked the other prospector, "or you just blowin' hot air?"

"Sure do," Adams replied, handing him the only remaining nugget from Smith's leather pouch.

"Take a good look. Feel how heavy it sits in your hand. That's solid gold, my friend."

"Beautiful," the man responded. "Just beautiful."

He hefted the nugget appreciatively, trying to judge its weight. He enjoyed watching the light of the fire's orange flames reflecting off its irregular surface.

"No matter how often I handle a piece of gold," he mused quietly, "I'm always surprised that such a small chunk can be so heavy."

Adams brow wrinkled and he turned red at his collar. "Small!" he snorted.

The other prospector laughed. "Now don't take offense," he said. "This nugget's a beauty. It's the biggest I've ever seen, that's for sure."

"I know where there are lots more like this one," Adams boasted. Exaggerating, he added, "Nuggets that are two, maybe three times as big."

Nine years had passed since Andrew Adams had just barely survived his trip from Zigzag Canyon. Since then, his lust for gold had grown stronger and his desire to return for the buried coffeepot full of nuggets was gradually overcoming his fear. Nearly every morning he awoke imagining his return to that gold-filled canyon. He dreamed of relocating the diggings, which he had come to refer to as his.

It was 1846. His old friend, Landrew, had gone his own way, but Adams continued to prospect in New Mexico and to bide his time. Someday, when he felt it was safe, he would mount a full-scale expedition into the Apache lands, back to that canyon — his canyon — of gold. For now he waited impatiently, telling his story to any who would listen.

This night, sitting beside the fire, his companion stared at the nugget. It was real enough; he wasn't sure about the rest of the story though. Adams hastened to reassure him. "Gold's there, I tell you! Only reason I haven't gone back for it already is this Apache called Red Sleeves. When he's dead and buried, then's when I'll go back! I aim to live to enjoy that gold."

He snatched his nugget, stood up, and strode off into the darkness.

The other prospector stayed by the fire, contemplating Adams' story and the heft of the nugget. He decided there must be some truth in Adams' account.

For the next seventeen years, Adams led an increasingly lonely life. He was now thirty-four and had prospected throughout New Mexico, always careful to stay clear of Apacheria — which was becoming better known as Arizona since the time of Emory's expedition. He managed to find enough gold to live on but he, like so many other prospectors, seldom found enough to buy more than the essentials. Periodically he took odd jobs to make ends meet and to earn enough extra to grubstake one more prospecting trip.

During one of those lean times Adams was in town thinking about taking a regular job again. Standing in front of the general store, his eye caught a neatly dressed cavalry sergeant marching across the street to the veranda in front of the sheriff's office. The soldier stopped in the shade.

"Attention!" the uniformed man barked. Several men paused to hear what he had to say. "The United States Cavalry is recruiting livestock tenders and teamsters for a new outpost west of here. Job pays room and board, plus negotiable allowance, depending on experience. Anyone interested should make application now. At the sheriff's office."

The sergeant relaxed and with a pleasant grin nodded to those who had gathered. Then he strode off down the dusty street to repeat his message throughout the little town.

Seated nearby in the shade, Adams listened with considerable interest to the sergeant's announcement. Prospecting had been pretty poor lately, he conceded, and a man had to eat.

He considered it for a few minutes, then squaring his shoulders, stepped off the shaded porch, walked to the Sheriff's office, and signed on. The following morning he left with the patrol headed toward Fort West located twenty-five miles west of Silver City, under a four-year contract as a mule tender. Adams was no longer a free man.

At age sixty-three, Mangas was still regarded as the most formidable Apache alive. The years had not dimmed his eyes, slowed his reflexes or weakened his body. His prowess was undiminished but he had tired of war.

He grew more reclusive. Unlike the old days, he seldom gave his warriors charms or readings about their future. His burden as leader of his people weighed heavily on his mind. He longed for needed rest, but there was none to be had.

Nevertheless, the war that preoccupied him was still going well and he felt more confident with each passing year. The Apaches had defeated the Mexicans easily, and now they were waging a successful war against the United States Cavalry and lingering settlers the troopers were supposed to protect. Yet Mangas knew from his visions that change would eventually come, and neither he nor any other Apache could prevent it.

This morning he had meditated for a long time, and it was past sunrise when he left his tepee. When he stepped out into the fresh morning air he paused to watch his youngest and loveliest daughter as she listened attentively to the conversation of warriors preparing for a raid Mangas had planned.

Mangas had fathered only one son and that could have depressed him but his three daughters had all turned out to be formidable women and he had astutely married them to neighboring tribal leaders, thereby strengthening the alliance of the regional Apaches tribes, bringing prestige to the Mimbres and power to his own position as a respected intertribal leader.

Mangas walked to the nearby spring seeking Dancing Horse. He found her visiting with several squaws who were cleaning their warrior's battle garb. In a rare moment of relaxation he watched contentedly from the shadows for nearly an hour, enjoying their furtive giggling. Mangas was proud of his people.

When the sun was high in the sky, he walked to the water's edge and, standing beside Dancing Horse, spoke quietly, facing into her reflection in the water. "Leave your work and walk with me. We must talk."

They walked in silence for hours. Dancing Horse wondered what troubled her man, but she chose to enjoy his company and the beauty around them in silence; he would tell her, if he chose.

Several miles from camp they came to a cliff overlooking a wide mesa. Mangas chose a vantage point with a picturesque view, sat, then drew Dancing Horse onto his lap.

"You see the beauty of this place?" he asked. "It looks much the same as it did three years ago when we came here, but it has changed. Everything changes. Remember the lone ponderosa pine that once towered above the junipers on this mesa?"

Dancing Horse gazed across the mesa. She nodded, remembering the majestic tree, gone now — felled by a violent storm in the dark of night.

Mangas continued in a reverent tone. "Things change but life goes on. That tree is gone but the forest remains. The forest must live on as long as possible."

Adams carried the newspaper headline with him the rest of his life.

"REIGN OF TERROR ENDS MANGAS COLORADAS IS KILLED!"

The newspaper was dated January 25, 1863. The official version was that Mangas had been captured in a cavalry raid near the Santa

Rita copper mines. The article noted that several troopers had given a different account of what had happened. According to the official report, Mangas was lured to Fort West on the promise of making peace. There was much more to the story.

Mangas Coloradas had led a band of warriors in an ambush on a cavalry supply train. After years of success he had grown arrogant and this time he was careless. The cavalry had set a trap. When Mangas and his braves attacked the wagons, mounted troopers charged from hiding in the nearby trees. The covered "freight" wagons, it turned out, held more troops. All brought deadly firepower against the unprepared Apaches.

Mangas was badly outgunned and outpositioned. Several braves were killed in the initial barrage of gunfire. Others were seriously wounded. He knew they had to retreat. His only path of withdrawal lead into a box canyon. As the Cavalry closed the trap, Mangas' men declared that they were ready to die, rather than surrender.

It didn't come to that. The officer in charge of the Cavalry proclaimed his well-rehearsed lie, "Mangas Coloradas, we have found your village. If you and your braves will surrender, we will spare the rest of your people. You will be treated fairly."

None of this was true. The cavalry had not found Mangas' encampment and they had no intention of treating Mangas, his warriors or any other Indians fairly. Regardless, Mangas could not gamble with his peoples' lives. He surrendered and was taken to Fort West where he was bound hand and foot and thrown into a dark cell, alone.

Fearing that other Mimbres might try to rescue Mangas, the commanding officer completed his plan, calling four of his best men to his office. "Mangas Coloradas will not be rescued and he will not escape. Do you understand?"

The official report of Mangas' death summed up the entire affair in two words: "Attempted escape."

Adams was at Fort West when they brought Mangas in. And although the formidable Apache wore handcuffs and leg chains, being so close to the now-legendary warrior chilled Adams to the bone. He watched with satisfaction and relief when Mangas was thrown into the brig.

That night Adams was unable to sleep, knowing the Apache warrior was imprisoned only a few yards from where he lay. He hoped Mangas would soon be moved somewhere far away.

Long after midnight Adams fell asleep, only to be awakened in the predawn hours by the sounds of wood splintering, glass breaking and men screaming. Adams envisioned Mangas single-handedly tearing down the brig and escaping.

By the time Adams reached the barracks window the racket had died down. He saw two soldiers stumbling out of the brig, each carrying a large club.

The officer of the guard came running. After listening to their explanation, which Adams couldn't hear, he ran to the infirmary. A moment later the post doctor ran to the brig. After a while two bodies and one obviously badly injured man were carried out on stretchers.

Two days later the trooper was buried. At the funeral, Adams listened to the story of how the man had given his life trying to prevent Mangas' escape. Adams knew it was a lie. He had a good idea what had really happened.

Adams was surprised that Mangas' death did not bring him satisfaction or relief. Somehow Mangas' death reminded him of another senseless slaughter he had witnessed long before.

That night Adams sat in the civilian barracks contemplating all that had happened. "Now, at last I can go back to the diggin's," he mused.

Another mule tender, not quite asleep in the next bunk, stirred and stretched. "What'd you say?" George Davidson asked.

Davidson, at twenty-one years was tall, strong, and emanated youthful prowess. He had more mule savvy than anyone Adams had ever met. Davidson, a Greek immigrant, was not yet a naturalized U.S. citizen, but he spoke the language well.

Adams handed Davidson the newspaper.

"If we could get out of our military contracts," Adams said, "we'd be rich!"

Davidson gave him a look of puzzlement.

"Remember that zigzag canyon I told you about?" Adams asked.

"The one with all the gold?"

Davidson nodded, still not understanding.

"Don't you see? Mangas is dead," he explained. "Now it's safe to go back there!"

Davidson brightened at the thought of getting rich, especially if it was going to be as easy as Adams claimed.

"Well," he offered, "our contract with the cavalry expires in sixty-seven. From what you tell me, we don't have much worry that anybody will go in there ahead of us. And even if they do, they'll never find that pot of nuggets you keep hinting about. We can wait. Sixty-seven will be soon enough to be rich."

It was a hot, sleepy day at Fort West in the summer of 1864 when the news of the outpost's closing was announced. The Civil War was beginning to wind down and civilian positions in that part of the country were being eliminated wherever possible. All non-military personnel at the fort were given the option of transfer back east or release from their contracts.

Like most of the others, Adams and Davidson chose early release. The two excitedly began to make plans for their upcoming expedition. "Just like the Army," Adams quipped. "We've been taking our own sweet time with preparations for our adventure into Arizona and now, all of the sudden, we have to hurry and get ready to go!" Adams had always intended to urge Landrew to go back with him, when the time came. He didn't suppose there was much chance Landrew would go, but he felt obliged to give his old friend the chance. Now, with this change in plans, there wasn't time to try to locate the Frenchman. Last he had heard, Landrew had signed on with Emory's expedition and was heading for California.

After twenty-seven years of self-imposed exile, Adams, now forty-four, was finally preparing his return to the beautiful green valley that had haunted his dreams through the years. He made his plans known around the fort. There were plenty of soon-to-be-unemployed frontiersmen hungry for wealth and adventure. The way Adams told it, finding the "little hidden zigzag canyon" would be a cinch!

"I'll send for my cousin, Jay Davidson," George volunteered. "He's a Mountain Man. He ain't no Jim Bridger but he can take care of himself. I've heard tell he knows how to deal with Indians, too."

That night Adams related the story of the coffeepot full of gold to the men he hoped to recruit.

"Every evening those men brought all the gold they'd collected that day to the cook's table. Smith would check each man's take," Adams explained. "That was fair enough. It was Smith's expedition and by agreement half the gold they discovered was supposed to be his. I never heard a whisper that any of the men might've been cheating Smith, either. There was too much gold to be tempted with such foolishness! Well, anyway, every evening Smith would pry up that heavy flat stone in front of the fireplace, pull open the lid of a big coffeepot he had buried there, and dump in the day's diggings. Then he'd put the lid back on the pot, put the stone back over the hole, and brush dirt over the stone. Shoot, before we'd finished supper a man couldn't tell anything was there.

"I'm positive those heathen Apaches never found it. They were too busy looting the camp and burning the cabin, amongst other things . . . " his voice trailed off. After a few moments he continued. "That old pot's been sitting there since thirty-seven. I estimate there are three hundred pounds of gold right there! And plenty more for the diggin'! Fellows, that much gold's worth more money than the lot of us could earn if we lived to be a hundred!"

All were enticed by Adam's nugget and the story he told. Each man dreamed of gold and riches. Each wanted a share of the easy wealth Adams promised was waiting near a hidden zigzag canyon.

On July 15th, 1864, twelve men with gear and loaded pack horses were ready to depart. Participants on Adams' first return expedition were: Andrew Adams, George Davidson, Jay Davidson, Ray Peters, Charley Bowers, John Gehog, Peter Von Strat (the German), John Grant, Steve Low, Pete Bucklew, Bill Snow, and John Brewer — who was better known to the members of the expedition as John Wingate.[3]

Brewer had acquired his nickname during his days as a scout and guide at fort Wingate, in northern New Mexico. He was freighting from the new state of California into Arizona Territory, when he heard the Adams story from a soldier in Tucson. News that Adams was at Fort West recruiting for an expedition led Brewer to make his way there and sign on with the group. He was put in charge of provisioning.

The men set out, ignoring the blazing summer sun, expecting to reach Arizona Territory within a day or two. On their second day out they reached the Gila River. Adams was certain he would have little trouble finding his way. He directed the group to head west, downriver.

They made slow progress. Adams had forgotten just how rugged the country was. It took three days for the group to reach the San Francisco River, which Adams believed was the river he had traveled nearly thirty years before.

In early 1838 the Gila had been swollen with spring runoff and Smith's group was forced to detour around the junction of the San Francisco and Gila rivers. Adams never knew the San Francisco existed.

Late in the summer of 1864 the Gila's flow was subdued and gentle. Adams' group easily followed it to the mouth of the San Francisco River, which the group's leader mistook for the Prieto.

"This is the river, boys. I remember for sure that it was the first big river that ran into the north side of the Gila. Let's make camp here for the night. We'll get an early start in the morning."

The following day they headed north on the San Francisco. Within two days they had traversed the richly mineralized region that would soon become the location of a thriving copper town, Clifton, Arizona. They camped in the wide valley there.

Adams was unusually quiet.

"George, something's not right," he confided. "This canyon is different from what I remember."

"Well, Andrew," Davidson responded, "that was a long time ago. You were pretty young and they kept you pretty busy tending livestock and looking after camp chores. Maybe you didn't have the time to take stock of the surrounding country. Twenty-seven years is a long time, Andy. Maybe this isn't the right canyon. Still, let's give it a fair look-see before we move on to another."

Adams agreed. The next morning the group got an early start. By afternoon they had reached the junction of the Blue River and the San Francisco and Adams was thoroughly confused. With every turn of the river's course, he hoped to see some landmark, something he would recognize. But he never did.

When the river split, the Blue River coursed to the northwest, Adams again spoke to George Davidson about his misgivings.

"George, I don't know what to do. The country here looks sort of right but I don't remember any split in the river. We've come far enough from the Gila, we should be there. I know we're close, but this isn't the right place."

The next morning he assembled the group and said, "Men, this will be our base camp for a few days. I've been hoping to recognize some landmark but I haven't yet. I figure we've come far enough from the Gila, we should have reached the spot we're looking for. It's a canyon that takes off to the east and is really hard to see, but I don't think we've passed it. We should spend some time here to be sure. My plan is to scout the area from this camp for the next few days."

Some in the group voiced concerns that Adams was lost. But he answered them with the sound of confidence that he didn't really possess. "Look fellows, I was only there one time," he said. "That was twenty-seven years ago. This country looks right . . . if only there were more trees . . . and we've seen a bit of color in our gold pans, haven't we? It may take a few days but we'll find it."

After a week of fruitless searching, provisions were running low and Adams sent John Brewer and Peter Von Strat to the settlement of Pueblo Viejo, somewhere about forty miles to the southwest.

"We need to keep as many horses as possible, so we can do more searching. That means you'll have to walk back. Take three horses with you for pack animals," Adams instructed. "The trip shouldn't take more than two weeks at the outside. We'll do a little hunting and fishing. Jay Davidson claims he can keep us from starving, and with luck we'll make you rich before you return."

For two weeks the prospectors made ever-widening searches, often spending nights away from camp. Adams grew more certain he had taken a wrong turn somewhere.

"George," he said, "either we have to try higher up on one of these rivers," he gestured to the San Francisco and the Blue, "or we have to go back to the Gila and look for another river. This just isn't the right place."

"All right," Davidson agreed. "Besides," he continued, "it's past time Brewer and Von Strat were back with supplies. It's been over two weeks. I reckon we ought to go looking for them, don't you?"

Adams sighed heavily. "I think you're right. We'll head out at sunrise."

The following morning Adams announced the plan to the group.

"George and I are going to ride out and look for Brewer and the German," he said. "Jay can keep you men fed and you can all use the rest. I hate to admit it, but I think we've taken a wrong turn somewhere. George and I will go find Brewer and then we'll decide whether to head back down to the Gila and look for another river or try farther up one of these rivers. If we don't find Brewer and Von Strat we'll go back to Pueblo Viejo and bring back supplies ourselves."

With that, Adams and George Davidson rode out of camp, leaving the eight others grumbling. They were disgusted with Adams' inability to find the canyon and the promised treasure, and they were more than a little tired of their diet of fish.

A few miles down the San Francisco River, Adams and Davidson found two of the pack horses, dead, their loads gone. Nearby lay the decomposing body of Peter Von Strat. Brewer and the third horse were nowhere to be seen.

Scenes of the past flooded Adams' memory. Visions of marauding Apaches stirred panic in him.

"Come on George, let's get the hell out of here."

"We can't just leave," replied Davidson. "We have to go back and warn the others."

With great difficulty Adams controlled his hysteria. "You're, right George, but then we leave, quick!"

Adams and Davidson turned their mounts riding hard, back to the camp.

The warning they carried came too late. The bodies of their comrades lay scattered around the campsite. None there had escaped the massacre. Terrified and sickened by the grisly sight, Adams and Davidson fled, continuing north along the Blue River. They rode as fast as they dared, hoping the cruel pace wouldn't kill their horses before they reached safety.

They followed the River all that day and hid in the trees along its banks that night. The next day they turned loose their exhausted and crippled mounts and headed west on foot. Late that evening, they came to the headwaters of another river — the south fork of the upper Salt River. Traveling down this river, they arrived at a cavalry outpost four days later, dehydrated and malnourished. The post physician at Fort Apache, Dr. Spurgeon, took them in and cared for them, undoubtedly saving their lives.

As the two recovered under the expert and kindly care of Dr. Spurgeon, Adams told the doctor what they had been searching for, and even showed him his keepsake nugget.

Over the next few days, Adams told Dr. Spurgeon all he could remember about his lost canyon. Though still weak and shaken by the most recent massacre, he was stubbornly determined to go back.

"I've waited twenty-seven years to get back to that gold," he said. "I'm not going to let the Apaches win. Besides I need to find out what happened to Brewer."

Doctor Spurgeon was a sensible man. He persuaded Adams to wait until he was fully recovered. "There are not enough troopers at this fort, Mr. Adams, to mount an expedition just to look for John Brewer and you are not well enough yet to guide such an expedition. Anyhow, I suspect your friend is either dead or has already found his way to safety."

Adams didn't argue. He had to admit to himself that he wasn't really ready to return. After all, by only the slimmest margin he had now escaped two massacres! Even the best of luck runs out eventually, he reasoned.

Adams never learned Brewer had escaped the massacre. Leading a lame horse and lagging some distance behind Von Strat, he saw the Indians who attacked and killed the German. Brewer assumed the camp had already fallen, and after hiding in the trees beside the river until dark, he escaped and returned to Fort West.

Many times in the following years Adams tried unsuccessfully to recruit a new party to return with him to his canyon of gold. No stranger escaped his persuasive attempts.

"I'm telling you," Adams claimed, "there's enough gold in that canyon to retire an army."

His latest "victim" was Captain Charles Shaw, who had served in the Union naval forces during the War Between the States.

It was now 1874, thirty-seven years after Adams' first narrow escape and ten years since his second. He was fifty-four years old.

Captain Shaw, an adventure-loving man, was impressed with Adams' persuasive story and where easy riches were possible Shaw was as eager as the next man. Soon Adams, Shaw and fourteen other men were headed into the wilderness, spurred by dreams of a zigzag canyon filled with gold.

Despite Adams' lust for gold, he wanted no part of any more Apaches. "Never again," he swore. Accordingly, at the first sign of Indians, the group returned to civilization, disbanded, and gave up the search before they had really begun.

A year later, in 1875, Adams traveled with Captain Shaw to San Bernardino, California where they organized another expedition.

This time the band was unfettered by Indians. However, Adams was unable to recognize any landmarks and they spent fruitless months combing the area of eastern Arizona Territory and western New Mexico Territory looking for a zigzag canyon and the remains of a burned-out rock-walled cabin.

All summer they traveled up and down the Gila looking for the right river. On their second trip back down the Gila, without knowing it was the very river he sought, Adams decided they should try the Prieto. "I'm sure this isn't the river. But let's travel upstream and see what we find," he suggested.

The group agreed. After traveling several miles, Adams stopped. "Nope, this can't be it. There were more trees there. And another thing, I remember having trouble right away because we couldn't get the livestock across the river. The water was too deep. We've crossed this river three times now and have hardly gotten our feet wet!"

The same changes that had slowed the flow of other rivers in the region had reduced the Prieto to a trickle, except during the spring snow-melt and following hard rains. Where once a pristine river had splashed and rumbled through a lush valley, periodic flooding had stripped all the splendor from the canyon floor, leaving bare rocks for the meager trickle of water to wet. This canyon bore no resemblance to the one in Adam's memory.

Tired and discouraged, the group turned around and headed back to the Gila, unaware of how close they had been. Dissention grew within the ranks of Shaw's second expedition. Most of the men were convinced Adams was simply inept. When he proposed the group go back up the Gila to the San Francisco River for the third time, even Captain Shaw became disgusted and withdrew his support. "No more am I going to follow an idiot!"

Adams was despondent. He returned to California to recuperate from the hardships of the trip and to eventually make new plans.

Later that same year Adams befriended a man named C. S. Stevens. Adams was still telling his story to anyone who would listen and Stevens was certainly interested, believing he had figured out a clue that would lead him to the pot of gold Adams now spoke of freely.

Two years later, without consulting Adams, Stevens recruited men to form an expedition of his own. He was certain he would find Adams' lost canyon.

On April 3, 1877 Stevens, Jack Simms, Bill Morris, Zack Zoubrouth, and a man called "Dutchie" pooled their meager funds and left Silver City on foot, leading three burros and inadequately prepared. Two months later after searching the headwaters of the Blue River they arrived in the now thriving community of Clifton without food or money. They hadn't eaten a proper meal for thirteen days. They knew they were lucky to be alive and none of them ever again tried to find Adams Lost Diggings.[4]

CHAPTER 18
SANDERS' DISCOVERY, 1879

It was 1879, and Nana was seventy-nine years old. He was still a formidable figure, and he was determined that no white man's reservation would hold him. In the spring he and a small band of Apache braves simply rode off the San Carlos reservation. They began their retaliatory crusade of destruction by setting fire to a homestead located on Cherry Creek near its juncture with the Salt River, about one hundred miles northwest of Clifton.

"We shall never return to the reservation!" Chief Nana shouted to his small band of braves. "Would our great chief, Mangas Coloradas, have allowed his people to be put on the white man's reservation and to be treated like dogs? We are Apaches and we will push the white-eyes from our lands!" The warriors who followed Nana shouted their support for his strong words. But Nana remembered Mangas' prophesy and knew in his heart this would never be.

They roped four steers and killed the other livestock. While the ranch burned they butchered and roasted a calf for a quick feast. Hours later they headed west, into the foothills of the rugged Sierra Ancha Mountains, herding the steers along with them.

Private Sanders and the rest of the patrol had been following the trail of this band of renegades for two days when they saw smoke from the burning buildings of the ranch. Cautiously the troopers advanced to investigate. From a hill overlooking the ranch they could see the devastation. Sanders spotted the small band of Indians disappearing into the rugged mountains to the west.

They had been on Nana's trail for days, and they had mixed emotions about being so close to a dangerous group of marauding renegades. Nevertheless, locating and tracking renegades was their job and they were under standing orders from the post commander to gather information on hostiles or suspected hostiles, but to "avoid engagement." They were too small a group for combat operations against even the smallest raiding party of Apaches. Too many soldiers had already been lost that way. The standing orders were clear, "Reconnaissance patrols — usually less than twenty men — are forbidden to initiate action against suspected renegade Apaches." The group Sanders was with was just such a patrol and they were to gather information, nothing more.

Despite the soldiers' orders not to engage any Apaches, the Indians were under no such constraints and could be expected to attack if given any opportunity. Ambushes set by the cavalry more often than not turned out to be ambushes set by the Apaches! They always seemed to have the upper hand.

"I counted seven riders, sir. Looked like four animals in tow," Sanders reported to his lieutenant.

Lt. Severn was young and eager to take useful information to his superiors at the post. "Sanders, you, Jones, and Dobson are appointed field scouts," he said. "I want the three of you to cut a trail south of the one Nana took and stay on the flank of the mountain. Somewhere over there is Coon Creek," he gestured to the west. "From there you should be able to see several miles in every direction. I want to know where that band is headed. I figure they'll skirt around the flank of the mountain higher up, where they won't be so easy to see. Eventually if they keep heading west they'll cross Tonto Creek, around twenty miles from here. But they could turn south and head for the Salt River. We need to know which way they're headed. If you reach Coon Creek without cutting their trail, we'll assume they're headed for Tonto Creek. If so, head back to the post at full gallop. If you cut their trail before you get to Coon Creek, turn back immediately and report to the fort."

The young Lieutenant grew even more sober. He gestured toward the smoldering ruins below them. "We'll see if there is anything we can do here and then head back to the post. It will be too late to pursue the hostiles today, but we can have a full regiment ready in the morning. The fort is about five miles northeast. We'll be waiting for your information. Good luck, be careful, and *no heroics*. That's an order."

Lt. Severn and the rest of his troop mounted and rode toward the ranch, Leaving Sanders, Jones, and Dobson trying to gather the courage to complete their assignment. "I wonder what I did wrong?" Sanders muttered.

"Didn't have to do nothing wrong," Dobson answered, "'cept join this man's Cavalry."

They were in no hurry to leave the safety of the rocks just to pursue hostile Apaches. But eventually the appointees mounted, rode across Cherry Creek, and found a fresh trail leading west. The going was surprisingly easy on the south flank of the rugged Sierra Anchas. Sanders figured they had traveled about three miles west of Cherry Creek when Dobson and Jones decided they had gone "far enough."

"I'm not going any farther!" Dobson whispered. "We've done our duty. We haven't seen hide nor hair of them heathens and I'd like to keep it that way. You and Jones can do as you please but this trooper is hightailing it back to the post!" Not waiting for a reply, Dobson turned his mount and rode away at a trot. Jones didn't hesitate. Without a word he reined his horse behind Dobson's.

Sanders sat there with only his horse, Jasper, for company. He sat motionless, surprised at the sudden departure of the others, trying to decide what to do. He felt a duty to continue, and he felt certain the Apaches couldn't be very close or he would have seen them.

Reluctantly he rode on at a deliberate pace. He hadn't gone more than a quarter of a mile when he spotted a fresh trail, complete with still-steaming manure, heading to the southwest!

"Oh my God," he whispered, as if Jasper could understand. "How did they get past me?"

With the hair on his neck standing out, he turned Jasper and headed straight south at a gallop. He figured he could get to the Salt River soon enough and from there he knew he could ride east and make good time back to the fort without riding along the skyline and without backtracking. He knew the old Apache trick of turning the tables and following an unsuspecting enemy.

He had the information his commander wanted. At least some of the raiders were heading southwest, toward the Salt River. Sanders was ready to report.

He rode hard heading south down the bottom of a gentle swale, toward the river. As he continued, canyon walls formed and rose steeply on both sides of him. He felt trapped. He didn't like the feeling, but he believed this was better than riding exposed on the skyline.

The further he rode, the more concerned he was that he had gotten himself into a bad situation. He tried to convince himself it was unlikely the Apaches had already come this far south. In any event, he wasn't about to go back the way he had come. His only good choice was to continue down the deepening canyon although minute by minute that course seemed like less and less of a good idea.

Jasper, the big bay horse Sanders had been issued at Ft. Apache, was strong and surefooted. He was glad to have such an animal under him now. The two got along very well, and Jasper had proven himself invaluable in more than one tight situation.

"We can't stop yet, Jasper," Sanders said as he patted the horse's neck. "I know you're tired and hungry, I haven't given you any rest all day. But we can't stop now. I have a bad feeling about this here Coon Creek. And I don't want you to be the main course of an Apache feast! It can't be more than a couple of miles to the Salt River. When we get there you can slow down for a spell. But for now. . . ."

He tickled Jasper's flanks with his boot heels, bringing the well-trained horse into an easy gallop. For several miles the going was easy in the grass-covered, sandy bottom of the creek bed. Eventually, though, the terrain changed and Sanders had to slow Jasper to a careful walk.

"This canyon is getting too rough for my liking. I don't know if we can make it to the river or not, Jasper."

Fear gripped him. He imagined Indians spying on him from the high cliffs that loomed ominously on both sides of him.

He felt like an idiot. "How could an experienced trooper get himself into such a mess? This canyon would make a dandy trap, that's for sure!"

Rounding yet another turn in the creek, Sanders heard the unmistakable sound of crashing water.

"That must be the river," he prayed. "We must be close now, Jasper."

But it wasn't the river. A few hundred feet farther he reached an impasse. He could see the wide river bottom only a stone's throw away. Yet between him and the river was a twenty-foot drop, where the water of the creek poured through a narrow opening and fell into a large pool. Neither horse nor rider was in any mood to examine the beauty of the spot. Jasper repeatedly shied back as Sanders tried to survey the situation. Much as he trusted this horse, he dared not dismount with Jasper acting so skittish and with nowhere to tie the reins.

Finally Sanders realized he had to go back up the canyon, and look for a way out. Traveling a short distance up the canyon, he was surprised to note something he hadn't seen on the way down. The cliff on the east side fell away sufficiently to allow a possible way out. He patted Jasper on the neck and dismounted. "Maybe you'll soon be getting that rest I promised."

He tied the reins to the saddle and headed Jasper up the mountain, holding onto the horse's tail. Both man and beast were winded when they neared the top of the canyon wall.

Sanders whoaed and Jasper stopped, obediently, just short of the skyline. While the two caught their breath, Sanders noticed a glittering rock formation.

"What do you suppose that is?" he wondered aloud.

Walking to the outcrop, he picked up a handy rock and broke off a large slab of quartz. Sander's heart jumped. What laced the crystalline rock was unmistakable — gold.

"Jasper, I'm a rich man!" he blurted out, suddenly oblivious to the immediate danger of his situation. "No more chasing Indians, no more cavalry!"

His spoken words reminded him that he had two more years to serve in the cavalry, which in turn jerked him back rudely to reality. Remembering stories of fool's gold he now questioned whether what he had found was really gold. He knew the test. Breaking out a piece of the yellow stuff he bit down on it hard. When it gave way easily to his bite without shattering he knew it was the real thing.

He remounted, and leaning low in the saddle he galloped over the top of the mesa. Soon he slowed Jasper to a walk. He picked a trail down the steep escarpment to the river bottom. Once there, Sanders turned Jasper east and rode at a gentle trot until he came to Cherry

Creek.

The sun was low in the sky. It would be a moonless night. Sanders knew he could not make the cavalry post that evening. He turned north and headed toward the burned-out ranch. He would have preferred the safety of the fort, but he reassured himself with the thought that Apaches would have no reason to go back to that ranch.

The sun was setting as he neared the remains of the still-smoldering ranch buildings. Riding through the evening shadows, he contemplated what might have happened to the settlers living there. He wondered how many new graves he might find.

But Nana hadn't discovered anyone at the ranch. In truth, the old man hadn't looked very thoroughly. He wasn't in a killing mood. He was just looking for a good steak and a chance to thumb his nose at the U.S. Cavalry. So, while the ranch burned, his braves roasted a calf, had a quick feast, then moved on.

Daylight was almost gone when Sanders dismounted and walked Jasper into the circle of smoldering buildings. He was startled by movement behind the water trough, near the well. Drawing his revolver he hollered, "Who's there?"

"Over here," came a meek voice. "I'm at the well."

"I see you," he said. "Who are you and where did you come from?"

"My name's Jennifer. Jennifer Hardy. I live . . . I used to live here."

Sanders walked over to the young woman, who had been washing the smoke and soot from her skin and her tattered dress. She appeared hardly more than a teenager. Her badly torn undergarments revealed a lovely body. She seemed unaware of her immodest attire.

"A group of Apaches rode in earlier while I was in the root cellar. It's a rock cave by the end of the house," she explained. "I hid in there. My stepfather and mother went to town this morning so I was here alone when the Indians came. The fire singed me some and I like to've choked to death once, but I'm okay now. After the fire died down I heard someone picking through the rubble so I stayed hid until after I heard them ride away. When it started to get dark I figured maybe it would be safe to come out. Take me away from here, please," she pleaded. "There's a spring and a cave up at the meadow. There's plenty of grazing for your horse there, too."

As Sanders raised her petite body into his saddle, he was acutely aware of her as a woman. He couldn't help himself. She had almost nothing on and she curved in all the right places. He gathered her wet dress and led Jasper away from the ruined ranch.

Following her directions they soon came to a large cave. He helped her dismount, again enjoying the softness of her supple body. Then he turned to the job of unsaddling his horse and preparing his bed. He had trouble keeping his eyes off her, yet he was embarrassed by the stirrings he felt.

As Jasper moved off, feeding hungrily, Sanders gathered several armfuls of twigs and branches and carried them into the cave, where Jennifer huddled in the deepening darkness.

"Do you think it's wise to build a fire?" she asked.

"Well, I think so," he said. "If those heathens were following me, they would already be here. The last time I cut their trail they were miles west of here, still heading southwest."

"I guess it's all right, then," Jennifer sighed. "It would be wonderful to get warmed up. I could sure use some hot coffee, if you have any to spare." Then with a little smile she added, "Just a few hours ago, I thought I'd had all the hot anything I ever wanted!"

Soon a small fire was warming the cave and the smell of boiling coffee filled the air. For some time Sanders listened to Jennifer tell about what had happened. His eyes followed the shadows of the firelight that danced on her skin. He had long since given up trying to ignore her provocative curves under the thin and torn material of her undergarments. Her heavy cotton dress, draped over the branches of a tree, would not be dry for several hours. He was not sorry for that. He was so taken with her loveliness that he failed at first to notice she was shivering and hugging her shoulders against the night chill. Then, ashamed of his oversight he offered his heavy jacket. "My apologies, miss. Should have thought of this sooner."

"That's all right, Private," she said. "I didn't even notice I was chilled until now. I guess I'm more upset than I'd realized."

"That's not surprising. Now, you'd better climb into that bedroll and get warmed up," he said. "No reason to catch cold."

She hesitated to take his bed but realized he was right. She didn't want to spend the night in the cold dark cave with no cover at all.

As she slipped into the warmth of his bedroll, he walked to the opening of the cave. She watched him, studying the outline of his broad shoulders against the fading light of the evening sky. She thought of her late husband.

She hadn't been with a man since his death. Tonight she longed to be held. If Private Sanders was willing, it would be fine with her. More than that, she wanted it. Something about her brush with death awakened a need in her.

While his back was still turned to her, she found the strength to say what she was thinking.

"I don't want to sleep alone tonight. After what happened I really need to be held. I haven't been with a man since my husband died a year ago," her voice quavered.

As Sanders turned to face her, she hesitated, then asked softly, "Will you share this bed with me?" He made no reply and no movement toward her, he only stared at her in disbelief for several moments. "Please, will you hold me tonight?" she repeated.

Sanders couldn't believe his ears, or his luck! This was easily the strangest day of his life. He had started in pursuit of renegade Apaches. Later he had ridden down a deep canyon where he'd been terrified, expecting to die. Next, he discovered enough gold to retire on, and now this!

Sanders was practically a virgin; he'd been with a black whore once, that was the extent of his experience with women. He hadn't even seen a woman in weeks. Now, the most beautiful woman he'd ever met was begging him to share a bed. How could he refuse a lady in distress?

He watched by the flickering firelight as Jennifer laid open the bedroll, sat up, and peeled first the top and then the bottom of her undergarments from her freshly washed skin. She crossed her arms over her chest to hide her nakedness but she couldn't cover the fullness of her breasts. Her modesty and the light from the dancing flames made her even more appealing to Sanders. He had never before seen such beauty. To him, the soft curving shape of her body was nothing less than a miracle. Her waist was tiny and her hips were full. He stood transfixed, staring . . . .

After several minutes of silence she pulled the blankets over herself. "Will you hold me?" she asked softly.

Even more shyly than Jennifer had, Sanders removed his clothes and sat on the blankets beside her. He was embarrassed by his arousal. He felt very awkward but he was losing his self control. "Are you sure?" he asked.

She didn't speak. Instead, she took his face in her hands and kissed him full on the mouth. He reached around her shoulders and pulled her closer, hugging her through the blankets with both arms. He held her like that for a long time.

Finally, he slipped under the blankets and after they had caressed each other for a long time he entered her and she moaned with pleasure.

Much later they pulled the bedding over themselves. He gathered Jennifer into his arms. They slept through the night and when he awoke she was still in his arms. Again he felt a stirring. Again she welcomed him with her body.

Eventually, they dressed to face the day. She wasn't sure just when her parents would return. She wanted to intercept them on the road before they got to the ranch, to give them the bad news and to let them know she was all right.

He caught and saddled Jasper and they set off. Jennifer rode comfortably behind Sanders as they moved slowly down the trail toward town. For those few hours he forgot he was a soldier. He was only a man, enjoying the feeling of a woman's ample breasts pressing against his back.

It was late morning when they met Jennifer's folks. Sanders explained what had happened at the ranch and let Jennifer explain that there was nothing left to salvage.

The stunned couple considered what to do. "There's nothing out there but more heartache and danger," Mr. Hardy whispered, sadly. "I don't think I have what it takes to start over right now, maybe next spring . . . . We'd best go back to town and see what happens." His wife nodded silently.

In spite of the devastating news, Mrs. Hardy was aware of a certain glow in both Jennifer's and Sanders' expressions. She could tell the two had slept together. But right now there were other things to worry about.

Jennifer thanked Sanders for his help, and with a long gaze each thanked the other for the stolen moment they had shared. Then Jennifer climbed into the wagon and the little family headed back toward town and an uncertain future.

For two years Sanders kept his discovery on Coon Creek a secret. Often, memories of his night with Jennifer filled his dreams, that, too, was his secret. Then in 1881, he was discharged from the cavalry. "Goodbye, Lieutenant Severn. I'll be seeing you around."

"What are your plans, Mr. Sanders?"

"I don't know exactly," Sanders lied, "but I think I'll stay out west. By the way, is there any chance the cavalry could see fit to sell me a good saddle horse?"

"Which one did you have in mind?" the lieutenant asked with a crooked grin. "As if I didn't know!"

An hour later, Sanders rode Jasper out through the gates of Fort Apache. In spite of what he had told the Lieutenant he had a specific plan and a clear goal.

Two days later Sanders arrived at Picket Post, a stage stop west of Globe, Arizona. "How are ya doin', Hunkydory?" Sanders yelled as he walked into the grocery.

"Just fine, trooper!" the storekeeper replied. "Come on in and have a cup of java and a bite to eat."

W. A. (Hunkydory) Holmes ran the stage stop. He was a short man with a rounded belly that jiggled when he laughed. To Holmes, there were no strangers. "It looks to me like you're a free man," he said. "What plan have you got for yourself now that the cavalry don't own you?"

Sanders leaned close to him. "Hunkydory, since I've known you for a long time I'm going to tell you exactly what I'm going to do!" He unwrapped the now-polished slab of quartz and handed it to the storekeeper.

"You have to keep this a secret," Sanders implored.

"Why, that's the real thing!" Hunkydory remarked in a loud voice, clearly impressed. He held out the slab of rock and turned the polished side toward the light from the window. Sanders grabbed the rock out of the storekeeper's hand, but not before several customers had turned to see what had Hunkydory so excited.

An old man stood up and walked over to Sanders. "Looks like the real thing to me, too," he said. "Forgive my curiosity. My name is Andrew Adams. I've been prospecting the country east of here most of my life. Where did you get that sample?"

"That's none of your damn business, old man," Sanders retorted. He quickly wrapped the slab in his bandanna and held it in his left hand, his right hand coming to rest on the butt of his horse-pistol.

"I have to know," Adams insisted, Sanders' face paled with tension.

"Wait, wait, boys," interrupted Hunkydory. "Sanders, Adams means no harm. The old man claims to have lost a rich placer deposit somewhere in Arizona."

"Lost his gold," Sanders laughed, relaxing slightly.

Adams persisted, "Did your gold come from around Clifton?"

"No, it didn't," Sanders answered stiffly. "And, as you saw, it isn't placer gold, either! It's lode gold, and I know exactly where it is."

Adams sat back down and lit a cigar. "I have no designs or your gold, young man," he said. "I've been trying since before you were born to relocate a placer deposit I was at in 1837. I'd like to tell you my story."

"I haven't got time to listen to any stories about lost gold," Sanders snapped. "I have work to do."

Dejected, Adams left the store.

Later, after a few beers, Sanders told Hunkydory the story of his discovery. He described Coon Creek, and gave the details of how he had chanced on the outcrop.

CHAPTER 19
SANDERS' EXPEDITION

It had been a long, hard ride from Picket Post, and a driving rain had been pelting him for hours. Sanders was wet, tired, and anxious to find shelter. Since he was familiar with the practices at cavalry posts, he knew what to expect at Fort McDowell. The sentry was probably a malcontent being disciplined for some transgression or was simply incompetent to do any more complicated duty. It always amazed Sanders that such a critical post should be manned by the least trustworthy soldier in a barracks.

"Open the gate," Sanders hollered. He watched with self-satisfaction as the bleary-eyed private, who looked to be suffering from a nasty hangover, slowly opened the wide timber fashioned gate. The slickered private reluctantly only opened the gate partway and as Sanders rode through he gave the gate a good kick, sending the sentry sprawling in the mud. As he chuckled to himself Sanders looked around the grounds and concluded, "Not much going on here today."

Just then his old friend, John Bogdonovitch came out of the mess hall, braving the cold drizzle to meet him in the courtyard. "Terrible weather we're having isn't it, John?" Sanders shouted. "Haven't seen it rain like this since that day back in seventy-eight."

Bogdonovitch remembered that day all too well. He had been one of three wagon masters freighting supplies for the cavalry in the pouring rain when out of nowhere Apaches attacked. The freighters had had no reason to expect trouble. When the supply train came to a narrow stretch of road, the troopers who had been riding guard on both sides of the wagons and were unconcerned with anything but the weather fell back to follow the third wagon.

Bogdonovitch was the best teamster so his wagon was second. He carefully held his teams back to give the lead wagon time to maneuver between the boulders in the narrow section of trail. The less-experienced driver behind him let his lead mules push into the back of Bogdonovitch's wagon. Knowing the young driver was having trouble controlling his animals, Bogdonovitch jumped his teams to pull his wagon out of harm's way and to give the young teamster enough room to bring his mules under control. Bogdonovitch's sudden lurch forward probably saved his life. The other two drivers were less lucky. Both were killed in the initial wave of arrows.

Several arrows passed so close behind Bogdonovitch's head that he could hear the fluttering sound of the shafts cutting the air. He heard the thunk of others as their razor sharp flint heads slammed into the oak sides of his wagon.

With its driver slumped across the seat, the lead wagon was careering out of control as it bounced clear of the narrows that had slowed the group's progress. Bogdonovitch felt something slap the heavy leather of his left boot, but there was no time to give it much thought.

He whipped his lead mules with everything he had, praying he could safely make open ground. Once through the rough narrows he deliberately steered the teams sharply, intending to overturn the wagon. When the wagon tipped the hitch-pin failed and the terrified mules ran for their lives.

Bogdonovitch held fast to the reins, allowing the mules to pull him away from the toppling wagon. When he knew he was clear, he loosed the reins intending to run for cover behind the overturned wagon. But when he jumped up his left foot gave way with a throbbing pain. He looked down to see an arrow protruding from his boot. He scurried to the wagon dragging his injured leg behind.

The toppled wagon provided good protection. The troopers had taken cover at the far end of the boulder field he'd just driven through. The Apaches were between them hiding in the rocks.

He and the troopers had the Indians in a pretty good cross-fire. He wasn't able to get a clear shot at any of the renegades, but he fired his Winchester Rifle with enough accuracy to keep them pinned down. He was running out of ammunition though, and he looked back down the road to see what the troopers were doing.

In horror he saw they were mounting up. They were deserting him!

"Hey! Don't leave me here!" he screamed.

The last trooper stepped into the saddle, turned his mount, and flashed Bogdonovitch a wide grin that showed through the rain, across the considerable distance that separated them. For a moment

Bogdonovitch thought the man was sneering at his predicament. Then the trooper wheeled his mount and charged straight through the rocks past the cowering Apaches toward the overturned wagon.

Bogdonovitch marveled at the trooper's skill. He rode at full gallop, standing tall in the stirrups, reigns in his right hand, Colt .45 Army revolver in his left, firing as he rode past the ambushers.

The Apaches, too, must have been impressed with his shooting, for they all took cover, hiding among the boulders long enough for Private Sanders to help Bogdonovitch into the saddle, and for the two to ride double — back through the boulder field unmolested.

Later, Sanders was decorated for valor. Bogdonovitch believed it was insufficient compensation for what he had done. Sanders just shrugged and laughed when the teamster mentioned it. "I was just doing my job!"

Sanders' courageous action initiated a warm friendship between the two men. Now, three years later, he had come to tell Bogdonovitch of his gold discovery and to offer to take him in as an equal partner. Bogdonovitch was delighted. "Never cared to work for a living, anyway!"

"Can you find any good men to ride with us?" Sanders asked.

"I know of two. Both are experienced in mining, too. They're in the mess hall right now."

They walked into the dining area where Bogdonovitch made introductions.

"Bill Peterson, Sam Stone," he said, pointing to the men as he named them, "this is my good friend, Sanders. I guess I'll die without learning his given name. But anyway he saved my life once. I've told you that story. He has a job offer I think you boys might be interested in. Wait 'til you see the slab of rock he has!" He turned to Sanders, "Well," he drawled, "are you going show it to them, or do they have to beg?"

Sanders opened the flap on his wet saddlebag and pulled out his oil-skin wrapped treasure. He looked around warily. When he was satisfied the four of them had the dining hall to themselves, he unwrapped the gold-laced slab of quartz and passed it to John.

Peterson gasped. Stone's eyes grew wide.

"I've hunted all over southern Colorado, up in the San Juan

Mountains," Stone said in awe. "That's the best specimen of gold ore I've ever seen."

Peterson agreed. "Sure looks good to me," he murmured.

"Pass the coffee and I'll tell you my plan," Sanders said. "First, let's settle the details. There's plenty of gold for everybody. We'll be equal partners. We'll share the work and the profits. Any man doesn't do his share of work can figure on getting nothing. I've waited and planned for two years for this opportunity and now its time to make it pay off." Sanders gulped coffee, savoring its warmth. "Are you men in?" All three nodded eagerly.

"Good. We'll ride to Camp Reno," he went on. "That's the last stop on the trail. We'll purchase our supplies and pack animals there. No sense carrying anything farther than we have to.

"The way I figure it, we should take the time to build a cabin so we'll have shelter from bad weather and a protected place to sleep. The outcrop is on a steep hillside, and I sure don't want to be working there if it's raining or wet. By the time we finish the cabin the ground will have dried out pretty good, if it ever stops raining."

"What about those renegade Apaches we've been hearing about?" Stone asked.

"I'm not afraid of any gol-danged Indians," boasted Bogdonovitch. "Them heathens tried to kill me once and failed, I've got a right pretty flint point I dug out of my left foot, to prove it! Anyway, they'd best look out for us with old dead-eye Sanders along!"

"I hope you don't have to eat those words, John," Sanders said mildly.

The next day the rain stopped and the group left for Camp Reno, intending to stop over at Fort McDowell on the way. Sanders fairly jumped into the saddle and leaned forward, patting his horse on the neck. "Okay Jasper," he whispered, "let's show these civilians how to cut a trail."

After two days of hard riding the four arrived at Camp Reno. They were greeted by Lt. Davis, the fort's intermediary officer. Since it was his job to aid, assist, and advise civilians, he was anxious to inform Sanders' group of new trouble in the region.

"The sentry tells me you men came in from the west," Davis said. "If you intend to continue traveling east, I'd advise you not to do so at this time. Nana and a large band of renegades are on the warpath again. Best we know right now, he's out in New Mexico Territory somewhere. But his moves are totally unpredictable. No one is safe. If you must continue east, for God's sake, wait until we are certain that Nana has moved out of the region!"

"I knew those Apaches were going to be trouble," Stone grumbled.

Stone and Peterson held a quick conference. Peterson then spoke, "Sanders, we aren't in any hurry to die. If you intend to keep going, even when the army is saying it isn't safe, we're going to have to stay behind. Be glad to join you later, if you'll still have us."

Bogdonovitch, his expression sour with disappointment, spoke up quickly, "I'm in, Sanders, if you're still going."

"Oh, I'm going," Sanders responded firmly. "Can't blame you two, though. I know what Nana can do. I've seen him in action. He's all crippled with arthritis and he's already lived longer than any man has a right to live, but he just won't quit. But I've waited two years for this already and Nana or no Nana, I'm leaving just as soon as we can get the gear we need rounded up."

"Well, good luck then," Lt. Davis said. "Maybe if I had better information, I could detain you. I can't say for sure whether Nana is out there. Some think he's already heading south. You're grown men." His voice carried a warning tone, "Hope you make it to whatever is so important that it can't wait a few more weeks."

The morning of their departure the sky was clear and bright, a good day to travel, cool and no rain in sight. The ground was still wet enough in places to be hard on the horses' feet so the two men walked most of the first day. They didn't mind. They talked excitedly about what lay ahead.

During a brief break, Sanders walked over to Jasper and patted him on the rump. "John's a good man, and I'm glad to have him along, but you're the one I know I can depend on, old friend," he said softly. "We've been through a lot together and you've never let me down."

As they had anticipated, the going was slow. The three pack horses were heavily loaded and the country was rough. Day after day they struggled, moving over one small pass and then another, inching closer to the gold on Coon Creek.

On the third evening Sanders said, "John, tomorrow we'll leave the Salt River and climb out to the north over that black mesa to our left. Just beyond the top, I'll show you more gold than you've ever imagined!"

Just as Sanders claimed, the next day, less than a mile beyond the top of the mesa, they dropped into a canyon that drained toward the east. After about a mile the canyon they were following turned to the south, but they continued riding east, through a heavy thicket of giant prickly pear cactus, climbing a gentle slope which led onto the top of another, lower flat-top mesa. As they neared the top Sanders pointed out the well-preserved remains of an ancient stone-walled Indian ruin.

"See those stone walls over there? Old ruins like those are scattered all around this country. Some day I'd like to investigate these." Sanders was stalling, his heart was pounding with excitement. He was almost too anxious to continue. Would he find his ledge of gold-strewn quartz so easily? They rode south along the top of the mesa. Looking eastward, Bogdonovitch noticed a deep narrow ravine running north to south. Sanders guided them close to the west edge of that gorge and abruptly reined Jasper to a stop. The exhausted pack animals stopped in their tracks, glad for the rest. Sanders sat motion-less and erect in the saddle.

After a long silence Sanders spoke. His voice carried such intensity that, although his words were measured and whispered, they seemed to echo in Bogdonovitch's ears, as though they had been shouted.

"There it is," he said, pointing across the canyon.

On the opposite hillside was an outcrop of white quartz. Even at several hundred yards, Bogdonovitch could make out golden streaks, and could see the entire outcrop ablaze with the golden, gleaming light of the setting sun.

Bogdonovitch sat frozen, overcome by the glory before him. "This is richer than I ever imagined!" he whispered excitedly.

Sanders stared at the beautiful sight for several minutes, happy to see it was as he'd remembered it. Finally he spoke.

"We'll have to ride back north to get across this canyon, but I wanted you to see this now. Truth is, I was anxious to see it myself!"

They rode north, crossed a low saddle, and came to another

canyon that continued east. They followed this drainage into the canyon that held Sanders' treasure.

"We'd better make camp before long," Sanders said. "It'll soon be too dark for us to travel in this rough country."

As the two rode along, Sanders told Bogdonovitch the entire story of the day he had found his gold, omitting only the details of his memorable night with Jennifer Hardy.

"If we hurry down the canyon," Sander said, "we can see the outcrop up close before it gets dark. Then we can make camp on top of that mesa on the east side of the creek, or maybe at the river." His heart was still racing.

Before long, they were leading their horses up the wet and slippery side of the canyon. As they neared the top they stopped to get a closer look at the treasure. But by now the sun was too low in the sky. The spectacle was not what it had been earlier. They didn't linger. Sanders decided they had time to make it to the Salt River before full dark if they hurried.

That night they sat near the south bank of the river eating a simple dinner of canned beans, jerky, and hard biscuits.

"You know, that was the prettiest sight I've ever seen," Bogdonovitch said. "The way the sun reflected off that outcrop, I mean. Just thinking about something so beautiful makes a man forget the misery of this country. You know, Sanders, we've eaten a lot of meals together in the past three years. But I haven't enjoyed any as much as this! That outcrop is quite the thing . . . but I want you to know, I treasure your friendship even more than that."

Sanders was touched by his friend's words. He didn't reply immediately. When he did speak, it was about the future. "Let's build us a cabin right here, John," Sanders said. "There's a fresh water spring and plenty of wood. That's why I wanted to cross the river in the first place."

"This is a great spot for a cabin," Bogdonovitch said, nodding in agreement.

CHAPTER 20
NANA'S GREAT RAID, 1881

Some one-hundred miles from where Sanders and Bogdonovitch were planning their future, Nana and his men were traveling north toward the San Carlos Apache Reservation.

"Do you think we will see the Dreamer?" a young warrior asked. This was Kochera, he was Nana's second-in-command. He was also Gotch Ear's son.

"If it is meant to be," Nana replied. "I want to see the Dreamer because I know he can help me. But it is not always good to get what you want. There is a price. The things I learn through the Dreamer may bring sorrow along with answers. The Great Spirit is all-wise but we are not. Sometimes where he guides us is not where we would choose to go."

Gotch Ear had joined the Mimbres shortly after the Massacre at Zigzag Canyon. Because of his knowledge of the ways of the white man he soon became a mentor to the tribal elders. As Gotch Ear's eldest son, Kochera held an honored place in the tribe.

Nana had settled his band of women and children in the Sierra Madre Mountains of northern Mexico, hundreds of miles southeast of the San Carlos Reservation. Now, at the peak of his war of vengeance, he set his course toward the hated reservation. Nana hoped to see Noch-ay-del-klinne, the Dreamer, an Apache who was said to possess a special power.

Where Noch-ay-del-klinne got his power no one knew but there were reports among the Apache that he could summon the dead. If any Apache questioned the Dreamer's power before Nana's visit, none questioned it afterwards.

Kochera sought out Noch-ay-del-klinne and escorted him to the mountains where Nana and his men waited. "You wished to see me, great Chief?" the Dreamer asked.

"Yes, I have heard of your power to summon the dead and I

come to ask you to summon an old friend for me, this night. I must talk with Mangas Coloradas.

"I have seen eighty winters. I am tired and crippled. My old friend Mangas was truly wise and strong. I seek his strength and wisdom to continue."

In the month since Nana and his band had begun their raid, they had traveled more than two thousand miles and had engaged in seven major battles against superior numbers of hardened, well-trained, and disciplined soldiers. They had attacked twelve ranches, a handful of mining camps, one town, and several freight wagon trains. Along the way they had taken every opportunity to bring hardship and destruction to the "white invaders" who were entering the ancient Mimbres homeland in ever increasing numbers. Nana was totally victorious in every one of these engagements.

In an official report explaining that the U.S. Cavalry had been powerless against Nana and his band of warriors, a decorated Civil War General summed up thus: "Nana is undoubtedly the greatest military tactician who ever lived."

Noch-ay-del-klinne listened to Nana's request. "Come to the river tonight," he replied.

That evening Nana and his warriors found the Dreamer and three Apache braves already at the river, dancing in the bright moonlight. Through the long cool night they continued their ceremonial dancing until the sky began to lighten in the east.

Noch-ay-del-klinne, Nana, and most of the braves walked up a small hill in the predawn light. When they reached the crest the Dreamer stopped and lifted his arms in prayer. After a short incantation he spoke to Nana. "I shall guide you to the place of the dead. But first we must disguise ourselves so we do not frighten our spirit friends."

Under the Dreamer's instruction, the warriors blackened their faces with charcoal from the fire and tied eagle feathers in their hair.

When they had done this, the Dreamer gave Nana "strong medicine." He told Nana, "When you drink this, you will die, but your spirit will not go far. Your journey will bring you to him whom you seek. Your time among the dead is limited. Do not tarry. You must not stay beyond your time or you can never return; you will be lost, neither here nor there."

Moments after the old chief had swallowed the strong medicine, the unmistakable form of Mangas Coloradas rose slowly from the earth and stood, towering over Nana.

The trembling warriors bowed respectfully before the legendary chief, then followed Noch-ay-del-klinne as he silently motioned them off the hill, leaving Nana alone with his departed friend.

"Mangas, my friend, I have longed for this moment."

"You have aged, my friend," Mangas replied. "Still, it is good to see you. I have watched with pride as you have brought vengeance upon those who invade our lands. We both know our young braves shall never again hunt and live the way we and our fathers did. The old way of life is dead, there will be no more generations of free Apaches. Still, we must never give up this fight or our people will vanish from the earth.

"The Great Spirit created this earth for us to dwell on. He gave us game to hunt, rivers to bathe in and springs to drink from. It is not his will that our people should vanish from the earth. There must never come a time when our songs do not fill the air, when people will say, 'There are no more Apaches'."

"Mangas," Nana said, "my memories of you have always given me strength to continue. Now I need your knowledge so I can be certain I follow the right path. I have tried to live a life worthy of the gift you gave me, but now I grow old and tired. I am afraid I will not know when to stop fighting and take our young brothers home, before all are slaughtered, leaving our women and children with none to guard them." Nana paused then spoke sadly, "The whites are overrunning our lands. Their appetite for gold is never satisfied; they stop at nothing to get it, scarring the earth, killing the forests, and driving the wild animals from the land."

Mangas turned to Nana. "You will know when it is time. There will be a sign." Each man lifted his half of their shared power crystal toward the new day's sun. The morning light created a prism of colors in an unbroken band, uniting the two halves. A golden glow illuminated both men's faces. They stood, still as statues, until this golden light faded. "You must go, your time

*runs out. It will be many years until we are together again but I shall be at
your side always."*

Nana watched as the visage of Mangas faded away. He wondered what the promised sign would be. Strangely strengthened, he
rejoined the living, turned, and danced his way off the hill. He
scurried down the hill gyrating in a stylized dance. The energy he
mustered after a sleepless night inspired the young braves and they
soon joined in, their dance initiating the closing chapter of Nana's
vengeance war.

"The ceremony is complete," Nana said at last. "We must leave
this reservation swiftly. We will travel northwest to the Salt River. The
white man's cavalry has already gone south, thinking we are heading
for Mexico. Instead we will ride toward the Sierra Ancha Mountains,
fooling the white dogs one more time. From there, we will go south to
the Gila and follow it east into our ancestral tribal lands. From there
we will travel south into Mexico."

Army authorities believed the Dreamer was deliberately stirring
up trouble. They made it known he was to be killed at the first
opportunity. Shortly after Nana's visit the Dreamer heard this and
tried to escape the reservation. He was ambushed and killed by
waiting soldiers.

Nana's visit with the Dreamer coincided with Sanders' and
Bogdonovitch's arrival at Sanders' golden ledge. The two started
building their cabin. They worked hard for four days and were
nearing completion of their log shelter and a simple corral. In the
stillness of their fifth evening on the Salt River, the prospectors rested
on wood stumps inside the cabin, leaning against the wall, and facing
the canyon where the gold outcrop lay.

"Well, John," Sanders exclaimed. "This cabin isn't much but it
will keep us dry. Tomorrow we can get to work on the outcrop."
Sanders played with his specimen of quartz, admiring the polished
surface he had worked onto one side and the new inscription it bore.
"How's this, John? I've carved my name out of pure gold. Now isn't
that a pretty sight?"

Bogdonovitch sat back on his stump of wood and laughed.

"It truly is," he said. "Isn't fair, though! My name's too long to be carved on anything we're likely to find and if we did find a solid chunk of ore big enough, who would carry it?"

Sanders laughed. "Yes, I guess Bogdonovitch is a mite too long," he mused lightly. "Well, shoot, just use John!"

A muffled sound outside the cabin startled Sanders. "Jasper sounds restless, I think I'll have a look."

An uneasy feeling followed him as he walked to the log corral. "What do you say, boy," he spoke to Jasper. "Let's saddle you up and look around the area." Sanders swung into the saddle and rode into the growing darkness. As he disappeared beyond the bend in the now well-beaten trail, three Indians kicked open the cabin door.

Bogdonovitch was almost dozing. He came to with a start. "Bastard savages!" He grabbed for his Winchester laying on the wood slab in front of him, but was seized by two of the Indians before he reached it.

The third Apache walked over to the struggling Bogdonovitch, enjoying the terror in the white man's eyes.

"Sand . . . ."

Bogdonovitch's last word, the name of his friend, was cut short and turned into a dying scream as the Apache thrust a long flint knife up from under his rib cage.

Riding toward the river, Sanders heard the scream. He jerked the reins to wheel Jasper around but before the horse could respond Sanders was deafened by a rifle's report. Jasper jerked under him, reeled, and came crashing down on his right side, blood oozing from his nose.

"Oh, my God!" Sanders shrieked, working his leg out from under Jasper and groping for his rifle. But hearing footsteps all around, he knew it was too late. He rose, prepared to run, but found himself surrounded by Apache warriors. Among them was one old man he recognized instantly.

"Nana!" Sanders spat. "You murdering, heathen renegade!" Sanders lunged at the old chief, grasping Nana's shirt-front with both hands and in the scuffle breaking the rawhide cord hanging around the old man's neck.

"Mangas, my friend, this is for you," Nana said calmly. Then he ripped a long knife into Sanders stomach jerking it upward with all his might, slicing Sanders from naval to chest. Sanders' eyes revealed a moment of terror before he stumbled backward, dead, on top of his fallen horse.

"Burn that cabin," Nana commanded. "Kochera, you and Kaytennae look around this area and see if you can find what these men were doing here. Chief Juan José told me once that there was squaws metal near the Sierra Ancha Mountains," he gestured to the north. "I expect that's what you'll find if you follow the trail of these men. If you find it, hide it well. If you find any that's already been mined, hide it like we hid the gold we took from Zigzag Canyon."

The other braves saw the grand the old man wince in pain as he mounted his horse. Crippling arthritis was taking its toll.

"O Great Spirit," Nana muttered. "I hope my time is coming soon."

In victory Nana and his warriors rode south, into Mexico.

Advance scouts told the tribe, hidden high in the Sierra Madre, of Nana's latest triumph. When the others arrived in camp, they found those there in the midst of a great celebration.

Nana, however, felt the need for solitude. "I will be back soon," he told the celebrating Apaches. The tired old chief limped as he climbed the hill where he often meditated. He reached inside his outer shirt for his pouch with the crystal, only to discover it was gone.

"O, Great One," he prayed, dismayed, "what have I done? I have lost my crystal, my friend's precious gift. What can this mean?"

The question was hardly formed before Nana knew the answer. This loss was the sign Mangas' spirit had foretold.

Sanders was Chief Nana's last victim. The great, shrewd, and feared Apache war chief died in 1896 just before his ninety-sixth birthday. In his final years, he saw his people humiliated time after time as they were shuffled from one reservation jail to the next.

CHAPTER 21
ADAMS' FAREWELL, 1886

On the morning of May 29, 1886 Adams again found himself on his way to Clifton. He'd begun to wonder if he would go to his grave leaving a fortune buried in the Arizona wilderness. His failed searches had become personal defeats. He hated failure.

At age sixty-six he was hoping to muster one more group of prospectors to search for his lost treasure. The stagecoach ride from California was too long for the aging man to make without a break. He laid over in Prescott, Arizona for one day.

There he took a room at the board and bath on Main street, bought a newspaper, then went to the spartan dining area and seated himself. The dining area was under a veranda at the back of the main structure. He ordered coffee while he waited for his simple dinner of roast beef and biscuits with gravy.

Steaming coffee arrived promptly and he leaned back in his comfortable chair, perusing the paper, sipping the strong brew. It was impossible to bypass the front page headline in the Prescott *Morning Courier:*

APACHE VICTIMS FOUND

"Blasted Apaches! The Cavalry will never be able to stop them, mark my words," Adams muttered to himself.

There was more truth to this than he knew. When the Apaches finally were subjugated, it was Pima Indians and not the U.S. Cavalry who were primarily responsible.

Adams read the article carefully.

In 1882, J.G. Barney, W.H. McCullough, and a Mexican headed out together from Alma, New Mexico on a prospecting trip. They were known to have been heading into Arizona Territory in search of the "Lost Adams Diggings."

Their remains were recently identified by family members who were able to identify several possessions which were found in the vicinity of the bodies. The cavalry officer in charge of the investigation stated that these deaths were almost certainly caused by Apaches but he could give no further detail. When asked about the time of death he said, "It looked like several years ago. Hard to tell, all there was left was bones and clothing." He went on to describe that scars on the skull of one body, "probably the Mexican," were indicative of scalping.[5]

Adams put the paper down and frowned into his empty cup.

"Say," he motioned the waiter, "could I get another coffee, please?" Adams thumped the paper. "Sounds like the Apaches are still killing folks, just like in the old days!"

"Those devils would cut you open just to see your heart beat," the waiter said innocently, and with unintended irony. "This isn't the only account of late. Those men were probably killed in eighty-two, but there have been plenty of other killings before and since. Two men were killed a few years ago down on the Salt River near Cherry Creek. The rancher who found their remains figured they were probably killed in eighty-one or eighty-two. One was a feller named Sanders and the other had one of those names nobody could pronounce. Folks around these parts say Chief Nana himself did that job. One of the bodies bore Nana's trademark — a split belly. Hard to say what happened to the other one. His remains was pretty well fried in the fire the Injuns set."

The waiter brought Adams' meal and a full pot of coffee.

"Anything else you need before I head home, Mr. Adams?"

"Why no, thank you," Adams answered. "You said one of those men was named Sanders? And Nana killed him?" He continued without letting the waiter answer. "Down on the Salt River, eh? You know, I met a man named Sanders back in eighty-one, up at Picket Post. I saw some of his gold, too. Impressive specimen. He sure was an unfriendly sort of fellow. Old Nana must have gotten to him shortly after I met him. Too bad, a young man like that and all."

"Where are you headed, Mr. Adams?"

"Clifton, I reckon," Adams answered. "Years ago I found a gold strike in a canyon somewhere in that area. I haven't been able to relocate the place. You know, young man, I'm sixty-six years old and I've had some pretty close calls in my day. I'm afraid this may be the last time I get to search for that zigzag canyon. Sounds like I'm going to need luck on my side again with the Apaches still on the warpath."

The waiter poured Adams a last cup of coffee and hurried home. He wasn't interested in listening to another lost gold story from another "old timer."

Adams left Prescott the next morning, as always believing this would be his lucky trip. During the long stagecoach ride though, doubts began to gnaw at him. Hearing of Sanders death and reading about the deaths of another group of "Adams prospectors" brought back long-buried memories. Adams had hoped Mangas' death would end the campaign of terror the Apache Nation had been waging against settlers and especially against prospectors. Clearly it hadn't. Old Nana still carried on and there were younger chiefs coming along to continue the wars.

After nearly two weeks on dusty trails — the stage line advertised them as roads but Adams couldn't imagine why — the stage rolled into Clifton.

Stepping from the coach, Adams was struck by all the changes he saw. His first trip up the San Francisco he'd seen nothing but empty river bottom. On his second visit, a tent city had sprung up along the river's banks. What he saw now was a mining boomtown, complete with streets, boardwalks, stone and wood buildings, a jail, saloons, churches, hotels and boarding houses. There were little shacks plastered along the river bottom and on the steep canyon walls on both sides of the river. The smell of people and the mining smelters spewing their hazy brown smoke combined to fill the air with an obnoxious stench.

Adams didn't like what any of what he saw, not even the "ladies" on the saloon balconies. He longed to find the wilderness he remembered. He could not bring himself to admit that it was men like himself, those who searched the wilderness for minerals, who were responsible for bringing the changes that destroyed the wilderness he loved.

As usual, Adams bought a paper and went to find a room with a good bed, a hot bath, and somewhere to eat a hearty dinner. He couldn't stop the changes so he might as well enjoy the civilized comforts they brought. Tomorrow he would go in search of recruits for one more expedition.

At breakfast Adams struck up a conversation with a leathery old cowboy sitting on the next stool.

"My name's Adams, Andrew Adams," he said, offering his hand to the tall stranger. "Wonder if I might have a word with you?"

"Sure, Andrew. Name's Dud Eldridge. Call me Dud. What can I do for you? Wait a minute. Did you say Adams? You're not connected with this cock-and-bull story about the Lost Adams Diggin's, are you?" Eldridge snickered.

"Yes sir. One and the same," Adams boasted.

"No kidding!" Eldridge shook his head in disbelief, the pitch of his voice raising in excitement. "I've been running cattle in these parts for forty-two years and I've been listening to people tell different versions of the 'Adams Diggin's' story most of my life. Ain't no two of 'em alike! I'd love to hear the real story, right from the horse's mouth. Do you have the time?"

Did he! There was nothing dearer to Adams than an interested listener. He popped the snap on the left side of his shirt, lifted the flap, and dug into the deep pocket over his heart. "Just have a look at this. I've been carrying this nugget around for fifty years," Adams said. "It's the only one I was able to save from my diggings. Had to use the others over the years to grubstake prospecting ventures."

Adams told his story with relish, scarcely mentioning the details of his escape with Landrew. In fact, as time wore on, he often confused that escape with the long ride he and Davidson made, after the second massacre.

When first telling a prospective partner his story, Adams usually left out certain details. The part about the buried pot of gold was reserved for serious prospectors. Adam's secrecy was foolish. After the expeditions with Shaw the "pot full of gold story" was well known.

Adams told Eldridge about the zigzag canyon, the waterfall, the half-breed guide, Gotch Ear, and all the gold in the canyon just waiting to be picked up.

"We had hardly scratched the surface," he exaggerated. "There's plenty of gold left there, just waiting to be claimed!"

Then Adams broached the inevitable question. "I'm going out again and this time I'll find it. Know anybody who might be interested in going in with me, as a partner? How about you?"

Eldridge had already heard enough to figure that Adams had absolutely no idea how or where to find the canyon. "Not me," he replied matter-of-factly. "I've been working cattle all my life and I aim to keep doing it until it kills me. I don't aim to go chasing after gold. Especially gold that's already lured dozens of men to their deaths from what I hear.

"Anyway, don't you see how this country's changin'? Copper and gold strikes everywhere. Why, we're right in the middle of the biggest gold rush since the forty-niners hit California Territory. Rich companies are buying up all the claims worth a stitch. Going after your gold would be like me fighting the big cattle outfits up Montana way. Those big boys use hired guns, you know. Besides, they claim copper is where all the money's at now, at least in this territory.

"I can understand how you feel, though. Dreamed of a big cattle spread myself once. Isn't the same with gold, is it? I mean, I can make a living on the little spread I work. Prospectors haven't got anything 'til they strike it big, and from what I've seen around here that's pretty rare.

"No, I'm not interested in helping you look for your lost canyon. Thanks for the offer, though. Maybe twenty years ago, but not now.

"I do know a man who might be interested in talking to you. He works for the railroad. I've heard tell he searched for your lost canyon once, quite a few years ago.

"Something else you should know, Adams. Two months ago Geronimo and Nana surrendered. Old Nana is still on the reservation, but Geronimo escaped with a few renegades. A small band of Apaches can raise a big ruckus. You should have been here when Nana made his last raid!"

Adams laughed softly and flashed a wry grin.

"What's so funny?" Eldridge asked.

"Why, nothing," Adams replied, "just wondering what makes you think that was Nana's *last* raid?"

Eldridge frowned, cocked his head and both men broke into laughter. "Well, I guess you're right on that point!" Eldridge exclaimed. "Guess I should have said *latest* raid."

"Anyway," Eldridge continued, "old Nana and twenty braves caused more trouble around these parts than three hundred Apaches should have been able to. Cavalry couldn't do anything to stop them, either."[6]

Adams interrupted. "I reckon I know about Indians! Nana and I are well acquainted. I watched him flick a tomahawk once . . . . Besides, those damn Indians will always be the plague out here, I'm too old to worry about that any longer. Who is this fellow who works on the railroad?"

"His name's Stevens, I think," Eldridge answered.

Adams searched his memory. "Stevens . . . C. S. Stevens! I haven't seen him in a coon's age. He and I discussed my diggings over a beer once, in Silver City, as I recall. Never thought I'd see him again. I sure didn't know he was anywhere near these parts. By golly, I'll go look him up this very day! Thanks for the information, Dud. Been good talkin' to you."

Adams headed straight to the train depot and walked up to the first railroad worker he saw. "Excuse me, mister, do you have any idea where I might find Mr. Stevens?"

The young man scratched at the stubble on his chin and gestured. "Down at the main railroad office, I think."

Adams walked across the vacant lot and into the building. There sat Stevens. Despite the many years since their talk, they recognized each other immediately.

"Adams, you old goat," yelled Stevens. "You look a lot better than you have any right to! Why, I been telling people you died back in seventy-eight. How ya been?" Nudging Adams he grinned and asked, "You here after that gold again?"

"Well, I thought maybe I'd have another look for it," Adams admitted. "Are you interested in having a look with me?"

Stevens rolled his eyes and grinned from ear to ear. "Not a chance! Not me! I've been on that wild goose chase once. That was one time too many. I've got a good job and I'm not wasting any more of my time looking for something that's lost. After that talk we had in Silver City I made my own try, in seventy-seven. It was an embarrassing fiasco. I nearly starved to death! I learned to hate cornbread, but I didn't learn much else, except that I'm not cut out for that sort of life. I've given it up. This is still dangerous country to be traipsing around in. Even if a man is lucky enough to find something and the Apaches or Mother Nature don't get him, he would still have to compete with the big mining companies. I've watched one 'lucky' prospector after another make a good strike and then be forced to sell out for practically nothing. Back in the sixties none of us recognized it but right under our noses a big gold rush was developing here in Clifton. It really got going in seventy-two."

"Yes, I've read about it and I see the results," Adams said sadly. "Nevertheless, I think I'll stay around here a while longer. A man never knows when he might get lucky."

Adams stayed around Clifton for eighteen months, and was last seen by C. S. Stevens in 1888. Finally, discouraged that he couldn't get anyone to go in with him, he left for California and literally disappeared from history.

CHAPTER 22
CLIFTON, 1899

"**S**tevens, C. S. Stevens? He works on the Longfellow Narrow Gauge spur in Clifton," the conductor answered. "I've been told he moved here way back in seventy-seven. He's the town expert on local history. He'll tell you plenty of stories about the mines in this area. I've got to warn you, though. He's windy as an old bellows. Once you get him pumping you'd better stand back. He'll talk all night."

As the train rolled into the new Clifton depot, Luke Longmore gathered his baggage, thanked the conductor, and headed for the Clifton Hotel, since it had been recommended. After registering he cleaned up, then crossed the street to the Copper Queen Cafe for supper.

He ordered the house special, with coffee. Then he asked the pretty Mexican waitress, "Do you know where I might find a Mr. C. S. Stevens?"

She laughed pleasantly and pointed to the next table. "He's the red-haired man with his back to you," she replied.

Longmore introduced himself and joined Stevens who was just finishing his meal. "I'm told you know a lot about the mining history of this region," Longmore began.

"Yes I do," Stevens boasted. "What do you need to know, young man?"

"Well, to tell the truth, I'm mostly interested in the Adams Diggings," Longmore replied. "My friend Milo Morris tells me his father and a man named C. S. Stevens hunted for the Adams back in 1877. Milo's father was named Bill, Bill Morris. Are you the same C. S. Stevens, sir?"

"Well, yes I am," Stevens answered.

"I was hoping you could tell me what you know of the Adams story and one other thing. Do you know anything about General Kearney's military expedition of 1846? I read in Emory's notes from that adventure that they camped at the mouth of the San Francisco River."

Stevens ignored Longmore's questions.

"How did you find me?"

"I came into town on the new railroad. Being a railroad man myself, I know railroaders usually know just about everything," Longmore replied with a friendly grin, finally answering the question. "The bald conductor told me where to find you. He also said you were an authority on the history of mining in Clifton."

"Mr. Longmore," Stevens said, "I'll be glad to tell you what I know about the Adams. But I warn you, if you're thinking of looking for the Adams Diggin's around here you'll be wasting your time!"

Longmore furrowed his brow. "Why's that?"

"The Scottish companies have everything all claimed up!" Stevens explained, "My God, son, this is 1899. Clifton has been a mining boom town for over sixteen years now. If the Adams were around here and anyone ever located it, they'd have to fight the big mining companies to keep it. The Scots have owned the Arizona Copper Company since 1883. They're working hard to consolidate all the little mining claims in the region. Oh there are a few lone-wolfs left around here but they're being squeezed real hard. Every time an independent prospector makes some piddling little discovery the big companies find some way to grab it from him. Usually they just wait until he's good and broke — for some reason it seems to be real hard for an independent to find men or supplies to work a claim. Then they buy him out for next to nothing."

Longmore interrupted. "Let me explain myself. My interest right now is primarily in Adams' story. You see, I'm writing a book on old mining lore. When Milo Morris told me you and his father hunted for the Adams I figured there was a chance you could tell me more about Adams. Did you know him personally?"

"Yes, I did," Stevens replied. "Met Adams back in seventy-five or seventy-six. We shared a meal and a beer over in Silver City. In seventy-seven I came to this area on an expedition with Bill Morris and three other men. You can read about that in the local newspaper. They have all the old issues down at the city hall. A few months after that inglorious expedition, I moved to Clifton. I've lived here ever since.

"For several years I maintained a strong interest in Adams story and in the stories of others who searched for his lost diggings. He didn't really have any friends, he was just too dedicated to finding that lost canyon of his. But I guess you could say I knew him pretty well.

"He came through town several times and we always visited. The last time he came here was in eighty-six. Said he wanted to make, 'one last search'. As far as I know he never did, though. Everyone had heard his story and the truth was he had no idea where to look. Last time I saw him was early in eighty-eight. Said he 'was heading back to California'. The wilderness he remembered was gone and he didn't like that."

The conductor had been right about Stevens. He babbled on. "As early as seventy-two there were already three big mining companies in the area. But Clifton was still wide open to the lone prospector. This country was wilderness like you young folks will never see. And now look!" he exclaimed. "The mills and the mines employ three hundred workers — mostly Mexican and Chinese. Clifton has become a bona fide city with every service a man could want, including saloons and whores. Even some white women! Now that's something we never had in the old days."

"That's all very interesting," Longmore commented dryly, trying to get Stevens back on the Adams story, "but I'm more concerned with the gold-mining history and especially the Adams story."

"Well, copper has always been king in Clifton," Stevens continued. "Gold and silver are important but not like copper! The smelter at Clifton is going constantly, day and night. Why, the Scottish Arizona Copper Company is producing ten-thousand tons of pure copper every year! It's hard to imagine that much copper!"

"Tell me about Adams," Longmore insisted. "What was he like? Do you think he really had a mine?"

"There's no doubt in my mind," Stevens replied. "Adams was an honest man. I've always been certain his story was true. It never changed over the years — well not the important parts anyway. If you'd heard him tell it, you wouldn't have had any doubt. He always carried this gold nugget he claimed came from his 'little zigzag canyon'. I've heard some claim he was a promoter looking to see how much money he could get out of folks with his wild story, but that just wasn't true. He didn't want money. He wanted partners to help him search for his lost diggings. I've never heard of him making a penny off anyone. As he grew older he grew more frustrated because he couldn't find his way back to that canyon."

"Why do you think he couldn't?" Longmore asked.
Stevens sat back, crossed his arms and stared thoughtfully across the table.

"Well, that's a good question. My guess is he was looking for something that didn't exist anymore."

Longmore's brow wrinkled and he asked, "What do you mean?"

"Adams waited nearly thirty years before he came back to look for it the first time," Stevens explained.

"Thirty years?" Longmore asked. "I thought he made his discovery in sixty-four."

"Oh no, it was a lot earlier than that, back in the thirties," Stevens clarified. "Anyway, things changed a lot in that time. For one thing, while Adams was gone Mountain Men had killed off nearly all the beaver. You better believe that changed things! In 1884 there was a flood here in Clifton, washed practically the whole town away! Old timers said the river never had flooded like that until the beaver were killed out. Makes sense. All those beaver ponds used to hold back a lot of flood water.

"Another thing, the vegetation around here has changed since the old days. Why, when I first came here there were still a few old pine stumps. No live trees, but there were some stumps. Even those are gone now. It's all cottonwoods and sycamores these days. Dud Eldridge told me that in the old days this valley was lush with grass. Look at it now!"

Longmore was tiring. The subject seemed to keep wandering away from Adams. "Mr. Stevens, I sure thank you for all the information. Sounds like you know more about the Adams than anybody else I've met."

"Yes, for all the good it does me," Stevens complained, smiling. "I have a good job with the railroad here and I aim to keep it. Chasing lost mines is no way to live these days. Working for those who have the big mines is the only chance a poor man has for a decent living!"

"Well, you may be right about that. But I'm still fascinated with stories of lost mines. I've chased the stories all over the Southwest for years. The Adams story is my favorite. Have you heard from the old man since you saw him in eighty-eight? Do you have any idea where he might be now?"

Stevens shook his head, "I don't even know if he's still alive. If he is, he would be close to eighty. All I know is he was living in California then. He headed back to California when he left here."

Longmore signaled the waitress for refills on coffee, staring at the pretty young girl's figure and her swelling neckline as she leaned forward to refill their cups.

"I've always liked the way Mexican señoritas dress," he nervously told Stevens, "especially when they're well filled out."

Stevens laughed. "I'm a married man, son. Anyway, I'm getting a little old for that sort of thing. But I do remember what it was like when I was your age. A sight like that would cause a real stirring. Maybe you ought to try the saloon over there," he gestured to the building diagonally across the intersection. "I've heard their girls are the best in town."

Longmore's heart raced but he shook his head and focused his thoughts. "Later, perhaps. Do you know Adams' full name? I've read accounts giving several different first names."

Stevens hesitated and then said gropingly, "An . . . Andrew, I think. Yes, that's it, Andrew Adams. You kind of threw me there. I always called him Adams, just like folks calls me Stevens."

"What about his partner?" Longmore asked.

"You mean the Frenchman?" Stevens asked.

"Frenchman? I thought his last name was Davidson, that doesn't sound French," Longmore said.

"No son, you're confused. You've been listening to that nonsense old Doc Spurgeon was telling folks. Adams and Davidson were partners on Adams return trip back in sixty-four. He didn't talk much about his first escape, but he did tell me it was in the thirties and he and a Frenchman survived. He mentioned the man's name but I don't recall it. I do remember he said his friend couldn't read English. That's about all I can tell you about him."

CHAPTER 23
LONGMORE'S INVESTIGATION

Longmore and Stevens talked long into the night. When the young writer returned to his modest room at the Clifton Hotel it was 3:00 a.m. but there was still plenty of activity in the prosperous town. He opened the outside door and stood at the top of the insubstantial exterior stairway that led to his second floor room. He paused to look down the moonlit street toward the river. He considered, just for a moment, looking for a little entertainment at the establishments across the street that were still full of life. But he was too tired, and he stepped back into his room. Next to the kerosene lamp on the vanity he found a fancy cardboard box of safety matches with the hotel's name printed on it. By the light of the waning quarter-moon, he struck one against the built-in striker on the side of the box and watched the match flare up and then settle to a small even flame. He touched the flame to the lamp's wick, setting the light in front of the mirror on the vanity. As he placed the chimney back on the lamp's base the fire flared and a sooty flame smoke blackened the glass.

"I *must* be tired," he mumbled. "Been a long time since I forgot to trim the wick before putting the chimney back on."

At best, this small lamp provided little light for the darkly finished room. With its chimney smoked it cast little more than an eerie yellow glow on the dark, wood-trimmed plaster walls and the faded flower print of the ceiling paper.

Longmore picked through his maps. Wanting to have another look but fatigue won out. His mind was exhausted and he knew his eyes needed rest. He turned the lamp wick down until the flame flickered. As the lamp cooled in the next few minutes, the flame slowly diminished, giving him just enough light to get undressed and into bed before it died.

He lay down, watching the flickering last rays from the lamp dance across the ceiling and contemplated what he had learned. Earlier that month he had traveled to Fort Leavenworth where he had read a rough copy of Emory's notes from the 1846 expedition. He had noticed that in those notes the maps of eastern Arizona showed various rivers entering the Gila and he realized that several were not in the proper locations. He also recalled Emory's reference to an illiterate Frenchman by the name of Londeau.

It wasn't until Longmore was almost asleep that he grasped the importance of a very interesting piece of new information Stevens had given him: The massacre had occurred in the 1830s. Longmore sat bolt upright in bed, rose and relit the lamp, cleaned the chimney and mounted it.

He arranged his hand-sketched copy of Emory's map and several government maps of the region on the vanity, then located his notes of Emory's story. He dug through the notes until he found Emory's reference to Londeau's story. Longmore had copied it verbatim because it was a direct reference to a lost gold deposit.

The thought that had awakened him was now clear in his mind. Like everyone else at the time, Longmore had assumed Adams' trip up the San Francisco River with Davidson in 1864 was the trip when Adams had discovered the rich placer deposit. That was what newspaper accounts of the time had claimed.

But Stevens knew Adams. And Stevens said otherwise. The 1864 trip was a *return* trip; on the 1864 trip Adams was trying to *relocate* a placer deposit he had first been to in the 1830s, in the company of an illiterate Frenchman. Here, on the vanity right in front of Longmore, was a copy of Emory's quotation from an illiterate Frenchman who claimed that a group of prospectors had found gold along the banks of the Prieto River in the late 1830s and were later massacred by Indians.

How many large groups of successful prospectors could have been massacred in that region in the 1830s? It seemed clear to Longmore that Londeau was describing the same massacre Adams had survived. Further, Londeau was an illiterate Frenchman, one who seemed to know a great deal about a wilderness massacre and Adams' surviving partner was described as an illiterate Frenchman. There were just too many coincidences and Longmore didn't have all that much faith in coincidence anyway. "Londeau must have been Adams' partner," he mumbled.

Now, if he could only make sense of Emory's maps. The government maps were no help. Every updated issue from the era showed rivers in somewhat different positions and often as not the names switched places or changed entirely. Nobody around Clifton seemed to know any more about the old names for the rivers than Longmore did. "Yes, young man, those river names were all messed up back then . . ." he muttered, parroting Stevens. "That's a great help!"

He trimmed the lamp's wick until the light from the low uneven flame danced in the chimney. Before long the lamp died. Longmore stared through the darkened room at the lace on the window shade visible in the moon's glow. It was an eerie sight for his tired eyes and troubled mind. It had been a long, long day and now a long night, piled on top of a week's hard travel. He fell back into bed and closed his eyes. He was asleep before he knew it.

Luke Longmore had just turned twenty years of age. He had a sharp mind, which he occupied gathering all the information he could find on lost mines and treasure legend. Even his dreams often involved searching for some lost mine. Tonight he dreamed of the Adams Diggin's: *Two young men running for their lives along the flanks of a pitch black river . . . .*

When he turned fourteen, Longmore had left his home in Louisville, Kentucky and traveled west, alone. A few months later he rode into a mining camp in New Mexico Territory, where he took his first job as a water boy. In the years since, he had moved from one mining or railroad camp to another, working when he had to and gathering information when he could on the many lost treasure stories of the southwest region. They had been six full years and they seemed like a lifetime.

Of the myriad legends he heard around campfires, none fascinated him as much as the Adams story. By the time he had first heard it there were already several versions. It seemed to Longmore that every telling held some new variation. Trying to sort out what was truth and what was embellishment was a big problem. When Longmore got to Clifton he spent considerable time at the local newspaper office reading every article on the Adams he could find. And there were plenty.

Now, while he slept, the diverse versions of the Adams story wove themselves through Longmore's dreams, like colorful yarns. At times they wove into a beautiful tapestry; other times they tangled into hopeless knots.

He was sleeping soundly when, as he had requested, the desk clerk roused him.

"Sir, Sir." The desk clerk rapped loudly on the door. "It's seven-thirty. You asked for a wake-up call, this is it!"

"What?" Longmore responded, fighting his way from deep sleep. "Oh yes. Thank you, I'm up."

He dressed in his cleanest clothes and packed his saddlebags. His month's leave from a new job on the railroad in Tucson — one hundred miles southwest of Clifton — would pass quickly. He didn't want to waste precious time sleeping!

As he packed, he considered his good fortune at being able to get so much time away from work.

"If old man Meyer wasn't such a history buff, he'd never have given me this time off to do research, even if they are over-manned right now. I'd better get started on finding Londeau. It's not likely to be easy."

Londeau was Longmore's only real hope, since Adams was nowhere to be found. "Even if I could find him," Longmore concluded reasonably, "what good would it do? He already tried the San Francisco River, thinking it was the Prieto. I can't tell much from these maps, but its pretty obvious Londeau wasn't referring to what's now called the San Francisco."

He grabbed his satchel and saddlebags, paid his bill and hurried over to the Copper Queen Cafe for breakfast.

"Good Morning, Señorita." He smiled as he greeted the attractive young woman who had served him the night before. "I'll have coffee, two eggs, bacon, and biscuits with lots of gravy, please."

She smiled back. He enjoyed watching her move gracefully toward the kitchen. He liked to see her work. He had returned there hoping to see her again. He knew he liked her looks and the way she dressed even before he knew she was called Katie. In fact, he liked everything about her. Too bad the train was leaving within the hour.

Katie saw him yawning and fighting to keep his eyes open, and she made her third trip to Longmore's table to refill his coffee cup.

"You must have had a late evening," she said, with a sly smile, and then blushed. Then looking at his bags, she added, "looks like you're leaving town. The morning train?"

"Matter of fact, I am," he replied. "I just got into town yesterday. I've been on vacation for two weeks, starting with a trip back east to visit my family in Kentucky. On the way back to Tucson I spent some time at Fort Leavenworth, Kansas, doing a little research for my book. When Kansas was separated from Missouri in 1861 the Fort's address changed. That confused me a bit. Anyway, that brought me here. I was hoping to find some new information from old timers or old newspapers, but I've had no luck. I'm heading for California next looking for a man who was last seen in San Diego half a century ago!" Longmore finished his outpouring with a rueful smirk.

"My goodness, Mr. Longmore," Katie exclaimed, "you've been busy, haven't you? You've also got a lot of faith! Not many folks who were alive in 1850 are still with us. If the man you're looking for is still alive, it would be quite something if he were still in San Diego. I wish you luck. It sounds like you'll be needing it."

Longmore was intrigued by the friendly young woman's intelligence and understanding.

"Miss Katie," he said, "I'm in a hurry. The morning train leaves in fifteen minutes. I've hardly had a chance to visit with you. I don't mean to pry or be too forward but I have noticed you are single."

He paused, suddenly aware of a lump in his throat. Wondering why the room had grown inexplicably so warm. He brushed beads of sweat from his temples.

"I was wondering," he continued in spite of his sudden discomfort, "when I come back through town, would you have dinner with me?"

Katie blushed at the sudden personal attention from the quiet, proper stranger. She didn't even know his full name, but she knew she was interested. She nodded a demure "yes." Then, somewhat flustered, she disappeared into the kitchen until Longmore was gone.

He left a small gratuity with his name and address scrawled on a slip of paper under the edge of his plate, then he hurried to the train depot.

"Is the morning train on time for the connection with the Southern Pacific at Lordsburg?"

"Yes sir, it is," the big round-bellied man responded. "Which way you headed from there?"

"California," Longmore answered.

"You're in luck. There's not much of a layover in Lordsburg for folks traveling westbound."

Longmore boarded and found a comfortable seat near the back of the rattling narrow-gauge car. Looking out of the smudged window, he considered the task he faced.

Fifty years is a long time, he thought. And if Londeau is still alive, how much will a man who has to be at least in his eighties remember after such a long time?

The odds were slim, but Longmore had to try.

Emory's notes gave him Londeau's name, and reported that the Frenchman had reached San Diego with Emory. It was a long shot, but maybe there would be more current information on Londeau at the military fort in San Diego.

The trip to California was long and tedious, taking him four hundred miles across the hottest deserts he had ever traveled.

The visit to San Diego was disappointing. He found nothing more in any of the military records there. He found no records at all of the Emory Expedition and the fort librarian informed him that all records from before 1850 had been moved to the Library of Congress in Washington, D.C.

Longmore spent a week in San Diego, following every possible lead, hoping to find someone who had at least heard of Londeau. He tried the local newspapers, the police, various civic organizations, and the Catholic Church, but with no luck. Two days before he was due back at his job in Tucson he boarded an eastbound train, thoroughly discouraged.

Back at work in Tucson, Longmore visited with his foreman, Milo Morris. In Morris, Longmore had a friend who enjoyed the old treasure stories as much as he did. He followed each of Longmore's narratives with much curiosity and demonstrated an investigative flair. Many years later Morris published Longmore's first book.

"Say, Milo, I found the man you told me looked for the Adams with your father, C. S. Stevens. He still lives in Clifton. He tells pretty much the same story you said your father did. Says he had no idea where he was going. He did give me some interesting new information on the Adams story though."

At lunchtime the conversation got around to prospecting stories again. "You say Londeau was known to have gone to San Diego with Emory?" Morris asked. "If that's the case, you should check the latest California census. It could take a while to go through the information, but if old man Londeau was there for the census that's the way to locate him. I've heard that many of those who went with Emory's expedition liked what they found in California and decided to settle out there. There's at least a chance Londeau is still there. Might even still be alive!" Morris suggested.

Longmore brightened, "Good idea! Why in thunder didn't I think of it? I don't give it too much hope, but it is worth a try."

Morris was Longmore's immediate supervisor, making it easy for Longmore to get a few days off. He wrote Miss Katie in care of the Copper Queen Cafe, telling her he was heading back to California to look for Londeau again.

Two days later he strode up the stone steps of the new court house in San Diego. He made his request and was handed the latest census file. Longmore paled, "Is there any order to all this?"

"Afraid not, sir, not yet at least," the clerk answered apologetically.

"It'll take me forever to go through all this," Longmore groaned.

Longmore took the massive book from the reference desk at the back of the lobby and found a seat at the nearest table. After a few minutes, he realized the situation wasn't as bad as it had first seemed. The forms were neatly filled in and all he had to do was look for the letter "L" in the last name column. After six hours of diligent searching, he had come on the names of three Londeaus. There were thirteen similarly spelled names that warranted further checking. None were old enough to be the Londeau he was looking for, but Longmore didn't want to miss any possible relatives.

Each time he was about ready to give up for the day he came upon another name with a similar spelling. He would copy all the information into his log, stretch, and go at it again. He was impressed with his own capacity for tedious research.

At three thirty two p.m., just twenty-eight minutes before the punctual courthouse superintendent would lock the doors, Longmore found the following entry: Landrew, Maurice, 785 South Plaza del Rey, 80, retired . . . . The age was right and the name was French. Emory had noted that Londeau was illiterate so that could account for the different spelling. "It's worth checking," he thought.

That afternoon, hoping against hope, he knocked on the door at 785 South Plaza del Rey. The door was answered by an old man.

"No . . . , no, I don't know any Landrew," the old man responded to his inquiry. "Frenchman, you say? Nope, sorry. Never heard of him. You might check with Mr. Dickens across the street. He's lived there for years and knows everyone in this part of town."

Longmore thanked the old-timer and crossed the street to inquire again.

Dickens didn't know if the Maurice Landrew who used to live across the street might have been the Londeau who was with Emory and he didn't know where Landrew was now. But wait. He did have a forwarding address. Somewhere.

"He had me write it down for him. He never did get the hang of writing or reading much," Dickens explained. "I never got no mail for him. He don't write nor read none, but 'You never know' he told me. Said he'd found a nice little cabin up in the hills. I'll be dogged if I can remember the name of the post office he gave. Let me find his address, you can read it for yourself. My eyes ain't none too good these days."

As Dickens tottered to his writing desk, Longmore's hopes flickered to life. "It must be the right man," he thought. "The age is right, illiterate, French — too many coincidences. I can't believe I get this close after so many years and he up and moves just a few months before I get here! But no matter. With a forwarding address I'll find him easy."

For several minutes Longmore watched as Dickens carefully picked through all the scraps of paper on his little rolltop desk, then rifled the drawers checking and rechecking every scrap of paper he could find. Long before the old man finally gave up the search, Longmore's stomach told him his easy answer was not to be. His face showed the defeat he felt.

"I'm sorry," Dickens said. "It was here. Can't imagine what happened to it. I'll keep looking until I find it. Where can I reach you, when I do?"

In extra large letters Longmore wrote down his name and address, thanked the man for his help, and left.

"There went my best chance," he mumbled.

He spent two more days combing the neighborhood for someone who might have information on the Frenchman's whereabouts with no luck.

When he returned to Tucson a letter from Miss Katie was waiting for him. Over the next few months he shared his frustration with her in correspondence. Her bright letters brought him much needed encouragement.

Longmore made three more trips to San Diego to check every lead from his list of thirty-two names. Not one person had heard of Maurice Londeau or Maurice Landrew, or knew of anyone who had been with Emory. At last he gave up and turned his attention to his job and to drafting the first manuscript for his book. He was surprised to discover just how much work it was to organize the papers, letters, articles, the notes he had collected, and to write down all the information he carried in his head.

Over the years Longmore moved from one depot to the next as track maintenance demanded. Although he had long since given up finding Londeau, his abortive search for the Frenchman was still stuck in his craw. "I came so close!" he often exclaimed to Morris.

Then one day, years later, the postmaster at the depot office hollered to him as he walked past the counter, "Luke, did you ever hear of leaving a forwarding address?"

"Well, sure," Longmore responded, "but there never seemed any point to it. Why do you ask?"

"If you had it wouldn't have taken two years for this here letter to catch up with you. As it is, if you didn't work for the railroad we'd never have tracked you down." The post master held out a faded envelope.

With all his moving he knew he had missed a few of Katie's letters. He was expecting this to be one of her's. But the script was wrong, he carefully opened the envelope. He unfolded a single piece of parchment. A yellowed scrap of paper wafted to the floor. He leaned over and retrieved it. It was an address.

Longmore read the note:

"Sir, in his will, Granddad asked that we watch for this piece of paper when we cleaned out his house after his death. He said it seemed very important to you. I don't know how much good it will do you after all this time, but here it is. It was stuck with pine pitch to the underside of a drawer bottom. It was pure chance we ever found it. We hope it is helpful . . . ."

There was more but Longmore didn't even bother to finish reading the note. He hurried home to pack.

Longmore's loud, insistent knocking startled the old man from the chair where he had been dozing . . . .

CHAPTER 24
FRENCHMAN'S CONFESSION

"**Y**es, Yes, I'm coming," the voice muttered behind the heavy timber door. "Be patient."

The door opened and Longmore saw an old, wrinkled and frail man. But his posture was erect, and the man's eyes still held a twinkle of youthful expectancy.

"Forgive me if I've disturbed you, sir," Longmore apologized. "Are you Maurice Landrew?"

The old man looked him up and down slowly. "Who wants to know? Who are you?"

"Forgive me, sir. My name's Luke Longmore and I've been trying to find Maurice Landrew for nearly ten years. I am a writer. I was doing research on the story of the Adams Diggings, when I came across the name 'Londeau' mentioned in the Emory Notes."

"Andy . . . Andy Adams!"

Longmore smiled broadly. "If you know Adams first name, you must be the man Emory called Londeau," Longmore said, his voice quivering with excitement.

"Well, maybe I am," admitted the old man. "Come on in and we'll talk on old times."

The Frenchman tottered to a heavy plank table and sat on a sturdy hand-carved wooden chair. He motioned Longmore to the only other chair in the one-room cabin. Longmore noticed several aged pieces of parchment with beautiful sketches of flowers hanging on the wall. He recognized the artist immediately.

"These are Emory sketches! They're wonderful! I've seen others, but these are some of the best!"

"Well, you've got me there!" the Frenchman laughed. "Yes, I was with Emory. I am Maurice Landrew." He pronounced his name as he had for Emory so many years before, with the subtle 'r' sound. "And yes, I knew Adams very well."

"You and Adams were the two who escaped the massacre on the

Prieto?" Longmore asked rhetorically.

"You ask as if you already know the answer!" the Frenchman exclaimed. "I've never told anyone I was on the Prieto. Did Andy tell you I was his partner?"

"No, sir," Longmore answered, "he didn't. In fact, much as I'd like to, I've never talked with Mr. Adams. I don't know if he's even still alive."

"Neither do I," the Frenchman said, emotion creeping into his voice. After a moment he cleared his throat and continued, "It seems you've already figured it out but tell me, how did you know it was me who escaped with Andy?"

Longmore laughed. "Well now, figuring that part out was simple. Finding you was the hard part . . . How else could you have known so much about a massacre that happened somewhere up the Prieto years before you told Emory about it? Who else but a survivor could have known the prospectors found gold on the river? Also, C. S. Stevens, a man who chased after Adams story, told me that Adams said his partner was a Frenchman who didn't read or write English. I'm surprised someone else didn't figure it out before now."

Landrew hesitated while a slow thin smile came to his wrinkled face. "Andrew would talk to anybody who would listen. It wouldn't have done any good to ask me about the Prieto back then. Except for Emory I never told anyone anything. I almost sent you on your way, but I guess it can't hurt me much to talk about it now. Let's get one thing clear though, I'll answer your questions on condition you keep what I tell you out of any story you write. Keep my name out of it, too. Give my old friend Andrew all the recognition. He saved my life and he deserves it. And I don't want a bunch of curious prospectors hounding me in my old age."

Longmore reluctantly agreed to print nothing of what Landrew was about to tell. The facts would help him build the story. He wouldn't have to use specific details and he could keep the Frenchman's account out of his book.

"As far as I know, Adams and I were the only survivors of that massacre, but I've often wondered what happened to Gotch Ear, our Indian guide. Never saw him that morning; he might have escaped, too, but I doubt it. I'm sure of one thing though, none of the prospectors survived. That horrid giant of a red man didn't take any prisoners, that's for certain."

Longmore wondered who this giant red man was but he had more important questions to ask. "I have so many things I want to ask you, Mr. Landrew. But first, please, tell me the story of you and Adams."

The old man grew quiet, his eyes transfixed, as though he were staring into distant, painful, memories. Longmore kept a respectful silence.

"I've lived a long time and I've never wanted to go back to that place," the Frenchman said. "I don't like to think about it and I've seldom talked about it." He paused, looking at Longmore for a moment, then asked, "Them Apaches still out there, boy?"

"They're mostly gone now," Longmore said. "There's hardly ever word of Indian troubles these days."

The Frenchman seemed unconvinced. Longmore tried to change the subject. "There's one thing I wish you'd help me get straight. You told Emory the massacre happened on the Prieto River, right?"

The old man nodded. "Yes, that's right."

"Which river did you mean? Emory got those rivers all mixed up on his maps. I can't make heads nor tails of which is which. I went to Clifton hoping to clear it up, but the folks there don't know any more than I do. And worse yet, no one around that part of the country now has ever heard of the Prieto River. I've brought some maps with me. Maybe you can point out the right river."

"Can't read English," Landrew complained, "but if you'll help me with the words, I can show you the river we were on, easy enough. Andy never was much for paying attention to where he was. If he had been, he could have gone back with no trouble."

Longmore brought out his newest map, dated 1899, and opened it onto the table. Landrew studied the lines and boundaries, frowning for several minutes as he familiarized himself with the markings, seeming to understand.

"You say that's the Gila running this way?" Landrew asked, as he swept his finger down the river's course. He paused and considered the map before him. "You say there's no Prieto River on here. This one you say is marked Eagle Creek — that's where the Prieto should be. No, this map's not right."

Longmore opened an older map and pointed out the New Mexico Territorial Boundary and the Gila River. Landrew ran his aged hand over the second, older map and pointed out differences between the two.

"This one is more the way I remember it," he commented. "At least those are the river names we used back in the forties. The Prieto is right where it's supposed to be — west of the San Francisco. That other map in young Lieutenant Emory's notes has the rivers all wrong. He was better with flowers."

Longmore was excited, hopeful that Landrew could help him. He pulled the older map closer to them, and asked again.

"Are you certain this is the river? I was hoping you would remember but it seems too good to be true!" he exclaimed. "On his searches for the diggings, Adams seems to have spent most of his time on the San Francisco River. Hardly any wonder he never found what he was looking for. He was looking on the wrong river!"

"I'm certain all right," Landrew scolded. "It was the next river west of the San Francisco. I'll never forget. No. I'll never forget that canyon with the gold where those heathens murdered and butchered all those prospectors. I still have nightmares of that big savage who tortured and then murdered the cook in cold blood. Despicable as that cook was, I don't see how anyone could have deserved what he got. It was <u>that</u> river, right there!" he exclaimed, touching the newest map where the stream named Eagle Creek joined the Gila.

For the next two hours, Landrew told his story. Once he started, he hardly paused to breath. He had kept the horror of his memories to himself for more than sixty years and now he felt great relief, as if he were confessing some terrible sin. He told every detail he could remember. Then he slumped in his chair, utterly spent.

Gently, Longmore asked Landrew to repeat the part about the cabin and the pot of gold under the hearth stone.

"Young man," said Landrew, "if you can find the ruins of that cabin, you'll find a heavy stone buried near its east end. That's where the coffeepot was. You'll know if it's the right cabin by looking for a little twisty canyon with a waterfall just upriver a few hundred yards. That little canyon on the east side of the river is where those men dug all that gold. There's more there, plenty more, still waiting to be mined from the sands."

"Mr. Landrew," Longmore said, "my hand is cramped and you must be exhausted. I think I've got it all written down. I wish I could tell your story in my book." Seeing apprehension in Landrew's eyes he added quickly, "But I won't."

He rose to leave. "I don't know how to thank you. I'd like to pay you something for your time . . . ."

"Won't let you do that," Landrew interrupted, "but you can do this for me: If you find any gold, send me the prettiest nugget."

Longmore glanced at Emory's sketches. Smiling, he nodded, and bid Landrew goodbye. As he walked down the path from the cabin door to the dusty road, Landrew yelled after him, "One more thing, young man. I know you don't believe those Apaches will cause you any trouble but I know better. The night after the massacre, when Adams and I were hiding on that ledge, I was so sick I thought for sure I was going to die. But I still saw that giant Indian. He was right below us yelling in Spanish for someone to come to him. He's still out there somewhere. He's the reason I never would go back."

Hearing the old man's irrational warning about a long-dead Indian chief, Longmore's heart fell. His confidence in the accuracy of what Landrew had told him began to waver. The old man seemed to believe some Apache had been guarding that canyon for sixty years, it was ridiculous.

Moments before, Longmore had been sure his years of patient searching had finally paid off. With the Frenchman's detailed information he had been certain he could find the right spot with little difficulty. Now he wasn't so positive about anything the old man had told him.

CHAPTER 25
LONGMORE'S EXPEDITION

Longmore returned to work in Tucson and, as was his habit, checked for mail. The postmaster handed him an ornate envelope with a Clifton postmark. The paper smelled of perfume and was, as he hoped, from Katie. The two had been exchanging letters for years. Today the smell of her perfume and her warm words were too much. Longmore decided they had written enough letters. He took a few more days off and went to Clifton where Katie was still working at the Copper Queen. Trying to maintain dignified restraint he ordered coffee and made his proposal in one sentence.

"I'd like a cup of coffee and I'd like you to marry me."

"Just a moment," she replied, then walked into the kitchen, leaving him feeling awkward and not knowing what to expect. But in a moment she returned, minus her apron, carrying a pot of coffee. She smiled. "From now on I'll be serving all your coffee and you'd better not be flirting with any more waitresses!"

They were married by the local Justice of the Peace. The folks at the Copper Queen gave them a small reception. Longmore took Katie back to Tucson, where they settled easily into domestic life. Katie was remarkably understanding about his fascination with prospecting and the research he had to do for his book.

Longmore used most of his spare time learning the country west of Clifton, preparing to hunt for the Adams. Now that he had a wife he had less time for his hobby. He was also busy working on his first book. It seemed it was taking forever to finish his manuscript.

In 1911, Longmore made his first serious trip to what Landrew called the Prieto, known around Clifton as Eagle Creek. The trip yielded little, but he learned the country was still wild and that numerous prospectors were plying the sands along the banks of every drainage around Clifton.

He planned a second trip the following year, but couldn't seem to save enough money. When he finally could afford to go, the United

States was involved in the war in Europe and his boss at the railroad could no longer give him the time off he needed.

Katie soon bore him two sons and a daughter. Because of his new responsibilities and the expenses of his growing family, it was 1920 before he was finally able to make a second trip. But he was ill-prepared and didn't have enough time to make a decent search for the ruins of a burnt-down, stone-walled cabin. Still, he was not discouraged. That pot of gold had been there a long time. It would wait a while longer.

In the fall of 1924, Longmore set aside almost a month for his long-awaited third trip to Eagle Creek. He needed a break from the chores of domestic life, his job, and writing his book, which was finally coming along nicely.

"Must you be gone for so long?" Katie asked.

"I'm afraid so," he replied. "My last trip convinced me that Landrew was right. The lay of the river is just as he described it. I am close to finding the answer to the 'Lost Adams Diggings' mystery. It's an important part of my book."

"I know how important finding the Lost Adams Diggings is to you," Katie hugged him as she spoke. "I just miss you when you're gone for such a long time. And I worry about you."

"This will be the last trip I'll make for a while," he promised. "I'm not planning to do any mining there, so no matter what I find I should be back soon. All that country is pretty much claimed up and it seems likely that somebody must have found Adams diggings long ago. Probably wasn't all that much left there, anyway. But a three-gallon coffeepot buried under a hearthstone with three hundred pounds of gold dust and nuggets in it seems to me to be worth searching for."

"You haven't even found the cabin," Katie sighed. "And what makes you think the coffeepot is still buried there?"

"Well, no one has admitted finding it. That would be a pretty big thing to keep secret. Someone would realize it was the Adams treasure and the story would surely have gotten out. Also, from what Landrew told me, it would be very hard to tell a cabin had ever been there, unless you knew where to look. And I do. This trip I'll have plenty of time to do a thorough search. Anyway, if I'm going to find it, it pretty much has to be this trip."

"What do you mean?" Katie asked.

Longmore was well aware that Phelps-Dodge, a mercantile company from New York, had bought all the mining properties in the Clifton-Morenci mining district in 1921. With the end of the war and the drop in copper prices they were now concentrating on buying all the good claims in the area. They had hired geologists and surveyors who were busy looking for other copper deposits in the region. If he intended to find that pot full of gold he knew he had to hurry.

Longmore endured one more long, boring ride from Tucson to Clifton. He was weary of the trip across endless, scorched stretches of Arizona desert. He arrived both tired and excited and made his way to the hotel. It felt like old times.

There were changes, of course. Electric lights had illuminated the rooms in 1920. But, in deference to the old timers who didn't trust electricity and as backup lighting — in case of electrical failure — the management had left the obsolete lamps in the room for the first few years.

Now the lamps were gone. Longmore didn't like the idea of having no emergency light, but he didn't worry about it too much. He wasn't planning to spend much time at the hotel!

He slept well and the next morning made his way to the livery stable to lease two horses for his trip to Eagle Creek. He was a good horseman and comfortable with most horses, but there were exceptions.

"If you rent me that Tennessee Walker you pawned off on me last trip," Longmore told the stable owner in a flat, certain tone, "he won't be coming back."

"Why, what do you mean?" The owner feigned surprised innocence.

"What I mean is this. That horse is a biter and I hate biters," Longmore replied. "If you rent me a horse that bites again, you'll likely lose a horse."

"Oh," the owner bellowed, "yeah, well we've had several complaints about that. Lots of Sunday riders like to use him because he's a fast walker. We keep him around for that. That's all he's good for anymore. Getting too old for rough use."

"Well, he might be all right for an afternoon ride, but when a man's holding a lead rope and trying to break trail, he's no good at all. He damn near bit my finger off last time."

"Sorry about that," the man said, pleasantly. "He was new in the string at the time. But I should have known better than to rent him out like that. I've got some better stock available since you were here last time."

Longmore gestured to a nearby bay. "Will this big bay pack?"

"Sunny? He'll ride, pack or drive," replied the stable owner. "Matter of fact, he's the best I've got for hauling gear out in rough country."

"How about that dun?" Longmore inquired. "How old is he?"

"That's old Billy. He's about fourteen. Sunny is ten. Both are good horses, but you can't pack on Billy. He don't like the back strap at all."

Longmore didn't like the idea of taking a fourteen-year-old horse out on a long and arduous trip. But he looked at both horses' teeth, checked their legs for soundness and, reassured that both were fit, paid the stable owner sixty-five dollars: Two weeks rental for two horses plus tack. That was a month's wages, and it hurt, but he paid it agreeably, considering the prospects it brought to mind.

Landrew had estimated the buried pot at close to three hundred pounds of gold. Longmore had calculated it out, "I guess it's worth a sixty-five dollar investment to find forty-eight thousand dollars worth of gold!"

He saddled Billy with a strong deep-seated work saddle and loosely laced both cinches. He would adjust the back cinch and tighten the front cinch later. He prepared Sunny with a heavier felt saddle pad to go under the sturdy pack saddle he specified. There were several extra straps and the livery man explained he often used that pack on a mule.

"Mules aren't shaped right for packing and you have to run extra straps around their tails and across their chest, or the saddle won't stay put," he explained.

Longmore tucked the extra straps under the saddle crosses and loaded a sack of grain into the bottom of each pack box, before he hooked those on the crosses. "Give him a chance to get used to the pack, and give me a chance to see how he does."

He led the horses across the street to the Garcia General Store and tied them to the hitch rack while he went inside to purchase supplies.

"Good to see you again, Francis," Longmore greeted the proprietor. "How's business?"

"Hello, Mr. Longmore! How are you? Longtime no see," Garcia replied. "We're doing pretty well."

The two chatted about the history of prospecting around Clifton, especially in the area west of town. "There's an old graveyard over on Eagle Creek," Garcia told him. "Used to be a few dying fruit trees there, too. Seems those people must have lived there for quite a while. I suspect they were mining in Eagle Creek; I don't know how else they could have made a living over there." Other customers came in and Longmore excused himself.

The livery man watched with curiosity as Longmore packed his oversized saddlebags. When he packed a short piece of small gauge track rail, the man couldn't keep quiet any longer. "What in tarnation you want with ten pounds of steel rail?"

"It makes a good anvil, just in case one of these nags you rented me flips a shoe," Longmore replied.

The livery man was impressed with Longmore's ingenuity. "What about the clock? What do you need with a clock out in the wilderness?"

Longmore laughed. "A little silly, isn't it? I like getting up at a certain time no matter where I am or what I'm doing. It's in my blood, after so many years working for the railroad."

With his saddlebags bulging and the bay loaded down with clothes, food, cooking gear, a bedroll, miner's tools, and a small spade, Longmore mounted the dun and rode south out of town, the bay in tow.

He followed the same trail he'd taken on his first two trips to Eagle Creek in 1911 and 1920. He traveled down the east bank of the

San Francisco River for several miles to a natural ford where the trail split. Longmore crossed the shallow water and continued west.

He camped that night at a hot springs close to the Gila River and bathed in the soothing waters. He hadn't ridden so much for several years and his aching bones welcomed the relief afforded by the hot, mineral-laden waters. The smell of sulfur clung in the air around the pools and especially where the steaming water bubbled out of the ground.

The second day was hard riding along the banks of the Gila River. He was forced to ford the river several times and rode many miles along the banks and in the shallows. Late that afternoon he reached the mouth of Eagle Creek or, as Landrew had known it, the Prieto River.

It had been a hard day's work for the horses. He made camp early, hobbling both Sunny and Billy but letting them roam more or less free in the tall grass. He didn't worry that the horses would run off; they couldn't go far without swimming and they wouldn't enter the water hobbled. He went to bed early, conscious of his sore backside.

By long habit, he awoke and shut off the ringer on his alarm a few minutes before it would have sounded, rising to meet the new day before the sun was up. Two hours later he had rounded up the horses, saddled and packed them, and fed each a ration of grain.

Bringing grain for the horses had been a great idea. Only two morning's rations and he had them hooked. After that, whenever they heard him making his breakfast they came bounding into camp as fast as their hobbled legs allowed. He chuckled. "Horses will do just about anything for a handful of oats!"

He mounted and rode up Eagle Creek. For three days he and the horses trudged through the harsh terrain. He found himself walking more than he rode. He was getting better at staying in the saddle without his backside aching but he still didn't know whether his knees hurt more after walking or after riding.

The travel was rough, much rougher than Landrew had described. This was because the beaver dams and all the flat bottomland was gone. There were boulders and rough rocky outcrops to contend with at every turn. His progress was slow, about six miles a day, he figured. But he had time.

His third morning on Eagle Creek he rounded a bend to see several grave markers on a little hill. He rode close enough to read several tombstones, all Mexican names.

"This must be the graveyard Garcia told me of," he mused. "I guess this explains all those old placer works I've been seeing downstream. According to the names and dates there must have been several families living here around nineteen hundred."

Longmore made two more miles that day before again unloading the pack boxes, unsaddling the horses, hobbling them, and turning them loose. He had been looking for a good place to let the horses graze, but grass was scarce and he gave up, figuring to feed them an extra ration of oats in the morning.

Once he had set up camp he gathered enough firewood for the evening's fire. Crouching before the blaze, he heard a faint sound. Suddenly the hair on the back of his neck stood out straight. He jumped to his feet and spun on his heels, staring into the evening sky. He saw nothing but a beautiful sunset.

"Who's out there?" He yelled.

He waited tensely, but there was no response.

"Guess I'm getting jumpy." The horses weren't acting skittish, but the feeling that he was being watched just wouldn't go away.

"What's going on here?" he wondered.

He stuck his Colt .44-40 revolver into his belt and checked the chamber on his Marlin rifle, which used the same cartridges. Empty as it should be, he noted.

He chambered a cartridge, working the finger lever sharply forward and back, then, alert and cautious, walked around the edges of the camp. There was no one, not even any other animals, and nowhere for anything or anybody to hide.

Convinced his imagination was running wild, he turned back toward camp. The horses were gone! He hurried to the top of the little knoll to see if he could spot them in the failing light. There was a faint, familiar odor in the air.

"That's sulfur," he thought. "There must be another hot spring close by."

Longmore recalled Landrew saying they sometimes smelled sulfur at night from their camp. Maybe he was closer than he realized.

"Where did the horses get to so quick?" he puzzled aloud.

It was late and there was little use looking for them in the dark. Either they'd come for their customary ration of oats in the morning, or he'd have some walking to do. He had never experienced hysteria in the wilderness and God knows he'd spent enough time alone in wild country, but he had to admit this place was giving him the willies. But what could he do? The horses were gone. He was just going to have to stay the night.

He built up the fire as much for courage as for warmth, ate a portion of hardtack, and climbed into his bedroll. He did not sleep well and lay listening to his clock tick the hours away.

Toward dawn he finally fell asleep, only to be roused a short time later by his alarm. He quickly dressed, armed himself, and headed out to look for the horses. Less than a hundred feet upstream he saw them feeding in a lush grassy patch. Then across the creek something caught his eye. Through the mist in the dim light of dawn, he saw the shadowy figure of a huge man. He cocked the hammer on his carbine and spoke. "I've got my rifle on you. Come closer and identify yourself. Move real slow now."

The shadowy figure never moved. There was no sound. As Longmore raised his Marlin to take aim, the figure simply faded from sight.

Longmore shivered, and not from the cool morning air. Again, he noticed that the horses were not agitated and the smell of sulfur stung his nostrils. He decided his mind was playing tricks on him. None too eagerly, he crossed the cold water to where he'd seen the shadowy figure and searched the sand along the water's edge. In the dim light he could barely make out what looked like two oversized footprints.

He decided not to wait until full light to prove to himself that these depressions in the mud were something other than footprints.

"I'm continuing up the canyon now!" he whispered gruffly.

Hastily he saddled and loaded the horses with his gear, then rode up canyon for several hundred yards at full gallop. Feeling less nervous and even a bit foolish now that the sun had risen, he slowed the horses to a walk and breathed a sigh of relief.

That day he proceeded up the Prieto, moving north, investigating every nook and cranny, any place where it looked like there could possibly be a hidden side canyon. He checked every mound of grass along the banks of the river for the remains of a cabin that might be hidden in the overgrowth.

He had found the ruins of two old stone houses before he got to the graveyard. This day he found another. It was located high above the creek, on top of a low mesa. The walls were almost completely gone. If he hadn't been really looking, he would have missed it.

Based on the Frenchman's description Longmore was sure it wasn't the cabin he was looking for. It was too high above the river and it was on the wrong side of the stream, to boot. He searched it, just the same.

With his hatchet he chopped away the brush that had overgrown the cabin's dirt floor, grateful that most of the rocks that had dislodged from the cabin walls had fallen toward the outside. That saved him the trouble of moving them.

Soon he had the floor of the single small room cleared. Charcoal-blackened and reddened stones of one wall showed clearly where the fireplace had been. He unstrapped his trenching tool from the top of the pack saddle and began to dig.

A strong breeze carried the smell of sulfur down the Prieto.

Before long he had excavated a good-sized hole but, other than a few pieces of charcoal, he found nothing. "Had to check," he mumbled.

Repacking the shovel and hatchet onto the pack saddle, he turned and headed up the canyon, one last time . . . .

CHAPTER 26
GOLD GULCH, 1929

Francisco Garcia had moved to Clifton as a boy. When his parents opened a small general store in town he was still a young man. The business prospered and Francis was kept busy working in the family business.

Francis Garcia was a lean, good-looking Mexican of surprisingly large stature and strength. He was well educated and spoke English better than most of his Anglo customers. One other quality shone through like a beacon to those who knew him. Francis Garcia was a totally honest man.

Affable, intelligent and inquisitive, Francis became an authority on the history of Clifton while he was still a young man. He enjoyed Luke Longmore's visits whenever the author came to town. They corresponded often over the years, Longmore usually seeking information on the history of the region and the more colorful characters who had lived there. Garcia smiled when he received this latest letter from his long-time acquaintance. "Wonder what he wants to know this time."

But instead of questions, the envelope held only a newspaper clipping and a short note, explaining errors in the article. "Just so you'll know the true story of the Adams. When people ask about it," Longmore wrote, tongue-in-cheek.

Garcia read Longmore's note, then read the clipping from the *Tucson Citizen* carefully.

THE LOST ADAMS DIGGINGS
Tucson Citizen, April 28, 1929

GOLDEN TREASURE OF "ADAMS DIGGINGS" BURIED IN 1875 IS STILL BEING SOUGHT. TON OF NUGGETS HIDDEN WHEN APACHES ATTACKED MINERS:
By F. D. Doucet

Clifton, April 27 — Renewed mining activity in the Clifton-Morenci district has once more brought up the subject

of the "Lost Mines," known as the "Adams Diggin's." Strange
mining men trek into the district in hopes of reviving some of
the many idle mines in this vicinity, some of them known as
rich producers before the big slump following the world war.

A number of interested parties arriving in Clifton the past
week have inquired of the famous old "Adams Diggin's," the
fame of which has spread from coast to coast during the past 50
years. One individual declares that he had heard it rumored that
these diggings had been located by a Clifton man.

This supposedly lost mine and treasure vault, which has
baffled prospectors for 50 years and more, is said to contain
more than a ton of gold dust and nuggets worth in excess of
$100,000. They were buried "somewhere north and east of
Clifton by prospectors who were about to be attacked by a
band of Apache Indians."[7]

Garcia laughed as he put down the clipping. "Buried in 1875!" he
sputtered. "According to what Longmore and Stevens told me that
date is off by nearly forty years!"

Again Garcia broke into laughter. "'Somewhere north and east
of Clifton?' Wonder why I've never seen any gold from northeast of
Clifton? The only good placer gold I've ever heard of comes out of
Gold Gulch and that's practically straight west of here. Longmore is
right, everybody's chasing old man Adams' return trip, thinking that
was when he made the discovery! So many of those old news accounts
tell about Adams' trip with Davidson and make it sound like that was
the trip where they made the original find! Longmore swears that is
wrong and I think he's right."

Not long after this letter arrived, hard times settled across the
United States. The stock market collapsed. Phelps-Dodge entirely
halted its operations in Clifton. Soon hundreds of people were scour-
ing the hills around town hoping to find enough gold to feed themselves and their families. Prospectors, out-of-work miners, and hundreds of others who knew nothing about searching for gold found
their way to the area, all hoping for one big strike, all praying to find

enough to keep themselves and their families fed. It had been nearly sixty years since so many people flooded into Clifton with such high hopes and so little to lose. Times had been hard then, too.

During the depression years landowners turned a sympathetic, blind eye to trespassers breaking their backs to feed their families. Besides, land boundaries meant little when the property owners lived far away.

The most popular place to pan for gold was north of town on the San Francisco River because it was convenient but also because there was good fishing. At least those looking for gold knew they would eat. There was also plenty of activity up both sides of Chase Creek, which ran into the San Francisco from the west where Clifton had grown up. But most of the prospecting was concentrated along Gold Gulch. This drainage originated west of Clifton and coursed west for several miles before entering Eagle Creek. In the two-mile stretch near the head end of Gold Gulch just west of the copper mines, there were dozens of new prospect pits, some hundreds of feet deep, bored into bedrock outcrops wherever desperate, hopeful prospectors saw any interesting color.

By June, 1932, unsuccessful prospectors and miners were leaving Clifton in droves. Four hundred families had already left town since the mines had closed. Most of these were Mexican workers who headed south on free trains furnished by Phelps-Dodge. But not everyone was giving up on Clifton. It was well known that things were little better anywhere else.

Just after Pedro Escaderas and three of his brothers lost their jobs with Phelps-Dodge they heard a rumor that a man named Blackburn had found gold in Gold Gulch by digging to bedrock and then cleaning out a pothole. Their parents back in Mexico were facing starvation, so the brothers decided to give Gold Gulch a try "for a few months."

They knew they weren't the first to ply the sands there, looking for gold. There were many stories about people panning there and it was, after all, named Gold Gulch for a reason, they reflected.

Their plan differed from most. Rather than spend time panning the surface sands for the occasional nugget and dust missed by generations of prospectors, they would do as Blackburn had done.

There were several large pools about half a mile above the falls where the canyon began to narrow. By working to the bottom of these pools they figured they had a good shot at finding enough nuggets to keep their families fed. They might even find enough gold to send some back to Mexico for their desperate relatives.

They had only hand tools to work with and their plan called for plenty of hard work. The first pool they chose was nearly twenty feet long and fifteen feet wide. They estimated that, by hand, it would take several days to dig out the few feet of gravel and a few weeks to pan it for gold.

They seriously underestimated the task. The hole was almost ten feet deep with nearly vertical sides. There was five times as much gravel as they had figured. In addition, there were numerous boulders in the hole too big to lift out by hand. Long before the gravel was all removed from the pool they were entirely underwater. They had to take frequent breaks to warm there aching bodies.

They spent valuable time gathering wood to keep a fire going so they could warm up occasionally. The large boulders soon choked their progress. They were stymied. It was Pedro who solved the problem.

He ran a loop of heavy rope between a high limb on a nearby cottonwood and a boulder on the opposite side of the hole. The rope passed through hand-made pulleys.

Large buckets were secured to opposite sides of the rope loop. The first was tied at the pool. The second was tied near the pulley in the tree. Pedro left enough slack in the rope loop so the lower bucket would sit on the bottom of the hole where they were working.

His ingenious system worked well. Those in the water set about loading a boulder into the submerged bucket. One or two of the brothers climbed the tree. After the boulder was loaded and tied into the bucket in the pool they hung from the second bucket. Gravity and sometimes a helping tug from a third brother at the edge of the pool did the work, lifting the boulder clear of the water, the pool and out of the way.

They were encouraged because they were finding some gold in

every scoop of gravel. They realized it would take many months to work all the gravel in that one hole. But long before they finished digging to bedrock, they had enough gold to make a trip to Garcia's store to pay their debts and purchase more supplies.

It was a Saturday afternoon when Pedro came through the door and handed Garcia a Coke bottle half full of gold nuggets.

"What do you think, Mr. Garcia? How much *oro* have we got in this bottle?"

"Pedro, that's the biggest pile of gold I've ever seen all in one place! Let's put it on the scales and see what it weighs!" he said excitedly.

They carefully emptied the contents of the bottle onto the scale pan and Garcia started adding weights.

"You have just over twenty-seven apothecary ounces here," Francis said. "Are you interested in selling it? I can't pay for it all today. Haven't got that much cash on hand."

"*Sí, señor, comprendo,*" Pedro replied. "My brothers and I have been working for months down in Gold Gulch to gather this gold. We need money to pay off our debt with you and to buy food and more supplies for our families."

"So these nuggets are from Gold Gulch?" Garcia inquired.

"*Sí, señor.*" Pedro responded.

"Well, I'll pay you market price for the gold," Garcia said. "Nuggets from Gold Gulch usually run about eighty-five percent pure. The miller gets the silver as payment for refining the gold. I'll give you eighty-five percent of the market value for your twenty-seven ounces. The price of gold is regulated by the government, you know."

"*Comprendo,*" Pedro said. He gestured outside, "Let me talk with my brothers, first."

He stepped out, spoke briefly with the others, then came back in nodding his head affirmatively. "We have a deal."

"With Phelps-Dodge closed down, every bit of gold you highgraders find helps keep this town alive," Garcia told him. "If you can come back in the morning I can have the money for you."

Pedro returned bright and early the next day. "Will you be able to keep this store open?" he asked, as Garcia counted out payment for the gold.

"*Sí*," Garcia replied, "God willing. Other people are leaving town, practically giving their properties away. They think Clifton is doomed. You know there aren't more than thirteen hundred left in town now. Five years ago there were more than five thousand. But I'm not ready to give up on Clifton or its people."

Garcia didn't see any of the Escaderas brothers again for many years. Then, one day in 1937 the store's bell rang and he looked up to see a familiar face.

"Well, lookee here!" he exclaimed. "Where have you been, my friend?"

"To be truthful," Pedro replied. "My brothers and I have been taking the *oro* we get from Gold Gulch down to Mexico. We sell it there. The price is not as good but food is much cheaper. Also, we can see relatives there. We sent our families back in *trenté y tres* — 'thirty-three — and my brothers and I spend the winters down there with them," he explained. "It's not perfect but it's better than living in tents or a borrowed barn during the cold winters in Gold Gulch."

Garcia brought Pedro up to date on what was happening in Clifton.

"The copper industry has begun to recover, have you heard? Three hundred and fifty men have gone back to work for Phelps-Dodge," Francis hollered from the back room where he was gathering some of the items Pedro needed. "You and your brothers might consider going back to work there," he suggested.

"*Sí*, Señor Garcia, I am one of those three hundred fifty *hombres*." He grinned, "I hired on today."

The two had a good laugh. "Good for you, Pedro," Garcia chuckled. "We'll be seeing more of you then."

By the end of the Great Depression, Gold Gulch had seen fifty years of placer mining by hard-working hungry prospectors. Untold amounts of placer gold had been taken from the sands of that ten-mile stretch of creek.

In 1942, Clifton's population had again reached the five thousand of its glory days. The lone-wolf prospectors, those who had sifted the sands and dug in the rock for meager wages during the Depression all but disappeared. Phelps-Dodge now owned all the land and mineral rights in the region.

With the reopening of the Phelps-Dodge copper mines and smelters, and with the prospects of a new war in Europe, jobs were plentiful. Clifton was a boom town again. Gold Gulch lay forgotten.

CHAPTER 27
KOCHERA, 1942

"Father" young John Kochera said, "I don't understand. Why does Apache gold belong to the whole tribe? If I find gold, why can't I keep it for myself?"

It was 1942 and John Kochera was fourteen years old. It had been four years since his father, Joseph Kochera moved his family from the San Carlos Reservation in eastern Arizona to Westville, Illinois, where Joseph's brother-in-law found Mr. Kochera work at a coal mine.

"Apache gold belongs to the tribe," the youth's father replied. "It would be wrong for one Apache to keep what belongs to all our people. Apache gold is to be used for the good of our people."

"Our people!" young John exclaimed. "Who are my people? My Mexican half didn't belong on the reservation. Neither my Indian half nor my Mexican half is at home here."

The older man listened to his son's angry words. He knew his children's mixed parentage had brought difficulties for them. There were always bigots. But he also knew facing up to those who would defame them had made his family very close. The results weren't all bad.

He waited for his son to continue.

"When we lived on the reservation, I heard the story of a secret place of gold, a place known only to tribal elders. It was said the Apache nation bought their great bulls and breeding stock with gold from a secret canyon, and that it was because of these fine animals the Apache tribes were able to build up such valuable herds."

"Yes, this is so," his father replied. "The elders of our tribe bought nearly one million dollars worth of prime breeding stock in 1914, I think it was. They paid in gold. At my job here I only earn five dollars a day. I'd have to work one hundred years to earn that much money! But this is the important thing. Apache gold is for the tribe."

John brightened at a new thought, continuing as though he hadn't heard his father's words. "I remember when I was very young on the reservation and Grandfather Kochera told me about a canyon of gold. Someday, when I'm older, I will return to him and find out where that canyon is."

"Okay," laughed his father. "I doubt that Elder Kochera will give you any information on hidden gold mines. He never told me anything. But you can sure ask him."

"Can we visit Grandfather this summer?" John asked eagerly.

"We'd better go soon if we are to see him again before . . . ." He loved his grandfather and couldn't bring himself to finish the sentence.

Joseph Kochera thought about his son's request. New Mexico was a long way off, and he really couldn't afford the trip or the time away from work. Still, he was an Apache. In his culture, time with tribal elders held special significance, especially for young people. He knew how important Elder Kochera was to his son.

"Yes, John," he answered, thoughtfully. "You will visit your grandfather this summer."

Tribal Elder Kochera was an ancient-looking man and, as the oldest surviving member of the Apache tribes, he was most revered. He had lived through catastrophic changes in the Apache's way of life and he carried in his heart and mind many sacred memories and tribal secrets.

When John and his father entered Kochera's lodge, they found the old Indian sitting cross-legged in front of a small fire of Utah juniper. This wood burned hot and clean with an intense blue flame. Though the fire was small, it warmed the room.

In a low, melodic voice, the old man chanted a song John did not understand. The youth recognized some words but they were separated by spans of sounds that held no meaning to his ear.

After a time, the old man looked up, smiled, and slowly rose to his full height. While he was not as tall as John had remembered, he was still a man of imposing stature, slender and erect. Age had shortened him, but it hadn't bent him.

"I have been thinking of you, my children," he greeted them. "It is good that we see each other again."

John ran to the old man and wrapped his arms around his grandfather's shoulders.

"Grandfather, I'm so happy to be back home."

Joseph Kochera joined his son and his father in an embrace. The three lingered there, warmed by the juniper fire and the glow of fellowship they had long been denied.

John stepped back and regarded his grandfather with fondness and with pride. The old man made quite a picture. He wore a red bandanna braided into his long white hair. A vivid, patterned blanket, a style usually worn by younger braves, was draped over his shoulders. His pants were white deerskin beaded with turquoise and fringed with soft golden deerskin. His concho belt of figured silver rosettes woven together with strips of fine red leather was fastened with an oversized oval silver buckle studded with turquoise and coral. John noticed his grandfather wore the buckle off center, to the left.

Around his neck, Elder Kochera wore a turquoise pendant, which held special meaning for the old man. It was made of gold and stone taken from a special place, which Elder Kochera's father had shown him when he was very young.

The three generations of Apache men sat around the fire for hours talking of the changes in their lives. The men talked of Mr. Kochera's new life in the east and how his family was adjusting to it. When they discussed world politics at some length, father and son were surprised to discover the old man knew as much or more about the situation in Europe as they did. Eventually the two men exhausted their animated discussion about politics and, seizing the opportunity of a lull in the conversation, John spoke.

"Grandfather," he began, "I have missed you. I have wanted to visit with you again before you . . . ." He stopped, embarrassed by what he had almost said, but the old man broke into a rolling laughter.

"My son," he said in mock sternness, gazing deeply into the youth's eyes, "I will die, as all men die. I am not afraid to die. Do not be concerned. It is good that you have come to visit with me before that time comes. Better to visit the living!"

All three laughed at the elder's dry wit.

"When I was a young boy you told me of the place where the stones and gold in your pendant came from, a hidden canyon of gold,"

John said. "Will you tell me that story again?"

Silence followed, the youth's words hanging unanswered in the stale air of the lodge.

"I have been told that only the Apache elders know of this hidden canyon of gold," John stammered, trying to eliminate the awkward silence.

The elder Kochera gazed into the fire as though he were gathering memories from the ethereal flames.

"This is so," he allowed. "Its location has been known by the tribal elders and the great ones for many generations before my father told me of it. Our tribe knows of many such places."

"Grandfather, tell me of the great ones of our tribe. Who were they and why were they great?"

The old man looked at his grandson. It was good that the young man wanted to know about his people. Nothing would give the old man greater pleasure than to tell his grandson the stories of Mangas, Nana, Geronimo, Victorio, Cochise, Cuchillo Negro, Spotted Elk, and the other heroes of the Apache Nations.

"John," his father scolded, "you ask too many questions and it is late. Your grandfather is tired and we must let him rest."

"No!" Elder Kochera interrupted. "It is all right. I want to share the Apaches' legends with my favorite grandson.

"The greatest Apache leader was Mangas Coloradas. He and Nana were friends from the time they were boys, long before Nana also became a great chief. When they were about your age, John, they went on a great quest to find their manhood. Together they killed a great sheep of the big horns, using only their wits and their bare hands. On their return home they discovered a canyon where the squaws metal gleamed, the place you ask of. It is said that Mangas' spirit still dwells at that place, waiting for a red-bearded man he saw in his visions."

John leaned forward, totally absorbed with his grandfather's narrative. The old man went on for two hours, reliving the tales, telling them in clear and rapid Apache as if they had happened only yesterday. At first John missed a few words here and there because he had not heard nor spoken Apache in such a long time. Soon, though, he found he could follow the stories. He relished his grandfather's ability to relate the ancient tales of Apache heroism and cunning in such vivid detail.

When his grandfather paused, John leaned forward and asked about the legendary Mangas. The old man rocked back, frowned and pointed to John.

"In 1864, when I was a young brave," he related, "Mangas was murdered by soldiers at Fort West. He had surrendered after the commanding officer promised his surrender would bring fair treatment to the Mimbres. I never met Chief Mangas but I knew Chief Nana well. In fact, I rode with him in 1881 on his last and most famous raid. He was already an old man, but he was still the greatest war chief of our people. He was even greater at planning battles than Mangas! After that raid Nana received a sign, something foretold by Mangas in a vision. Because of this sign, Nana fought no more. Mangas and Nana were great friends. Most of what I know of Chief Mangas I learned from Nana."

John listened patiently to his grandfather's recollections, his mind all the while fixed on a certain story, one about a canyon of gold.

"So it was Nana who told you about the canyon of gold?" John persisted.

"No," Elder Kochera replied. "My father, Kochera, took me there when I was very young."

"How did your father learn of it?" John asked.

The blazing fire had overheated the lodge. Elder Kochera slowly rose to his feet, went to the door of the lodge, and pulled back the elkhide drape. He tied it to the lodge post on the right side of the doorway with a leather thong. The old man turned back to face them.

"The answer to your question is something father was not very proud of," Elder Kochera explained. "As a young half-breed, he knew of the Apache people only from his mother, who was sold into slavery by her drunken, outcast father. Later, after she became pregnant, she found refuge in the white man's fort. They gave her food and a place to stay in exchange for work. So my father grew up knowing only the white man's way of life. He was about your age when his mother died. He knew the country well and became a guide so he could survive among the whites. When he was sixteen, he led a large group of white prospectors into the wilderness. One evening his spirit guide, a great eagle, led him to a canyon full of gold. He did not understand that what the eagle had shown him was for the Apache only and he showed it to his white friends."

"What happened then?" John asked, his curiosity mounting.

"That's the part father was ashamed of," Elder Kochera continued. "By Mangas' decree Nana was watching the prospectors. He knew Mangas held a special hatred for prospectors because it was a prospector who'd planned the massacre of our people at Santa Rita."

John knew the story of Santa Rita well. That event was a milestone in the relations between all Apaches and the invading whites. He had heard it told and retold around many a tribal campfire.

"What happened?" John pressed.

"When the white men entered the canyon, Nana and Mangas and their braves were waiting for them. The whites were all killed. Only my father's premonition of danger saved him. He left camp the night before the massacre."

Joseph Kochera spoke for the first time in hours. "Son, your grandfather <u>is</u> tiring now. We will come back in the morning. Tomorrow you can talk more."

"Just one more question," John pleaded. "Grandfather, will you tell me how to find this secret canyon?"

The old man turned and looked him straight in the eye.

"Son," he said gently, "for most of your life you have not lived the way of the Apache. I cannot pass this secret to you. The location of this canyon must die with the old men of the tribe. There are several reasons for this. The young Apaches do not understand the importance of using our riches only for the welfare of our people. Many seek personal gain and make deals with the whites for our resources.

"Also, when the whites began to settle near the canyon of gold, our tribe secretly removed much of the gold that was there. Under their government's law, the whites had a legal claim to that land and to that gold, but we removed it to a safe location. In 1914 we bought breeding stock with it. If the whites learned we had taken that gold they would claim we stole it from them. Right or wrong, under the white man's law we did steal it."

John nodded. He understood that his grandfather was firm in his resolve that the location of the secret canyon of gold would die with the old men of the tribe.

Elder Kochera, the last Apache who knew the location of the canyon, passed away in 1950 at the age of one-hundred and three years. His grandson, John Kochera, was then a twenty-two year-old U.S. Navy fighter pilot. John never lost his interest in lost treasure and gold mines. He read all the stories he could find on the Lost Adams Diggings and other famous lost gold mine legends. By the time he was discharged from the Navy in 1952, he had amassed a great wealth of information on the Adams legend and determined to investigate for himself.

Over the next several years he managed a few short expeditions into New Mexico looking for the Lost Adams Diggings. He never found anything that seemed to fit the story he had pieced together from the various lost mine and treasure books, but he had developed some specific ideas about the Adams legend.

Then one evening as he was relaxing in a bar in Milwaukee, Kochera met a man who told him a story that sidetracked him for years.

"Say, friend," the already tipsy stranger greeted him, "can I buy you a beer?"

Kochera turned and faced the man, studying his features carefully. "Why not," he answered after a pause. "But what's the occasion?"

"Ain't no damned occasion," the man replied, "I'm gettin' drunk and I want someone to drink with, that's all."

The stranger straddled the bar stool next to Kochera's and burped unabashedly. Finishing his beer in one deep drink the stranger slammed his drained mug down on the bar. "Haywood's the name," he said. "What's yours?"

Kochera studied the man's face intently. Finally the features came clear in the dim light. Haywood was an Indian.

"Kochera," he replied. "John Kochera. Call me John."

Haywood ordered another beer, "and one for my friend, John, here."

"I'm an Apache," Haywood declared, answering John's unspoken question.

"I'm half Apache myself," John replied. "My father is Mimbres. What is a full-blood Injun doing in this forsaken part of the country?" John asked Haywood.

"Working," Haywood replied. "Working and drinking! Wish I could get myself back to Arizona, I'd never have to work again." Haywood finished his beer in one large gulp and ordered another.

"Why's that?" John asked.

Haywood slapped John such a solid blow on the back that the younger man had to grab the bar to right himself and stay on the stool.

"I know where there's a fortune in gold, just waiting to be hauled out of the mountains!"

"Gold?" John inquired, choking on his beer, hoping his sudden interest wouldn't be too evident. "You don't say."

Haywood nodded grandly, as though he were already a wealthy man, and ordered another round. "Since you're part Apache yourself," Haywood said, "I guess it'd be all right to tell you about the gold. It was eighteen years ago, in 1942 that me and fourteen other Apaches went to a rich gold mine in Superstition Mountain, Arizona. We packed out hundreds of pounds of the richest gold ore you ever saw! The gold was to be used to pay the tuition for young Apache scholars to go to expensive universities. I was only sixteen then but I carried my share!" Haywood boasted.

John could hardly believe his good fortune. Here was a complete stranger confirming what his grandfather had told him so many years before: Periodically the Apache Nations retrieved gold from hidden mines.

John asked Haywood for more information about the location of the mine, but Haywood became evasive. John plied him with beer, hoping Haywood would let some detail slip. He could tell Haywood knew those mountains very well, but hours later he still had no further details on the mine's location.

Haywood was now very drunk. "Kochera," he hissed, "I ain't

telling you nothing more about that mine. Tell you what I will do though, I'll draw you a map. If you can get close enough to use it, the spirits must be with you." Haywood haw-hawed rudely.

The drunk Apache spread out a napkin on the bar and with a dull pencil drew a rough map, showing major landmarks and drainages.

"Right here is the mine," he said, stabbing the napkin with a pencil. "Before we left, we covered it with soil and brush and we planted some small trees."

Haywood belched loudly as he rose to leave. He found his legs useless and slid from consciousness onto the sawdust-covered floor of the bar.

John was certain Haywood had told him more than he would have if he had been sober. Perhaps meeting Haywood was a sign he should concentrate his search on something other than the Lost Adams Diggin's. Kochera knew the Lost Dutchman Mine was located somewhere near Superstition Mountain and now he had a crude map to a mine in that area. In recent years he had become increasingly frustrated by the Adams story, a story of lost gold that had no solid location, only the general description of the canyon where the placer deposit was found.

He looked down at Haywood, snoring noisily, pocketed the map, laid two dollars on the bar and walked out.

On January 6, 1962, after much enthusiastic talk and little planning, John and his older brother, Joe Jr., headed west to look for the mine Haywood had told about. En route, the brothers stopped at the small town of Reserve, New Mexico for the night. John had driven the entire day, but he was too excited to be sleepy when they arrived at the motel.

It was ten thirty p.m. They threw their packs in the room. Joe showered and went straight to bed. John took his turn in a cool shower and then lay on his bed, his mind going back to a drunken Apache in Milwaukee, the story that man had told and the rough map he had drawn. A half-formed thought gnawed at John's mind. He nearly recognized it, it was familiar; in fact, it had been pestering him for years. It came nearer, almost revealing itself, then slipped elusively away as John fell into an exhausted sleep.

He awoke a few hours later in the comfortable motel bed with a cool breeze from the open window blowing over him. He had been dreaming of the Adams massacre and of a half-breed guide named Gotch Ear.

Gotch Ear, Gotch ear-uh, Kotch-er-a, . . . Kochera!

John sat up abruptly. "That's it!" he shouted. "Why didn't I figure it out before?"

In the other bed, Joe started, awakened by John's loud exclamations.

"What are you carrying on about?" he muttered sleepily.

John took a deep breath and explained the great revelation that had come through his dream.

"Do you remember when I was fourteen and Father and I went to visit Grandfather Kochera? I was interested in stories of lost gold even then and asked Grandfather many questions. Grandfather told me the elders of the Apache Nations knew of many places of gold but he would not tell me where any of them were, saying only that Apache gold was to be used for the tribe, never for individual gain.

"He told me his father, Kochera, had discovered a canyon of gold, while guiding a group of prospectors. The prospectors were massacred by Apaches, only our great-grandfather escaped. Grandfather said the Apaches had later removed most of the gold from that canyon. It was later used to start the great Apache cattle herds. All these years I thought he just wouldn't tell me where the canyon was because he believed I wanted it only for myself.

"I was so disappointed in not being told where the canyon was, that I had forgotten other things he told me. Joe, grandfather talked of many places of gold! And Haywood told me he helped take gold from the Superstitions to pay tuition for young Apache scholars in the 1940's, right? I really didn't much believe Haywood's story but I figured to give his map a try just in case it was true.

"But what if Haywood's story is true? It fits with some of what Grandfather said, that there are other places of gold that the Apaches know about, too. Where does all this lead? It came to me just now in a dream. Remember the story of the half-breed guide named Gotch Ear who led Adams' party to a zigzag canyon of gold and how it was Nana who later warned them not to go above the falls? Grandfather said our great-grandfather, Kochera, led a group of prospectors to a place of gold where the prospectors were all killed in a massacre led by Nana and Mangas.

"Don't you see? The half-breed who led the Adams party was called Gotch Ear. Kotch-er. Kotch-er-a. Kochera. Gotch Ear was Kochera! The man who discovered the Lost Adams Diggin's was our great-grandfather."

Although he now realized it was unlikely the Adams Diggin's would yield any treasure, John Kochera again became obsessed with the Lost Adams Diggin's legend.

CHAPTER 28
NEW SEARCHERS

In 1968 Ron Feldman was lured to Arizona by the story of the Lost Dutchman Mine, said to be located somewhere near Superstition Mountain, about thirty miles east of Phoenix. Ron soon established a riding stable just east of Apache Junction in the foothills of North Superstition Mountain. It was a perfect location serving two kinds of clientele. Leisure riders who were unable to keep their own horses encountered scenic desert vistas. Lost Dutchman hunters — who were naturally attracted to a kinsman in the hunt — appreciated having pack animals and riding horses available and so close to the place of their dreams.

Times were lean but Ron's business showed signs of growth. He was busy but occasionally he had time to prospect. The bonding he felt with treasure hunters was the reason he kept his pack rates as low as he could. Nevertheless, he had to feed his horses, and the cost of hay had doubled in recent months. If he didn't maintain a fair price he would soon be out of business.

What was it that brought a half-breed Apache to Ron's stable one sweltering Sunday afternoon? Was it a common bond or conflict. Whatever it was it spanned the decades that separated their ages and Ron felt it when the brash older man drove into his yard.

"My name is John Kochera and I need the best price you can give me on pack horses," he announced. "I don't have much money, but I aim to get into the Superstitions early tomorrow morning."

Ron quoted his rates: "Pack horses are fifteen dollars a day and a wrangler is twenty-five dollars a day."

"How about ten dollars a day on the horses?" John countered.

With a wry smile Ron answered, "No. The price is fifteen per day per horse. Twenty-five per day for a wrangler . . . ." He explained why the rates were what they were. He had rendered variations of this speech so often that he rattled it off without even listening to himself.

"All right," Kochera agreed. "Can you be ready to pack me in at six in the morning?"

"Sure can," Ron replied. "Just have your gear and your warm body here."

"Tell me, Ron, have you ever done any prospecting?"

"I used to spend all my spare time looking for the Dutchman, but lately I've been concentrating on the Adams. The wife and I have been all over New Mexico and even a few places in Arizona looking for that placer mine. I haven't had any luck yet. But the legend has always intrigued me, especially the Apache connection. Even Gotch Ear, the prospector's guide, was half Apache."

Kochera's felt a thrill in his heart at the mention of his great-grandfather, just as he had when he'd first realized the connection between his family and the Adams story. But he never shared this connection with other prospectors. They wouldn't have believed him, he was sure of that.

"The Adams story depicts the Apaches as savages," Feldman continued. "But the whites were the invaders and they were raping the Apaches' lands. The Indians had every right to try protect their homeland."

John took heart in Ron's understanding of the Apaches' position. A friendship began to build between the two. The next morning he and Ron were on the trail bright and early, Kochera walking, Ron riding and leading two pack horses laden with camping and prospecting gear. Kochera took advantage of every opportunity to discuss prospecting and lost mine lore with his new acquaintance.

Eight miles inside the Superstition Wilderness boundary Kochera found a place to make camp. Ron unloaded the packs, then rode off, leaving Kochera alone in the wilderness until the appointed pick-up date.

Ten days later Ron packed Kochera's gear back out of the Mountain. On the trail, John was in a talkative mood. He wanted to know about Ron's family and he told about his career as a fighter pilot. In fact, they talked about many things but according to some unwritten code that most treasure hunters seem to follow one subject was not broached — What, if anything, john had found in the mountain. When they had finished unloading the pack animals back at the OK Corral,

Kochera asked, "Ron, do you have any idea why we do this?"

Feldman knew exactly what Kochera meant: Why do people like us spend time and money prospecting? Ron often asked himself the same question. "No, John, I don't. We're sure a different breed of animal, aren't we?" he said, laughing. After a pause, he continued. "Part of it is the search for the unknown, but that sure isn't the whole of it. I've always wondered if it was because of something missing in my life, like there was a part of my heritage I was trying to re-place . . . . Listen to me!" he exclaimed. "Truth is I don't know why I do it, and I sure don't know why others do it! My instinct says we're all modern-day adventurers, yet I suspect we each have our own personal reasons, too. Come on back to the porch. We can sit and watch the setting sun illuminate Superstition Mountain and maybe I can talk Jayne into fixing a pot of coffee."

Kochera nodded, and they were soon seated comfortably.

"I've always thought it maybe had to do with something missing in my past, too." Kochera picked up the conversation where Ron had left it. "My grandfather was an Apache elder. But my mother was Mexican and I never seemed to fit in anywhere. I learned a lot from my grandfather. He rode on Nana's last raid you know."

"Nana!" Ron leaned forward, his interest piqued. "He's the Apache named in the Adams story, the one who warned the prospec-tors not to venture above the falls."

Then they spent a few moments admiring the beautiful evening in silence before Ron continued about the Adams prospectors, "I wonder what was missing in those men's lives?"

The two chuckled.

Ron concluded, "I guess Adams and the rest were kin of ours, too."

The two again retreated into their own thoughts. After Jayne brought coffee, they continued their conversation for more than an hour. Ron was glad when Jayne rejoined them. He wasn't used to such intimacy with his clients, and he was always happy for his wife's company. As she handed him a second cup of coffee, he gave her a long glance, recalling nights of pleasure at campsites beside wilder-ness trails.

She'd gone with him on many trips into the Superstition Mountain Wilderness as he chased his dream, looking for the Lost Dutchman Mine, and she had accompanied him on every one of his Adams adventures. Tall, lean and strong she was an inspiration. Although she didn't claim to understand his need to explore, she supported him in his searches and, besides, she enjoyed every opportunity to spend time in the wilderness.

For three years, Ron and Jayne had hunted for the Adams. Traveling portions of four states, they had visited some of the most rugged terrain in the region while looking for that "little hidden zigzag canyon," described in every version of the Lost Adams Diggin's tale.

For a few minutes longer the two men sat on the porch, sipping coffee and looking east. They were quieted by the changing beauty of Superstition Mountain as the setting sun's rays colored it pink, then purple, and finally gray. Crevices on the western façade of the majestic mountain became more distinct, then faded into the ghostly silhouette of the mountain against the violet sky.

"Tell me more of your grandfather and Nana," Ron asked, breaking the silence.

Kochera leaned back in his chair. "My grandfather was Tribal Elder Kochera," he explained. "In the early 1880's, he rode with Nana on several raids against the invading whites. One story he told involved the massacre of two prospectors at a cabin on the Salt River near Cherry Creek."

"What!" Ron interrupted. "My prospecting partner and I have claims in that area. Do you know any details of that story?"

"Well, there isn't a whole lot to tell," Kochera said. "Nana and his braves killed the two prospectors and burned their cabin somewhere west of Cherry Creek. Grandfather said this was Nana's last raid. Right after that, Nana was given a sign that he should stop his vengeance war." Kochera paused and then continued in a different vein, "Where are your claims, anyway?"

"On Chalk Creek," Ron answered. "That's the second creek west of Cherry Creek. Coon is between Chalk and Cherry. A few years ago I discovered that some of the Spanish maps, the ones most Dutchman hunters call the Peralta maps, seemed to fit a portion of Chalk Creek, so I staked some claims there but we haven't found much yet. We keep getting conflicting assay reports on a low-grade deposit."

"Sounds interesting, I'd like to talk more about it sometime," Kochera stretched and yawned. "But right now it's late and I'm exhausted. I'd better be going," then he concluded with a twinkle in his eye. "I'm sure you and Jayne will be wanting to go to bed, too."

Ron had collected a fairly complete reference library through the years, and had read everything he could find on treasure and mining lore in the southwest United States. That evening he couldn't stop thinking about the two men killed by Nana near Cherry creek. Tired as he was, he stayed up searching through his treasure books. He was looking for corroboration of Kochera's story, or any reference to a lost mine near the Salt River somewhere west of Cherry Creek. He looked in Longmore's and Dobie's books — the standard references. Nothing there.

He looked through all his books that night and kept looking in other references when he got the chance. Many months later, he found the story he'd been looking for in an obscure lost treasure publication, a book titled *The Arizona Story:*

> In 1879, a young soldier by the name of Sanders was on a patrol chasing Apaches who had raided a small farm on Cherry Creek and rustled the livestock. He became separated from the other members of his patrol and, realizing his danger, he turned south from the flanks of the Sierra Ancha mountains and rode toward the Salt river. He rode down Coon creek until his progress was prevented by an impassable waterfall. Backtracking a short distance he found a path out of the east side of the canyon. Resting his horse there he spied an unusual outcrop . . . .

There it was! The story went on to tell how Sanders waited for his release from the cavalry and how, several years later, a local rancher discovered the remains of a body and a polished slab of gold-bearing quartz with the name Sanders inscribed on it. The author of the story was given the information by a man known as Hunkydory Holmes in 1892.

Ron phoned his prospecting partner, Mic McPherson, a graduate student teaching geology at Texas A&M University.

"Have you heard of the Lost Sanders Mine?" Ron asked in his usual brusk manner, getting right to the point.

Mic was used to Ron's out-of-the-blue phone calls about prospecting and investigating legends of lost gold mines and treasure troves. McPherson's background in geology had been useful to them in their prospecting ventures more than once.

"Well, let me think," Mic responded. "It sure doesn't ring a bell but give me a few details, I never was good with names."

Ron related the story as he had read it.

"No," Mic interrupted, "I haven't heard that story before but it sounds interesting."

"Well," Ron continued, "you're not going to believe this but it's supposed to be located on Coon Creek close to the Salt River. That's only a few miles from where we have our claims on Chalk Creek. Matter of fact, Chalk is the first creek west of Coon!"

"That brings me to the other reason I called," he went on. "How soon can you get over here to help me look for the Sanders?"

"I've got to talk to Peggy, I probably can make a short trip to look things over pretty soon," Mic responded. "I heard one airline advertising thirty-nine dollar round-trip fares from Houston to Phoenix and I've got a long weekend coming up. I'll call you back."

Since Mic was none too pleased with the way his graduate studies were going the diversion appealed to him. He talked with his wife, who agreed (in fact, insisted) he should go and he left immediately.

Mic left Ron's house early and drove to Chalk Creek. His plan was to walk south the few miles from their claims to the Salt River, taking samples and panning along Chalk Creek as he went. On the way back to the car he would hike up the Salt River to Coon Creek to look for a waterfall there.

Arriving at the claims, he shouldered his well stocked, seventy-pound backpack. By the time he entered the lower reaches of Chalk Creek he had collected a dozen pan samples and the pack was heavier — uncomfortably so. The canyon walls closed in on him. Towering cliffs rose on either side of the narrowing gorge. Bedrock became the dominant component of the creek bed. At each new turn in the creek, Mic searched for natural traps, places gold might accumulate.

He found a good pothole and busied himself digging with his bare hands in the frigid water to remove the accumulated debris. He set aside his backpack and took off his boots before stepping into the cold water, quickly realizing he had underestimated the depth of the pothole.

After he stepped out of the water he removed his pants and looked around before laying his belt and revolver aside. An unusual, misplaced thought came to him, this canyon is a perfect place for an ambush.

He gave up swimming in the icy waters before recovering the last few pebbles from the bottom of the hole. Instead, he panned what he had recovered and had lunch. He was glad he had brought a Pepsi; the pick-me-up from the caffeine was just what he needed. The soda was still cold after several hours in his backpack, a reminder that it was still early spring.

He shouldered the heavy pack again, glad that he had finally eaten. "Just think of all the weight I don't have to carry — at least on my back." He chuckled at the little joke, "I'd rather have it in me than on me."

A quarter-mile down the creek he came to a point where the canyon made a sharp turn to the west. He continued downstream observing that the canyon deepened and the sheer cliffs now towered more than one hundred feet above him on both sides. He could hear the sounds of rushing water. He must be nearing the Salt River.

After negotiating a few rough spots where recently fallen giant boulders jammed the bottom of the creek, he came to another bend in the channel. There the creek turned south. He rounded the bend and was stunned by the beautiful view.

The opening in the cliff in front of him was shaped like a

gunsight, tapering to a narrow notch where the waters of Chalk Creek rushed over the edge of an overhanging cliff before falling more than fifteen feet into a lovely symmetrical pool. He drank in the beauty of the place for some time before reminding himself he needed to move on. He could see the Salt River about a quarter of a mile to the south. To reach it, he would have to do a little climbing.

Mic clawed his way up the west face of the cliff rising to the west side of the waterfall. This wasn't highly dangerous but it put him in a messy situation, since the only path he could find down the other side was overgrown with vegetation. He was forced to remove the back-pack and drag it along behind him, all the while fighting to keep from losing too much skin to the Arizona flora. After a while he came to an area where he could stand up and again climb into his backpack.

"That wasn't too smart," he chided himself. "One thing's for sure, I'm not going back that way!"

With only a few hours left to look around he decided to explore Coon Creek where Sanders' lost mine was supposed to be. If he hurried he figured he'd have time to complete his twelve mile loop before dark. He set a quick pace up the north bank of the Salt River and soon noticed a likely place to ford the river. This was unusual, but he had no interest in the south bank of the river so he continued following the north shore. About two miles further east he came to a little creek flowing out of a wide, shallow channel into the Salt River.

"The topographic map shows Coon as the next creek east of Chalk. This has to be Coon Creek," he concluded.

He walked better than three miles up the gentle, wide bottom of the creek. The modest flow of water that had rippled down the creek bed near the river soon disappeared and the banks of the channel moved back, sloping off until he could hardly tell he was in a drainage. He came to Cherry Creek Road, looking at the south-facing flank of the Sierra Ancha Mountains straight ahead of him. Mic had a flash of inspiration.

"Sanders was wrong!" he exclaimed aloud. "He couldn't have been on Coon Creek, it doesn't have any waterfalls! He was on Chalk Creek!"

He returned to the OK Corral, anxious to share his discovery with Ron.

"Ron," he said, "Sanders was confused. Its Chalk, not Coon that has the waterfall!"

"Do you think there's a place a horse could get out of Chalk Creek on the east side?" Ron asked.

"Don't know," Mic responded. "I wasn't even thinking about that but it will be easy enough to find out. One thing's certain, if there is anything to the Sanders story, he was definitely not on Coon Creek. I could drive your car down Coon Creek all the way to the river! Ron, It's simple. Sanders either just didn't know which creek he was on or he deliberately lied. Either way, the story is wrong. As we've discussed before, lots of the old treasure stories probably have their place names confused. Remember, there were few maps, and landmarks were known only by local names. I'll bet there were plenty of times when a name got attached to the wrong place when the map makers put it on paper for the first time."

"Could be," Ron agreed. "I wish I had time to get up to our claims myself. Maybe next time you're back we can go together and prove one way or the other whether Sanders could have ridden out of Chalk Creek."

CHAPTER 29
VISION REVISITED

McPherson returned to Arizona during spring break. Armed with their new information, he and Ron were both ready to look for the Sanders' Mine.

"Mic, ever since you left I've been thinking about your belief that Sanders may have mixed up Chalk and Coon Creeks," Ron said. "I have to go and see for myself and I'm anxious to see that waterfall you said was so stunning. We can take Prince, Gunsmoke, and Griz. If we can't ride out of the east side of Chalk Creek, then Sanders couldn't have, either."

Mic reached over and scratched Griz on the head. "Do I get to ride the dog, or do I have to ride a horse?" Mic asked dryly.

"Nobody rides my dog," Ron retorted. "He's coming with us because he needs the exercise — but not that much exercise!" Ron loved his dog.

Griz was a common subject of their relaxed bantering.

Mic scratched the good-natured rottweiler behind the ears. "I was just kidding, Griz," he soothed. "We could outfit you in a pack saddle, though."

"Sounds as though you expect me to ride that miserable Prince," Mic complained.

"'Fraid so," Ron laughed. "Prince is the only horse I own big enough to carry you."

McPherson was a big man. Standing only five feet eleven inches he weighed a solid two hundred-thirty pounds. He was in the peak of health.

"Ron," Mic complained, "that isn't true! You've often bragged that Gunsmoke could handle my weight. Why don't you ride that ill-tempered Tennessee Walker? Let me take your beautiful, surefooted, under-worked, overpowered, gray Appaloosa?"

"Because Gunsmoke is my horse. That's why! Furthermore, he doesn't like to cross water and according to your description of Chalk

Creek we'll be doing plenty of that. Old Gunsmoke will usually follow another horse through water, but in case he doesn't want to, I'm a better rider than you are and I have a better chance of getting him to cross without getting dumped! I'll have to follow you."

Mic couldn't argue with that.

At four-thirty the following morning they pulled the two geldings from their pens, tied them to the hitch rack, and gave each a fair portion of grain and hay. After the horses had an hour to eat they led them to the horse trailer.

Loading was uneventful until they tried to close the trailer door. Prince's long body required every bit of the length of the two-horse trailer and he stubbornly refused to move his head into the enclosed nose section. When the door caught his tail he turned his head to the inside of the trailer, trying to make room to move forward. Gunsmoke, who had loaded first, reacted to Prince's invasion of his territory. A ruckus ensued and before the dust settled both horses had to be unloaded.

Gunsmoke loaded easily the second time, but Prince, soundly trounced in the fight, wouldn't load with Gunsmoke already in the trailer. Patiently, they unloaded Gunsmoke a third time. With no small effort the two loaded Prince, pulled his head forward into the nose section, tying it up short. Gunsmoke again loaded easily and they were ready to go, only thirty-five minutes after they had attempted to close the door on the trailer the first time.

Chalk Creek was about a four-hour drive from the OK Corral Stables. By the time they gassed up the truck, stopped twice for Ron to buy coffee, stopped again so he could relieve himself and so they could have breakfast, it was close to noon when they reached the creek and unloaded the horses.

Prince was still mad from Gunsmoke's trouncing. As Mic was saddling him he made an effort to vent his anger. Mic had turned and bent over to pick up the saddlebags when Prince made a try for his backside.

Ron saw the whole thing as he was tightening the cinch on Gunsmoke. He kneed his horse gently just behind the diaphragm, "Come on, Gunsmoke, you're holding wind on me. Let it out and we'll finish dressing you . . . Mic look out!" he hollered, too late.

Only Mic's tight fitting blue jeans and quick reflexes saved him from a mean bite. The sharp teeth just missed doing any serious damage and the horse was still in perfect position for Mic to catch him in the jaw with his best roundhouse punch.

"I think you may have a knockout! Look at his eyes! No, he's going to make it. It'll be a spell before he tries to bite you again. Did he draw blood?"

Mic examined the denim of his Levis and found only a few cut threads. He shook his head. With teeth clenched he tied the canteen and loaded saddlebags onto Prince's saddle. As he swung into it he kicked the big horse hard in the flanks and led out down Chalk Creek at a gallop. "Ron, I'm going to work some of the vinegar out of this horse today," he declared.

Soon the going was rough. He slowed the big horse to a walk. Already the canyon walls were closing in on them. Both men were admiring the beauty. "Much as I hate horses," Mic commented, "I'll have to admit the view is much better from up here."

The high desert terrain fascinated Mic. There were juniper, mesquite, willow, palo verde, the occasional poplar, prickly pear, saguaro, yucca, and other unfamiliar desert species to brighten the chalk, gray, rust, and amber colored hillsides. In the distance were angular peaks and barren slopes.

Farther down Chalk Creek the trail narrowed and the ever-present catclaw bush choked the path. It tore at their clothing. They were glad for their heavy denim and long sleeves. Still, both man soon sported plenty of bleeding scratches.

Unlike the riders, the horses' thick hides and heavy hair afforded ample protection from the sharp hooked thorns. The horses easily plowed through the catclaw thickets where, on his first trip afoot, Mic had scrambled and clawed his way to make progress.

The canyon narrowed and the cliffs rose to impressive heights on either side. The worst of the brush was behind them now. They rode a rocky trail. It was still early afternoon. All was going well, although Gunsmoke seemed more skittish than usual about crossing water. This day he balked at every puddle. In the places where the trail was in the creek bottom, Gunsmoke danced and slipped skittishly.

"Mic," Ron hollered, "let me take the lead. Next good pool we come to, I'm going to teach this son of a bitch who's boss!"

At a crossing where Chalk Creek gently flowed through a deep pool, Ron had his chance. The creek was at least twelve feet wide and deep enough so the horses would have to swim.

Ron spurred Gunsmoke right up to the edge of the creek. Griz tried to help by snapping at the horse's heels. Mic, for his part, had his hands full keeping Prince under control, in the face of Griz's barking and Gunsmoke's terrified dancing.

Ron sat twisted in the saddle, looking back with one hand on Gunsmoke's rump and the other holding the reins. He was screaming at Griz to shut up when the powerful horse gathered himself and lunged out over the deep water.

Only Ron's hand, braced against Gunsmoke's rear end saved him from being thrown. The horse nearly cleared the pool with his mighty leap — almost. Instead they landed in deep water. For a moment, only Gunsmoke's eyes and nostrils were visible. Then Ron emerged, soaked, and cussing his ill-behaved horse as they climbed onto dry ground. Gunsmoke shook so violently it rattled Ron's teeth.

Without a word, Mic walked Prince into the water and out the other side only slightly less wet than Ron, but a good deal less jarred. Looking calmly at his drenched and still-cursing friend, Mic drawled, "Well, I guess he knows who's boss now." They both laughed.

"I think you'd better take the lead again," Ron admitted.

Before long they came to the outsized boulders Mic had noted on his first trip there. The boulders blocked the horses' path to the falls.

"I can't be positive," Mic said, "but I'd guess these boulders haven't been here all that long. If they weren't here when Sanders was, he could have ridden right down this stretch all the way to the falls. Let's tie the horses up and look the area over. I want you to see the falls and the pool below them."

"That really is something," Ron declared, cautiously peering over the edge of the narrow overhang to look into the pool below.

"Mic, when you were here before, did you take samples from the gravel below the falls?"

"No," Mic replied. "I plan to do that this trip. Have you seen any place that looks like a man could ride a horse out of here?"

"Well," Ron responded, "there was one possibility in the last mile on the east side, not far upstream from where we tied the horses."

They paused for a small lunch and to enjoy the beauty of the place. A few minutes after they remounted and headed back upstream, they came to the spot Ron had noted. He pointed up the steep hillside.

Mic exploded, "Why, that's a mountain goat trail! Deer wouldn't even use that! You expect me to ride up that cliff!"

Ron grinned and turned his mount up what was more rock slide than trail. Mic had just turned in the saddle and was leaning to check his cinch when Ron spurred Gunsmoke. The powerful Appaloosa bolted up the imposing incline. Prince didn't intend to be left behind and he also bolted, with Mic unprepared.

Ron gained the crest of the hillside and reined Gunsmoke in hard.

"Whoa, boy," he hollered. "See, that was a piece of cake . . . ."

He heard Prince coming up behind and turned to smile at Mic as he spoke. Instead he found himself smiling at an empty, askew saddle.

Soon a winded Mic reached him. He straightened the saddle, tightened the cinch strap and wordlessly mounted Prince.

"Well, Mic," Ron said, trying not to laugh, "maybe *you* couldn't have ridden out of the canyon here, but *Sanders* or any other cavalryman worth his salt sure could have."

"Yes," Mic agreed. "If Sanders hadn't been a better horseman than me, he'd never have made it in the cavalry."

"What direction do you suppose he headed from here?" Ron wondered.

"My guess is he would have headed back toward the Salt River," Mic replied. "After all, he certainly didn't want to stay up on this ridge where he could be so easily seen. The trouble is, he could have headed down this side of the ridge, ridden straight across the top, or gone anywhere in between! Gives us about ten acres of hillside to explore in the next few hours."

"If the gold outcrop was still exposed," Feldman said, "there would be a gold mine here now."

"That's true," Mic agreed. "But if it were Apaches who killed Sanders, they might have discovered his mine and hidden that, too. Doesn't hurt to look but I doubt if we'll see anything today, Ron. We should plan to come back again with infrared film and your metal detector."

"Good idea," Ron said.

They tied the horses to a large bush, dismounted, and explored the area for an hour. Ron wanted to have a look at Coon Creek. "Let's ride over the top of this mesa," he suggested.

"That's a good idea," Mic said. "If there's anything to Sanders' story, we should be able to ride on down to the Salt River from here."

They mounted and rode toward the river. Ron quickly found a route off the mesa and soon they were at the river.

"Here's that ford I told you about," Mic said. "The water is higher now but it still looks like a man could take a horse across here."

"I saw it when we were riding down," Ron replied. "I'd like to go across and explore some for the cabin. It seems odd that Sanders would have built the cabin on the other side of the river but that's what the story claims. While I'm over there you can go to the pool under the falls and gather samples. We'd better trade horses, though."

Mic watched Ron ride across the river. When he'd reached the other shore, Mic turned Gunsmoke and rode back to the pool under the falls. The men planned to meet back at the ford at three p.m.

Ron rode up the south bank of the Salt, following a natural path along a gravel bar. He soon came to a fresh-water spring that issued from under a ledge of gravel. Minerals left behind as the spring's water evaporated had turned the gravel to solid rock. Ron was surprised to see crystal clear water springing forth so far from the jagged mountains that rose to the south.

He started to ride farther east across the sandy flats but had barely begun when he came across the charred remains of several logs rotting in the mud.

Tying Prince to a nearby sycamore, he began to explore. He

found a few old square-shaped nails stuck through the end of a small hand-hewn branch and discovered that one of the rotting timbers still had axe marks near one end.

He tried to quell his rising excitement. "That doesn't prove much," he told himself. "River could have brought this stuff here in the flood of sixty-four."

He continued to poke around. After a bit he came upon the well-pitted remains of a combination hammer-hatchet.

"This thing sure didn't float here!" he cried.

Satisfied that this could be the site of Sanders' cabin, he began to scour the area more thoroughly. After diligent searching Ron took a break, sitting on a muddy protrusion where a few waterlogged and rotting poles had trapped mud during floods.

He kicked a lump of mud at his feet casually turning over a clay-encrusted chunk of what looked at first like glass. He picked it up out of the mud. One clear facet protruded where the hard mud had broken off, and Ron knew he was holding something unusual.

He carried the clay-covered chunk to the spring and rinsed away the mud. As the cup-shaped object emerged, he saw it was no piece of glass. He held the crystal to the sun, admiring the rainbows reflecting off the facets and through the stone.

Mic arrived at the north side of the ford on schedule and had to wait nearly an hour for Ron to appear on the south bank. Ron spurred Prince across the river, obviously excited.

Reaching into the saddlebag, he pulled out the crystal and handed it to Mic. "I found this near some old hand-hewn logs over there!" He gestured across the river. "And look at this old tool."

McPherson looked at the hammer-hatchet. "Looks like 1860s," he estimated. He took the crystal in his right hand, cupping his left over it. "This sure is shaped odd. The fractures on one side make it almost look like glass, but on the other side is just regular quartz facets."

Mic examined the crystal closely, noting the rainbow colors showing through the gray-tinged quartz. "That's part of one big quartz crystal," he declared. "Let me see that hatchet again."

He examined the tool more closely, deciding it was hand-forged.

"Ron, it's hard to say for sure how old this thing is without lab analysis, but I'd guess it's from the 1800s." Glancing at his watch, he observed, "Right now we'd better ride or it'll be too late to get a look at Coon Creek. What took you so long over there anyway?"

"I wasn't gone that long, was I?" Ron replied.

They remounted, Ron back on Gunsmoke and Mic on Prince. Grizzly seemed happy to have his master on the proper horse. They rode east.

By dusk they had completed the circuit: down Chalk Creek, over the ridge to the Salt River, up the river, up Coon Creek, and back to the truck on Cherry Creek Road where they loaded the tired horses into the trailer.

"Loading was sure easier than last time!" Mic said gratefully as he closed the trailer door. "I guess they haven't got the energy to fight. And I'm sure glad, 'cause neither do I." After a moment of silence he looked at his friend quizzically. "What's the matter, Ron? You haven't said ten words since we left the Salt River."

"Oh, just thinking, I guess," Ron replied. "You were sure right, Mic. There's no doubt about Sanders having the creek names confused. Whether there's anything to the rest of his story or not, he didn't come to an impassable waterfall on Coon Creek!"

They threw their gear and the old rusty hatchet Ron had discovered into the bed of the truck. "I'll drive, as usual," Mic said emphatically.

"Real funny," Ron snickered, climbing into the passenger's seat. He knew Mic didn't think his driving matched up to his horsemanship.

On the long trip back to Apache Junction, Ron remained unusually quiet, sitting with his hat pulled down, covering his eyes. All the while his hands worried the crystal.

It was past midnight when they finished unloading and feeding the horses. Ron took time to lock the crystal in his safe before collapsing into bed, where Jayne had been sleeping for two hours.

Over their morning coffee he told her about the previous day's adventures — and misadventures — saving the best for last.

"Look what I found," he said. "It was covered in mud right next to where I found the burned logs and the hatchet. Look at the way the light plays in it."

Jayne admired the crystal and agreed he had made an unusual find.

It was a quiet day at the OK Corral and Ron was finally able to catch up on his backlog of chores. At the end of a long day he sat tired in his easy chair on the porch, watching the setting sun cast the changing shadows on Superstition Mountain, sipping a daily beer, and fondling his remarkable crystal. Night crept comfortably around him and his eyelids grew heavy, then closed.

He was no longer on the porch. The sun was long down and he was in a strange place staring at an apparition with upraised, blood-covered arms. A wave of terror came over him.

"No!" his mind screamed. "Get away from me! Who are you? What do you want?"

At last the apparition spoke. Its voice was soothing but its language was not Ron's language . . . . Ron was confused. He felt drawn to touch the apparition before him and he felt compelled to speak. But words would not come. He tried to gather his courage to embrace what was before him, but he could not.

He felt himself retreating into a dark cleft. He heard the low roar of rushing water. The cool wetness closed over him, the apparition faded, and he shivered, hearing the scream of an eagle.

CHAPTER 30
BREAKTHROUGH, 1989

Despite his feeling that much time had passed, it was still early evening when Ron awoke and went into the house. His skin was wet and clammy and sweat beaded his brow. He still clenched the crystal.

He poured himself a cup of coffee and sat at the kitchen table sitting where the cool air from the evaporative cooler blew across him.

For several minutes he sipped coffee and tried to figure out the unusual dream. He seldom remembered dreams, but this was more than a dream, more vivid than anything he'd ever experienced outside of consciousness. The longer he tried to analyze what he had seen the less he could remember. Soon enough most of the details evaporated. Only the strong emotions evoked by the dream remained.

Ron rose and walked to the bedroom door. The dim light of the hall threw gentle shadows on Jayne's body as she slept under the thin blanket in the waterbed they had recently purchased. He enjoyed watching the even rhythm of her breathing.

He undressed and crawled quietly into bed, cuddling. He was happy she had foregone her bedclothes. It wasn't long until he felt a strong need. She was sleeping soundly but he rolled her onto her back and impressed his urgent intention upon her.

Jayne, hadn't seen much of her husband for the past few days, and warmed quickly to his touch. She opened to his affection. She sensed that something was troubling him and she held him long into the morning.

Early the next day, Jayne turned off the alarm before it rang.

"Ron," she said, "you seemed so anxious last night. Is everything okay?"

"It is now," he replied. "Matter of fact, I feel great. I had a weird dream last night, out on the porch. I can't even remember it now, but it sure gave me a funny feeling."

She hugged him, threw back the cover, got out of bed, and dressed to do the morning chores. "I'll get the boys off for school and put some coffee on," she said.

There was no answer. "Ron?"

"Yes," he replied. "Seems like I ought to be able to remember the dream but I can't."

Ron decided to use the crystal as a paperweight on his desk. He admired it often and developed the habit of holding and turning it while he visited with clients or spoke on the phone.

He was toying with it one day when John Kochera phoned him.

"Hello, John," he answered, recognizing Kochera's distinctive accent at once. "How are you?"

"I'm still alive," Kochera chuckled. "I just got into town, planning another trip into the Mountain. I'd like to come out today and arrange for livestock, and argue price."

"Well, come on out," Ron said. "I'll be here."

Within the hour Kochera arrived and Ron invited him into his office.

"How's the fight going, John?" he asked, referring to Kochera's repeated attempts to give up smoking.

"I guess you know," he replied, patting his shirt pocket which held a pack of cigarettes. "These things are going to kill me someday. I plan on quitting as soon as I get out of the Mountain."

"Where have I heard <u>that</u> before?" Ron smiled.

"They've already given me emphysema. I'm only sixty-one years old and already I have bouts with it that make it hard for me to breathe . . . . Say, that's sure a nice crystal you have there," Kochera said, gesturing to the object Ron was holding.

"You remember when you told me about Nana's last raid and your grandfather?" Ron asked. "Well, I did some searching and came upon the Sanders story. Ever hear of it?"

Kochera shook his head. "No, it doesn't ring any bells."

Ron continued. "My partner, Mic, and I went up to Chalk Creek where our claims are, and we did a little looking around. I found what looked like the burned remains of a cabin on the south side of the river where that story said Sanders and his partner were killed in 1881, that jibes with the story your grandfather told you about Nana killing two men on his last raid. Nearby I found this crystal. It could have been where Sanders' cabin was."

"Can I look at that crystal?" Kochera asked.

Ron handed him the crystal. "Are you going in the Mountain tomorrow morning?"

Kochera nodded.

"You know, John," Ron said, as he took the crystal back, "I had the strangest dream last night."

Kochera sat back, pulled out a cigarette, and struck a match.

"No!" Ron exclaimed, "Not in here!"

"Oh, sorry, I forgot where I was." He shook the match out and sat with the cigarette sticking from between his lips.

"Are you still chasing the Adams?" John asked, as he inserted the cigarette back in the pack and buttoned the pack in his shirt pocket.

"Well, I guess so," Ron replied. "I haven't in a while but there are still a few possibilities left to look at. The stories in most of the treasure books leave the location of the placer deposit wide open. That's why I quit looking. I couldn't narrow it down to less than a few thousand square miles!"

"Well, Ron," John said, "I'm not in the best of shape and I've decided to concentrate on the Dutchman. If I have enough time left maybe I'll find that one before I go. Anyway, I'm giving up on the Adams. I've chased various accounts all over New Mexico and never found anything even slightly interesting."

"I hadn't decided this until right now," Kochera continued, "but when I get back home to Illinois, I'm sending you all my maps and notes on the Adams. Maybe you can do some good with them."

This conversation planted a seed in Ron's mind. By the time John's maps and notes arrived, Ron was thinking less of the Sanders and the Lost Dutchman and more about the Lost Adams story. He scoured his books and magazines, rereading articles of the Adams story and he and Mic were again talking about looking for the Adams.

"You know what, Jayne," he said wearily one afternoon, "I've looked at so much of this garbage in the old books on the Adams I'm beginning to think nobody knew anything for sure. Every time I pick up another book I find a different date for the massacre. Not a difference of a few years, mind you, but decades! Not only that, but different authors give Adams' partner any one of half a dozen names. Most versions claim it was a man named Davidson and put the date in the later part of the 1800s. Look at this," he pointed to Luke Longmore's account in the book *Desert Treasure*. "Longmore suggests that Adams' partner was a man named Landrew and the massacre occurred many years before 1846! Longmore quotes from a military report by a man named Emory about what Landrew said. If Longmore is correct, then the dates in all the other accounts are way off."

Later Ron called Mic, who was now living in Mesa, Arizona, only a few miles from the OK Corral, to talk about Longmore's account.

"Yes, I read Longmore's Adams account years ago. I remember there was something completely different from all the other versions," Mic replied. "Matter of fact, the differences bothered me so much I sort of ignored the rest of his account."

Ron continued, "Maybe we shouldn't do that. What if all the others are wrong and Longmore is right?"

"That's a good point," Mic answered. "The next thing we have to do is get a copy of the Emory notes, if they exist."

"Why's that?" Ron asked.

"Well, we have to know exactly what this Landrew character said. All we have now is what Longmore says he said," Mic replied. "That's not good enough."

After two months of searching local libraries for the Emory notes Ron called the historian at Fort Leavenworth, Kansas, who told him the Emory notes were available, and that he'd be glad to copy and send them. "It'll take a few weeks. There's no charge, but contributions to the historical society are always appreciated."

Four months later Ron found a bulging manila envelope in the post office box. Sitting in the truck while Jayne finished shopping, Ron thumbed through the stack of loose papers until he found the page he was looking for. When she came back and climbed in behind the steering wheel, Ron read her the passage quoted in Longmore's account.

"Jayne, it's exactly as Longmore said!" he exclaimed. "Landrew — well, it's given as Londeau here — tells the story of a massacre on the

Prieto River where very successful prospectors were killed several years before the Emory expedition. I haven't found anything anywhere else in these notes yet that suggests any connection to the Adams story. I wonder where Longmore got that idea, and why he changed the spelling of the Frenchman's name?"

When they got home, he rushed to clear off the kitchen table. Soon he had the Emory notes, his collection of maps, and Kochera's paperwork spread all around the room.

"Emory refers to the Prieto River — according to my English-Spanish dictionary that's another Spanish word for dark or black — and that's what Longmore said, 'Prieto or Black River' . . . " he was thinking out loud.

"Isn't the Black River the south branch of the Salt River?" Jayne asked.

"Well, yes it is," he answered, scratching his red beard, "but look at these old maps from the 1880s. They don't show any Black River anywhere. Several show a south branch of the Rio Salado or Salt River, but on those maps the south fork is unnamed. The Prieto is shown on the Emory map of eastern Arizona Territory but his map is all confused. There is even a footnote that was added later — evidently when the notes were published in book form — warning the reader 'the river names here are confused'.

"Emory shows the San Francisco, then the Blue, and finally the Prieto flowing into the Gila. But the Blue joins the San Francisco, not the Gila! Several other of these older maps show the Prieto River running into the Gila River in that part of the country but the Prieto and several other rivers change places from map to map!

"Best I can make out, the Prieto is a river that runs into the Gila west of the San Francisco River. On maps after 1899 that drainage is called Eagle Creek. Isn't that something? Evidently, legions of dedicated Adams hunters have spent years searching the headwaters of the modern day Black River assuming Longmore's 'Prieto' referred to the modern-day Black River!" Ron exclaimed. "They should have read the story more closely. Emory couldn't have been talking about that Black River. Longmore clearly explains that Landrew was talking about a river that ran directly into the Gila, somewhere in eastern

Arizona. I think it's time Mic and I took a trip east. Maybe he can help me figure this out."

Ron dialed and waited impatiently. "Mic!" he hollered into the mouthpiece. "You want to go hunt for the Lost Adams? Or should I say, how'd you like me to show you where it is?"

"Yes, to both questions," Mic replied. "Which state do you think it's in now?"

"I'm serious," Ron replied. "Remember we discussed a trip into the Black River country to look for the Adams? Well, come on over here. We're going to the Black River tomorrow, and it's not where you think."

"What?" Mic sounded confused.

"Never mind, just get here," Ron concluded, refusing to give any more information over the phone.

Late that afternoon Mic drove up to the OK Corral, he could tell Ron believed he'd made an important discovery. The grin on his face and the bounce in his step gave him away.

For several hours the two leafed through the information on the Adams'. Mic, playing devil's advocate, was trying to shoot holes in Ron's new theory. Finally he sat back in his chair.

"Ron," he said, "I think you've got something here. I think we've figured out several problems with the Adams stories. First, there's the historical confusion. Who was with Adams? When did they discover the diggings? Evidently several authors have confused two separate massacres, one that happened before 1846. That's when the gold was discovered. The other was around 1864. That's when Adams was trying to relocate the canyon. My guess is that confusion came from Dr. Spurgeon. Ever since the doctor's search, most Adams accounts have suggested the trip up the San Francisco River with Davidson was when they discovered gold."

Mic glanced through the Emory notes. "From what I've seen here, anyone looking for the Adams on the modern day Black River is wasting time. That can't be the river Longmore, Emory, or the Frenchman were referring to."

Ron nodded agreement and stared at Mic for several minutes.

"Ron, what are you thinking?" Mic asked.

"I'm thinking about the actual Adams Diggings. You know, if it was really as rich a placer gold deposit as Adams claimed, it had to be located close to a gold-producing region. The Morenci mining district just west of Clifton has produced lots of gold in the past one hundred years and it's the only mining district anywhere near the Prieto River."

Ron unfolded his topographic map and studied the area west of Clifton, again. "Looks like Eagle Creek cuts right across the western edge of the Morenci ore body," he said. "It has just about got to be the river in the Frenchman's story. This Gold Gulch drainage begins at the west side of the Morenci open pit copper mine and runs west to Eagle Creek. I don't see any other drainages that begin near the Morenci mine and run into the 'Prieto'."

"So you think this 'Gold Gulch' is where the Lost Adams Diggings is?" Mic asked.

"If Longmore was right, it just has to be," Ron replied.

"If it really is the Adams," Mic observed, "it couldn't possibly still be loaded with placer gold. People were all over that country around Clifton during the Great Depression. Any gold left after Adams' group was there would long since have been mined out."

"Yes, but that would be true no matter where the Lost Adams is located," Ron said. "With all the hiking, hunting, horseback riding, and motorcycle riding people have done all over this country, and don't forget the mineral exploration, someone has to have been to the Lost Adams Diggin's before now. There just isn't any chance it's really 'lost,' still out there somewhere, untouched since Adams' day."

"I agree," Mic picked up, "but if someone did find a hidden zigzag canyon with a waterfall — let's just assume for now that this 'Gold Gulch' fits that description — and it was full of placer gold, why didn't they realize it was the Adams?"

"I don't know," Ron replied.

"Wait just a minute . . . . What if prospectors did find the Adams Diggin's but there wasn't much gold?" Mic asked.

"Why wouldn't there be much gold?" Ron countered.

"What if Adams exaggerated? What if there really wasn't much placer left after the massacre? Or, what if Apaches took most of the gold from the canyon before prospectors returned?" Mic speculated.

"Ron, if someone found a canyon that fit Adams' description of the diggings perfectly but there wasn't much gold there, would they believe they'd found the Lost Adams Diggin's? Would anybody else believe it?"

"That's a good point," Ron said. "Most Adams hunters expect to find a canyon strewn with gold. If they walked into Gold Gulch and it matched Adams' account to a 'T' but the gold was all gone they'd assume it was the wrong spot."

"I think that may explain why the Lost Adams hasn't been 'found'." Mic answered, "But you and I are going there looking for a place that fits Adams description, where there could have been a rich placer deposit originally. If Gold Gulch matches Adams' story at all, we should really look around for the remains of a cabin and do some digging. That coffeepot full of gold could still be buried under the hearthstone."

"It has to be," Ron said. "If someone had discovered it, they'd have known it was from the Adams. Besides, if anyone found three hundred pounds of gold nuggets buried under the hearth of a ruined cabin, the story would have made national news."

"Not necessarily," Mic shot back. "Are you going to tell anyone when we find it?"

Mic drove home eagerly. Both men set early alarms and went to sleep, their bodies keyed up and their emotions running rampant. Their thoughts were filled with anticipation that tomorrow might be their day to solve one of the great mysteries of modern treasure lore.

CHAPTER 31
VISION FULFILLED

Long before sunup on November 21, 1989, Mic and Ron had started on their 180 mile trip to Clifton in Ron's four-wheel-drive pickup. In Globe they stopped for gas and Ron got a cup of coffee.

They rode in silence, each speculating what they might find in Gold Gulch and still wondering if Eagle Creek was really the same stream that the Frenchman had called *Rio Prieto*.

Ron was the first to break the silence. "I think we should try to retrace the path Adams took."

Mic agreed. "They would have followed the rivers," he said, thinking out loud. "Fortunately, according to my uncle Ed, there are jeep roads along all the rivers in that part of the country."

"If we head south from Clifton down the San Francisco and follow the Gila to Eagle Creek, or should I say Prieto River," Ron said, "we can drive up Eagle Creek Road."

At Safford they stopped to eat. Afterwards Ron was quiet again, staring across the table and beyond the couple at the next booth. His unsettling dream still bothered him. As he sipped his coffee he strained to recapture images but they wouldn't come.

"Give me ten dollars," Mic said. "Your turn to buy. I'll pay while you finish your coffee."

"What?" Ron responded, vaguely.

"Where are you?" Mic queried. "You seem to be off in another world."

"Yes, I guess I was," he replied. "I was thinking about that dream I had."

They drove out of Safford as violet fingers of light crept into the eastern vista. The purple and orange hues of the sunrise added to Ron's already rosy disposition. "A perfect beginning for the day we solve the Lost Adams mystery," he bragged, grinning from ear to ear.

Ten miles out of Safford they turned north on highway 666 heading toward Clifton. Thirty minutes later they crossed the Gila

River and soon they were approaching Clifton. On the southern edge of town they found the dirt road they were looking for.

They followed this road, down the San Francisco, crossed to the west side of the river and continued south until they reached the Gila. Upstream from its confluence with the San Francisco the Gila was nearly dry.

Back in the early part of the century, before all the dams were built, the Gila was the largest tributary to the Colorado River. There was more rain in the region before 1850.

"When Adams was first here he would have seen a lot more green than we do now," Mic told Ron.

They turned west. The truck bounced over the rough road, often jostling them violently. After several hours of this tortuous grind Ron pointed out the window toward the north. "That must be the Prieto there."

Mic turned north onto Eagle Creek Road.

"Do you realize we are probably retracing the route Adams took more than one hundred fifty years ago?" Ron said. "According to Longmore, somewhere about fifteen miles up this road," he gestured to the rutted dirt track they were following, "is where those prospectors made their discovery. We should start looking for the remains of a cabin before we go that far. Why don't we try a little panning right here?"

"Even if we found a little gold it wouldn't prove anything," Mic replied, driving on. "This river comes right through one of the richest mineralized regions in the Southwest. Anywhere we look along here we should find some gold. But the sun is moving and we have a long day ahead of us."

About an hour later they stopped to stretch their legs.

"I think I'll do a little panning," Ron said, still eager at the possibility of the excitement of seeing color in the pan.

"Won't hurt anything," Mic said, giving up.

Fifteen minutes later Ron was chasing "one more" trail of black sand around the pan when he uncovered a nice little nugget. It was smaller than a pin-head, but impressive as it glittered in the sun. "Hey, lookee here!" he said.

They examined the little chunk of gold for several minutes, watching the sunlight glint off the precious metal.

Ron was pleased with his good luck. "That's more gold than I've found in the Superstitions in all my years of searching for the Dutchman."

A few moments later the two were back in the truck with Ron driving and smiling to himself.

"Finding gold was a good sign," Mic remarked. "I'll bet this is just what the Adams party would have done. That's how Londeau described it, '. . . panned the sands as they went up the Prieto and were richly rewarded with gold . . . .'

"You know," he continued, "one thing that really bothers me about Longmore's story is that he changed the spelling of the Frenchman's name. Longmore had to have had a copy of Emory's notes, since other than the spelling of the Frenchman's name he quotes verbatim. So he knew how Emory spelled the name, yet, Longmore deliberately spelled it differently, Why?

"Emory claimed the Frenchman was illiterate, right? If Emory wasn't familiar with French, he might have spelled the name like the Frenchman pronounced it and maybe Emory got it wrong, but how would Longmore have known that?"

"Maybe he did *know* Emory spelled the name wrong," Ron replied. "But what difference does it make anyway?"

"But how could he have known?" Mic repeated. "And it makes all the difference in the world! Longmore wasn't a careless author. Yet he deliberately changed the spelling of a quoted source's name. Why?"

"Hey, what if Longmore knew the Frenchman!" Ron exclaimed. "That could be it. If Longmore knew the Frenchman, he would have known Emory spelled the man's name wrong. Matter of fact, what other explanation could there be for the different spellings? And if Longmore knew the Frenchman, he could have told Longmore the massacre recounted in Emory's notes was actually the Adams massacre. What else would convince Longmore a massacre on the Prieto sometime before 1846 was the Adams massacre, when everyone else claimed it happened after 1864?"

There was complete silence in the truck for the next few minutes as each considered the logic of their thinking.

"But," Mic finally said, "if Longmore's account is true, he would have found the Adams."

"What?" exclaimed Ron, bringing the truck to an abrupt halt. "How do you figure that?"

"It's simple enough," Mic replied. "Look at this one fact. If we're right, Longmore had all the information we have and maybe more; if we can find it, so could he!"

Ron slumped against the steering wheel.

"You're right!" he exclaimed, "Longmore's already found the Adams!" He pounded the steering wheel with both hands. "And if he did the pot of gold is already gone."

"That's an unfounded assumption," Mic replied. "In the first place, if Longmore found the pot of gold, why didn't he tell anybody? Second, we don't know if Longmore ever got here to look for it. This was still rough country in Longmore's day. Maybe he should have found that pot of gold but that doesn't mean he did! Furthermore, who cares? We're not here looking for any pot of gold, we're here to solve a mystery!"

"You're right," Ron agreed. "Hope springs eternal, though. Wouldn't hurt to get rich while solving the mystery, would it?"

For the next half hour the two rode in silence enjoying the beauty of the rugged barren cliffs as the truck crept along in the desolate solitude of the twisting canyon.

"Imagine," Mic said. "One hundred years ago, the Apache was lord over this country."

"Now," Ron observed, "they live on the San Carlos Reservation just a few miles west of here."

The road crossed the river again and they traveled along the north bank as the river headed east. When the road rounded a jagged cliff, Ron was looking through the side window and spotted something on a small hill.

"Look at that," he said, pointing to half a dozen stone monuments rising out of the dirt.

"It's a graveyard," Mic exclaimed. "Why do you suppose so many folks are buried way out here? Let's stop and have a look around."

"Look at these headstones," Ron said when they investigated. "Most are from the late 1800s and early 1900s. I'll bet these folks mined the sands of Eagle Creek for gold. If so, that's another good sign."

They spent several minutes at the graveyard contemplating the oddity of so many graves so far out in the wilderness. It was past noon when they got back in the truck. Mic took the wheel again and they eased up the rugged road.

"Its almost spooky, Ron. If Longmore were here, he probably would have seen those headstones, too. Matter of fact, he would probably have been looking for the same clues we are — the ruins of a cabin, a narrow zigzag canyon, and a waterfall."

"Let's watch for a good place to make camp," Ron suggested. "We can't be far from Gold Gulch and we better slow down and do some real looking, starting now."

At the first likely spot, Mic pulled the truck out into the low brush. They pitched the tent, then Ron gathered firewood and unrolled their sleeping bags while Mic climbed a ridge to look around.

"Ron," he hollered, "look at this. There's an old rock ruin up here."

They examined the tumbled-down walls, noting a hole dug at one end of the structure. They set up the metal detector but found nothing more interesting than a rotting soup can.

"I wonder if this digging could have been Longmore's doing," Ron mused aloud.

The two tried to visualize Longmore digging in the remains of the cabin.

Longmore chopped the brush and cleared the stones, looking for the spot where the fireplace had been, hoping to find what he was looking for, all the while knowing this was not the right cabin . . . .

Heavy thunderclouds rolled in and they hurried to get the gear moved into the tent. Flashes of lightning lit up the western sky and thunder rolled up the canyon. Mic hurried to build a fire before the rain hit. Soon beef stew and water for Ron's coffee were warming over the crackling flames.

They finished their simple supper just as the rain hit. The pair found refuge in the truck and waited out the two-hour downpour happy to have made camp high above the waters of Eagle Creek.

When the rain subsided, they left the truck and walked in the gentle drizzle to the smoldering remains of the campfire. Mic dug through the pile of driftwood and selected the least soggy pieces to add to the dying embers. Ron hovered over the smoldering remains, as if they might somehow warm him. Mic retrieved a can of lighter fluid from the truck, motioned Ron back, then doused the stack of wood.

"That sure doesn't smell like lighter fluid," Ron observed, making a face.

"It's lighter fluid alright," Mic confirmed, lighting a match and bringing a slow flame. "But I smell something odd, too," he frowned, sniffing the air. "I know what that is. It's sulfur gases. There must be a hot mineral spring nearby."

The storm passed completely, leaving the air fresh and clean. Evening came and the sky sparkled with the most brilliant display of stars either of the citified campers had seen in a while. It had been a long day. They turned in early and slept well.

Ron rose before sunrise and sat by the dead fire, surveying details of the surrounding country in the pre-dawn light. Parts of the wide valley were wooded with juniper, willow and huge cottonwood trees with oversized trunks whose branches carried only a few twigs. Cliffs towered on both sides of the river. As the sun rose, the growing light painted the salmon-colored cliffs red-orange. The waters of Eagle Creek played a gentle melody as they tumbled over the rocks and moved inexorably toward the Gila.

Waiting for the coffee to boil, the men sat on the tailgate of the truck breathing in their surroundings.

"This is the life," Ron mused. "It almost doesn't matter if we find anything here or not. The fun is the looking."

"There's a song lyric I like," Mic replied, "it goes something like, 'the pleasure's not the finding, it's the loving of the game'."

"Isn't that the truth!" Ron exclaimed.

"It would be fun if we could afford to do this more often," Mic was thinking out loud. "If we found that pot of gold, we'd be set to prospect full time. That wouldn't be too hard to take, would it?"

The two laughed with enjoyment — both in the moment and in the dream it held.

After a quick breakfast they continued up the river.

"There's that smell again," Ron noted. "The map shows a hot springs not far from Gold Gulch."

Jouncing along in the truck, they chatted about what Longmore might have seen when — if — he rode up the Prieto.

Longmore again smelled sulfur and noticed that a small canyon led down from the mountain to the west and joined with the Prieto where the river turned east and the valley widened. He tasted the clear water and spat, making a face. "So that's where that sulfur smell is coming from."

A few minutes later, Ron spotted something unusual. "That looks like a stone wall to me!" he hollered, pointing.

Mic stopped the truck.

When Longmore came to the ruin, just a short while after he again smelled the familiar odor of sulfur, he almost missed it because it was too obvious and because the ruin was no longer on the banks of the river as Landrew had described it. The river had cut away the mud that had lined the channel when Landrew was there, eroding until the water surface was ten feet below and fifty feet away from the cabin.

"Whoa, Billy," Longmore commanded, pulling back on the reins of the dun. "What's that over there, across the river?" Squinting hard he decided, "Looks like a stone wall behind that brush. Wonder why there's a stone wall against that dirt bank . . . ."

The two men jumped out of the truck and crossed the river to investigate. The Prieto was nearly two feet deep and calm where they crossed. The stone wall Ron had spotted was the remains of an old cabin.

Longmore rode the big dun across the river, leading the pack horse through the cool water. He got down and tied the horses securely to the nearest tree. After the incident of the night before, he made doubly sure of the knots.

He walked up the river bank and through the brush to where he found a complete stone wall built against the bank . . . .

"Do you think this is the cabin we're looking for?" Ron asked.

Could this be it? Longmore wondered.

"It either is or it isn't," Mic quipped. "Let's get the metal detector and give it a good going over. Looks like there were two walls of stone, the other two were probably completed with driftwood. Look over there," Mic pointed to a big rock fifty feet to the east. "Looks like they quarried these flat rocks from that boulder."

Longmore noted that both walls were constructed from flat slabs of rock that were quarried from a nearby boulder. The north end of the east wall had begun to collapse. Most of the floor of the ruin was exposed bedrock, but the east end and especially the southeast corner right next to the back wall, where considerable flood debris had accumulated, was soil.

They went back across the river, got their tools, and recrossed to the cabin. They immediately began digging in what seemed the most likely spot inside the cabin walls. Their digging produced charcoal and other debris from a fire.

Longmore got his spade, a pick, and a chisel from the packhorse and started to dig in the corner of the ruin. Soon he was turning over blackened sand and he knew he was in a fire pit. He attempted to drive the small shovel point into the floor further but couldn't.

"What am I into now," Longmore muttered. "It feels like solid rock."

Ron slowly swept the detector across what had been the cabin floor, lingering over fractures in the bedrock where soil had accumulated. The detector sounded and he bent over and pulled a long iron spike out of the dirt. Shortly, the detector sounded again. He called for help and Mic pried sod from the crevice with a trenching tool, turning up a short piece of corroded small-gauge railroad track.

"What in the world is this doing way out here?" Mic exclaimed.

"I've often carried a similar piece on the trail," Ron explained. "They make a great little anvil for emergency horseshoeing."

"That must be it," Mic said. "I can't think of any other reason for it being here. Longmore was a railroad man, wasn't he?"

"Yes, he was," Ron replied, getting more excited. "Just imagine, Mic, Longmore himself might have left this piece of track here."

"Why would he have done that?" Mic asked. Then answering his own question he said, "Maybe he had something more valuable to pack out."

Both men were getting caught up in the intrigue of their speculation.

"Don't talk that way," Ron scolded. "If that's the case we're out of luck! And I'm not ready to give up yet. Lots of old timers carried a piece of track as an anvil for emergency horseshoeing. This doesn't prove Longmore was here."

Longmore grabbed his oversized saddlebags, emptying their contents onto the ground . . . .

Besides the spike and the piece of track they found several rotted cans, a few carpentry nails, a horseshoe nail, and another hand steel that apparently had seen much use breaking rock.

"I'd say that horseshoe nail confirms the use of the track," Ron said. "Let's see what's in that fire pit you found."

In the pit they uncovered the rotted remains of an old boot and several more rotted cans. The detector indicated there was something big still buried deeper. Using his fingers to carefully clear the sand from around it, Mic cautiously pried the object loose.

"What is that?" Ron asked.

Mic beamed. "It's the remains of an old alarm clock," he answered. "My uncle Ed used to have one that looked like this."

All that remained of this clock was the cast iron case and the pewter ring that trimmed the opening where glass had once protected the face.

In the moonlight Longmore packed the big bay gelding. It was a heavy load, but the big horse could carry it for a few days. He threw the saddle, his bedroll, and a little grub up on the dun, mounted and rode out, leading the bay back down the Prieto River. It wasn't until he was several miles past the graveyard that he began to relax. At 5:00 a.m. there was no one to answer his ringing alarm clock.

"Whoever was here sure left a lot of gear," Mic commented.

"Yeah. I hope it *wasn't* because they had something more valuable to haul out of here," Ron said. Noting the position of the sun he suggested looking for Gold Gulch while the sun was still high. "I want to find out what that canyon looks like."

They gathered their treasures and took them back to the truck. Ron drove slowly alongside the river bottom. The road stayed on the same side of the river as the canyon turned to the north. Tall willows lined both sides of the road and partially blocked their view but they could easily see the beautiful sheer cliffs towering above them and closing in on both sides of the Prieto. They hadn't driven more than a few hundred yards when Mic hollered. "Ron! Stop! Look there!" Mic said, pointing to a narrow opening in the cliff on the east side of the river.

"That looks like it might be a canyon all right," Ron replied. "If it is, it has to be Gold Gulch, the maps don't show any other drainages coming into the Prieto from the east anywhere near here."

They jumped from the truck and rushed across the shallow water. There was in fact a narrow opening in the cliffs on the east side of the river. The towering cliffs turned sharply opening into a narrow, flat-bottomed canyon on the east side of Eagle Creek. The partners paused at the water's edge, taking in the view and wondering what they would find where the narrow canyon twisted out of sight. On the south side of the mouth of the side canyon a prominent bench jutted away from the cliff about fifty feet above the canyon floor — the very bench where Adams and Landrew had hidden while watching a massacre.

"Look there!" Mic exclaimed softly, pointing to the bench.

A bighorn sheep stared at them indifferently.

Ron drew an appreciative breath. "Look at the size of those horns! At least a curl and a half! He's a granddaddy for sure. Must weigh close to three hundred pounds. How do you suppose he got up there?"

"I don't know," Mic replied. "The way those things can climb, maybe he just walked right up the face of that overhanging cliff," he joked.

They watched the animal turn and traverse the cliff face as easily as if it were walking on level ground.

"Not a bad sign," Ron said.

"Sign of what?" Mic asked.

"I guess that this is a special place. I don't know. The thought just popped into my head," Ron said.

The two adventurers watched until the sheep disappeared, then entered Gold Gulch. The canyon stayed about fifty-feet wide as it slowly curved to the left. They soon came to where the canyon floor butted against a seemingly solid, sloping outcrop of rock. Beyond this they could see the canyon continuing, but with the canyon floor much higher than where they stood, it looked like the sloping cliff blocked their progress.

Ron hurried ahead of Mic, whose geological interests were captured by the abundant and beautiful, blue and green copper-rich minerals glittering in the gravel at his feet.

Ron continued until he approached the base of the rock wall that seemed to close the canyon, then stopped cold when he saw water issuing from the base of the cliff and heard the echoing sounds of falling water. As his eyes adjusted to the light and he studied the rock wall, he suddenly saw there was an opening where the water issued forth. "The hidden passage," he whispered.

His pulse quickened as he imagined what lay beyond, feeling almost as if he were the first white man who would see it. There was something else also, an emotion he did not understand. Besides the mystery of the Lost Adams Diggings, something else had drawn him to this place. He could feel it. "But what?" he wondered.

As he stepped through the portal, the walls on either side closed in on him, and he found himself standing in the entrance to a zigzag canyon. He looked up, stretching his neck, as if to catch his breath. Far above the overhanging cliffs forming the passage he now stood in, patches of evening sky and higher cliffs with a rosy hue glistened in the evening sun.

"We've found it!" he yelled. "This is Adams' Zigzag Canyon!"

He rested his backpack on a ledge of rock, and dug his crystal from the outside pack pocket. He stooped and washed it in the clear frigid waters rushing across his feet. Holding it, a glimpse of his strange dream drew near, but then eluded him.

"I know this place!" he thought, "I know I haven't been here before, but somehow I *know* this place!"

He was about to get his gold pan out of his pack and try a little panning when a thought struck him. "Where's the waterfall? There's supposed to be a waterfall."

Forgetting for the moment about panning, Ron stood and walked farther into the canyon, leaving his backpack on the ledge. As he walked along, the canyon walls closed in until he could reach out and touch, on either side, the damp walls that had never felt the sun's warming rays.

"I feel like I've entered an ancient world where no other man has ever ventured," he thought. "But, of course, the entire Adams party was here once, and lots of other prospectors, even Indians. That's right! Indians. Yes, Nana was here and gave warning to a group of prospectors." His head filled with the lore about a zigzag canyon, Ron looked around observantly. "There is a presence of something, or someone, here now. I feel it."

Standing in the long-sought "Zigzag Canyon" he was aware of a deep sense of kinship with all who had come to these wild lands before him, especially with those who had stood in this spot. His mind returned to the Indians who had known this place for many centuries and for whom it was sacred; to the explorers who discovered and tried to exploit the riches this place had once held; and to the hungry prospectors of the Great Depression, some of whom had found enough gold here to keep their families fed during that difficult time.

The details of his unsettling vision suddenly returned and flowed over him in an emotional torrent. He remembered the huge Indian with blood-stained arms coming toward him.

The sense of another's presence here, now, became overpowering. Abruptly Ron turned around, fully expecting to see the blood-soaked Red Sleeves.

"Show yourself!" he demanded, speaking to the empty air. Then, embarrassed at letting his emotions run away with him, he chided himself. "Look at me, talking to myself!"

He turned and hurried farther into the canyon to look for the falls he was certain he would find. Finally, there it was. The waters of Gold Gulch, swelled by recent rains, parachuted over the cliff above him and plunged into a beautiful pool at the end of the zigzag passage. Ron looked at the benched cliffs above the falls, his thoughts still on his dream. He remembered the accounts describing Nana standing on the cliff above the stooped prospectors and making his speech. "Maybe Nana spoke to the doomed prospectors from right up there."

With the crystal clutched tightly in his hand, Ron walked into the pool and through the curtain of water, oblivious to the chilling cascade. As he passed through the rushing water, the overwhelming sense of another's presence began to fade and was replaced by a feeling of peace and oneness with his surroundings. A great chief's vision from long ago was finally realized.

Ron stepped back through the waterfall, his trembling hands still clutching the crystal while distant words echoed through his mind.

"We truly are kindred spirits."

■

REFERENCES

Allen, Charles, *The Adams Diggings Story:* Hughes-Buie Co., El Paso, TX, 1935 (Pamphlet). Arizona Historical Society, Tucson, AZ.

Barnes, Will C., *Arizona Place Names:* U of A, Tucson, Arizona, 1935.

Brown, J. Ross, *Adventures in Apache Country:* Harper & Bros., N.Y., 1869.

Brown, Dee & Schmitt, Martin F, *Fighting Indians of the West:* Charles Scribner's Sons, N.Y., 1948.

Byerts, W. H., *Gold: The Lost Adams Gold Diggings:* (1915), Hollister, F., San Francisco, 1988 (Pamphlet).

Capps, Benjamin, *The Great Chiefs:* TIME-LIFE Books, Alexandria, VA, 1975.

Castenada, Carlos, *El Don Del Aguila:* Edivision, Mexico, D.F., 1982.

Comfort, Will Levington, *Apache:* E. P. Dutton & Co., N.Y., 1931.

Conroto, Eugene L., *Lost Desert Bonanzas:* Palm Desert-Southwest Publishers, Palm Desert, CA, 1963.

Corle, Edwin, *The Gila River of the Southwest:* U of Nebraska Press, 1951.

Dobie, J. Frank, *Apache Gold and Yaqui Silver:* Little, Brown & Co., Boston, 1939.

Dodd, Ed., *Ultramarathoning, the Next Challenge:* World Pub., Mountain View, CA, 1979.

Durrenberger, Robert W., *Major Floods and Storms of AZ, 1862-1977:* AZ Office of the State Climatologist, Tempe, AZ, 1978.

Emory, W. H., *Notes of a Military Reconnaissance from Fort Leavenworth in Missouri to San Diego in California:* U.S. Senate, Exec., Doc. No. 7, 30th Congress, 1848, also available from the Fort Leavenworth Historical Society, Leavenworth, Kansas: Wendell & Van Benthuysen Printers, Washington D.C., 1848.

Farish, Thomas Edwin, *History of Arizona:* Filmer Bros., Phoenix, AZ, 1915.

Foutz, Del, *Where is the Gold on the Colorado River: And How to Get it Out:* Self Published, Grand Jct., CO, 1982.

Griffen, William B., *Apaches at War and Peace:* U of N.M. Press, Albuquerque, N.M., 1988.

Hoig, Stan, *The Peace Chiefs of the Cheyennes:* U of OK Press, 1980.

Hough, Walter, *Antiquities of the Upper Gila & Salt River Valleys in Arizona and New Mexico:* Bureau of American Ethnology, Bulletin 35, Wash. D.C., 1907.

Lekson, Stephen H., *Nana's Raid — Apache Warfare in Southern New Mexico, 1881:* Texas Western Press, El Paso, TX, 1987.

Levinthal, Charles F., *Messengers of Paradise: Opiates and Brain Chemistry: The Struggle Over Pain, Rage, Uncertainty and Addiction:* Anchor Press, Garden City, N.Y., 1988.

Marrin, Albert, *Struggle for a Continent: The French and Indian Wars, 1690-1760:* Atheneum, N.Y., 1987.

McKenna, James A., *Black Range Tales:* Wilson-Erickson, Inc., N.Y., 1936; reprint, Rio Grande Press, Glorieta, N.M.

McLoughlin, Denis, *Wild & Woolly — An Encyclopedia of the Old West:* Doubleday & Co., Garden City, N.Y., 1975.

McLuhan, T. C., *Touch the Earth:* Outerbridge & Dienstfrey, N.Y., 1921.

Miller, Joseph, *The Arizona Story:* Hastings House, N.Y., 1952

Mims, Sam, *Trail of the Bowie Knife:* Guardian Journal, Hoer, LA

Mitchell, John D., *Lost Mines of the Great Southwest:* The Journal Company, Inc., Phoenix, AZ, 1933.

Mitchell, John D., *Lost Mines and Buried Treasure Along the Old Frontier:* Rio Grande Press, Glorieta, N.M., 1953.

Patton, James M., *History of Clifton:* Greenlee Chamber of Commerce, 1977.

Poston, Charles D., *Apache-Land:* A.L. Bancroft & Co., San Francisco, 1878.

Roberts, Dan, *A Story of the Centennial State:* Eagle Tail Press, Grand Jct., CO, 1976.

Ruxton, George F., *Life in the Far West:* Harper & Brothers, Publishers, 82 Cliff Street, N.Y., 1849, Rio Grande Press, Glorieta, N.M., 1972.

Santee, Ross, *Apache Land:* Charles Scribner's Sons, N.Y., 1947.

Storm, Barry, *Thunder God's Gold:* Southwest Publishing Co., Tortilla Flat, AZ, 1945.

Stout, Joseph A. Jr., *Apache Lightening — the last great battles of the Ojo Calientes:* Oxford University Press, Oxford, England, 1974.

Truscott, Lucian King, *The Twilight of the U.S. Cavalry: Life in the Old Army:* University Press of KS, Lawrence, KS, 1989.

Watkins, T. H., *Gold and Silver in the West:* Bonanza Books, N.Y., 1971.

Watts, Thomas D., *Alcoholism in Minority Populations:* Charles C. Thomas, Springfield, IL, 1989.

Wilkie, Katherine, *Man Who Wouldn't give Up; Henry Clay:* Messner, N.Y., 1961.

Wilson, Cunningham & Butler, *Arizona Lode Gold Mines & Gold Mining:* The Arizona Bureau of Mines, Bulletin 137, U. of A., 1967.

END NOTES

1. See Emory. Portions of what follows are taken directly from Lt. Emory's famous notes. We have followed exactly the significant events described therein with salient portions of the notes reprinted verbatim. We are indebted to the Ft. Leavenworth Historical Society for their help in procuring a reproduction of this key document in total.

2. See Emory. These are drawn from exact quotes. This was no idle boast. The combined Apache nations were the most powerful force in the region at that time and for many decades to follow. Because of Mangas' hatred for the Mexicans, due in no small part to the incident at Santa Rita, he would gladly have allied with General Kearney to wreck havoc on his unwelcome neighbors to the south. History does not tell us whether General Kearney seriously considered the offer. Kit Carson probably had it right; Mangas' alliance likely would have lasted only as long as it was beneficial to the Apache.

3. C. W. Hayman, 1934

4. Unattributed article. Phoenix Republican, April 4, 1924, taken from an unspecified article in the Clifton Gazette.

5. Copied verbatim from an unattributed original document found in the Arizona Historical Society archives at Tucson, AZ.

6. As it turned out, this was Nana's last raid. He and a few braves covered over three thousand miles in less than two months during the late spring and early summer and created great distress in the region. There is no evidence that Nana suffered even one casualty in all his raids even though the United States Cavalry had over three thousand battle-hardened troops in the region and managed to engage Nana on three occasions. This is one of the more salient examples of Apache expertise in "guerilla" type warfare.

Experts agree that two things led to the eventual defeat of the Apache nations in what is now the southwestern United States. First, the various Apache tribes could never agree on a uniform and consistent battle plan against the invaders and often worked at cross purposes with one another. Second, the Pimas, who hated the Apaches after centuries of near-subjugation by them, learned the Apache techniques of warfare and joined forces with the cavalry. Considering the resources at the Apache Nation's disposal and their skill as warriors, it is possible that without the Pimas' help, the cavalry might never have conquered them.

7. Copied from archives, Tucson, AZ.

SUNSTONE PRESS

Send for our free catalog

and find out more about our books on:

- ❖ The Old West
- ❖ American Indian subjects
- ❖ Western Fiction
- ❖ Architecture
- ❖ Hispanic interest subjects
- ❖ And our line of full-color notecards

Just mail this card or call us on our toll-free number below

_____

Name

_____

Address

_____

City   State   Zip

Send Book Catalog _____ Send Notecard Catalog _____

Sunstone Press / P.O.Box 2321 / Santa Fe, NM 87504
(505) 988-4418   FAX (505) 988-1025   (800)-243-5644